MAIDEN

OF IRON

A STEAMPUNK FABLE

To Bruce
Enjoy the great
adventure !

Blessing
Eli Wilder
An Olivia

ENDORSEMENTS

A steampunk fable at its finest. Melson is a master craftsman in her action-packed spin with Maid Marion and Robin Hood at the helm.

—**DiAnn Mills**, best-selling author

Edie Melson's steampunk adventure kept me turning pages long after I should have called my lady's maid to help me prepare for dinner. There wasn't enough tea in all of England to settle my nerves as Marion and Robin first matched wits with each other and then joined forces to stop a horrific evil from taking over the land. *Maiden of Iron* is a must-read for fans of the steampunk genre and a perfect first foray for those new to it.

—**Lynn H. Blackburn**, award-winning author

A superb retelling of Robin Hood—steampunk style! Edie brings the beloved characters to life in a whole new way that will keep readers feverishly turning the pages to find out what happens next. I can't wait for the next in the series!
—**Lynette Eason**, bestselling, award-winning author of the *Elite Guardians Series*

Edie Melson takes readers on a fantasy filled journey that is anything but mechanical. Marion, the *Maiden of Iron*, captivates the heart in her attempt to free children who are being held captive for nefarious reasons. And what better way to honor her embittered father, the former Guildmaster? A shocking twist of events will leave Marion, as well as readers, more confident than ever that steel and steam can never replace the heart.
—**Cathy Baker**, award-winning author

Set in a perfect steampunk world populated by automatons, grotesque hybrid machine/flesh beasts, and a mysterious illness infecting only children, this is the story of Robin Hood and Lady Marion the way it was meant to be told. Hard to believe it's not the original.
—**Zena Dell Lowe**, Writer, Producer, Director, Mission Ranch Films

Edie Melson's retelling of Robin Hood is a masterpiece of Steam Punk fiction that will keep you guessing through the turns and twists of sinister plots afoot in Victorian England. Immerse yourself in Maiden of Iron and travel to another time and to an incredibly crafted world.
—**Mary Denman**, Photographer, Blogger

EDIE MELSON

MAIDEN OF IRON

A STEAMPUNK FABLE

Elk Lake
PUBLISHING, INC.
PLYMOUTH, MASSACHUSETTS

Cover Design: Cheryl L. Childers
Interior Design: Cheryl L. Childers
Editor: Deb Haggerty
Published in Association with Christian Literary Agency

PUBLISHED BY: Elk Lake Publishing, Inc., 35 Dogwood Dr., Plymouth, MA 02360

Library Cataloging Data
Names: Melson, Edie (Edie Melson)
Maiden of Iron: A Steampunk Fable/ Edie Melson
342 p. 23cm × 15cm (9in × 6 in.)
Description:
Identifiers: ISBN-13: 978-1-946638-91-5 (trade) | 978-1-946638-92-2 (POD) | 978-1-946638-93-9 (e-book)
Key Words: Gaslamp fantasy, alternative history, fairy tales, fantasy, action/adventure, science fiction, Victorian Era
LCCN 2018940047 Fiction

DEDICATION

To My Darling Husband, Kirk.
My fellow traveler to unknown lands
of imagination and adventure.

ACKNOWLEDGMENTS

No book can ever see the light of day without an entire team of people moving it forward. That's especially true of this book!

First and foremost, I want to give a shout-out to my amazing husband, Kirk Melson. Without his constant support and encouragement—as well as his willingness to chip in with almost everything around the house—this book would never have happened.

I also want to thank those in my life who have given this project, and all of us involved, much needed—daily—prayer support. Cathy Baker, Candace Brady, Sheri Owens, Valorie Moore, Vonda Skelton, Beth Vogt, and Cynthia Cavanaugh. I also want to thank my Friday morning, More Than Sunday, accountability group. You guys are an inspiration. And I could never leave out my precious critique partners—Lynette Eason, Alycia Morales, Lynn Blackburn, Linda Gilden, Erynn Newman, Emme Gannon and Mary Denman.

A special shout out goes to the amazing (and in my opinion best agent in the world), David Van Diest.

Of course, I want to include everyone at Elk Lake Publishing, especially my talented editor, Deb Haggerty.

Additionally, no writer is ever able to move ahead without other writers to share the journey! Thank you to all the writers from my AWSA Mastermind Group, Cross N Pens, ACFW SC Chapter, and of course, The Light Brigade.

Finally a HUGE shout out to my sons and daughters, Jimmy and Katie Melson, Kirk and Weslyn Melson, and John Melson. You all have always believed in me and been among my staunchest supporters. I love doing life with you all!

CHAPTER ONE

Lady Marion Ravenswood leaned back on her elbows and kicked at the tunnel grate. The long, black leather duster had been a good choice, protecting her trousers from the dirt and chill, but she should have thought to bring an oil can as well. The humidity in these steam tunnels played havoc with iron, and things were always rusting shut.

"Come on girlie, put a little weight behind it." Gretta, also in men's attire, squatted in the tunnel behind Marion, looking more at home in the breeches than any lady of quality ever should. "We need to get in place."

Marion took a deep breath, made a conscious effort to ignore the stench, and kicked again, sending the metal grate tumbling to the floor. She righted herself and perched on the edge of the smaller, little-used access tunnel, barely a meter above the damp floor.

The only sounds were those normal ones—the hiss of steam escaping a rusted joint, the constant drip from the condensation formed by the hot pipes running near the ceiling of the large underground tunnels, and of course, the furtive sounds of the rats. She shuddered. *Why did there always have to be rats?*

"Quit admiring the scenery, and let's get a move on." Gretta gave Marion a gentle shove. The willowy blonde enjoyed the freedom of their forays into the underworld.

"Come on, Gret," Addison said. "Quit being such a bossy boots." Only Gretta's younger brother could get away with that nickname. Having just turned fourteen, Addison was now a permanent member of their gang—despite Marion's misgivings.

Using one gloved hand, Marion steadied herself before leaping from the small access tunnel into the larger one. She looked back at Gretta. "Now who's being slow?"

Her best friend grimaced and dropped to the floor, her soft leather boots making a small splash as she landed. She dusted her hands on her trousers and straightened the wool cap that did little to disguise her delicate features. She peered around. "You've chosen well for the ambush."

High praise, considering the source. Marion surveyed the area. Several wide tunnels intersected here, leaving them with options for a quick retreat. There were also several street grates, bathing the area with a misty glow in the early morning. Occasionally, the wagon wheels creaked in time with the shadows they cast as they rolled over the openings.

These tunnels were more than just a place to house the steam pipes that ran below London. They also offered access to the buildings above for trash removal as well as coal delivery. The surprisingly tall ceiling was swathed in darkness, almost inky black, but Marion could see the bottoms of the huge pipes. Perhaps next time, they should plan to attack from above.

The chrono clipped to her shirtwaist chirped once, a low sweet sound at odds with the surroundings. She checked the time, walked to a pile of trash against one dark wall and surveyed the oddments. "This should do the trick. We'll hide here while we wait." The other two joined her and began shifting the barrels and boxes to give them the space they needed. Marion toed a pile of newspapers, and a large rat scurried out. She leapt out of its way. At least she no longer screamed at the sight of the horrible rodents. Gretta raised an eyebrow at her antics but didn't comment.

Returning to her position, Marion noticed a growing odor of sulphur. *Great, what else?* She used the sleeve of her duster to cover her mouth. Her exertions had ruined the lace peeping beneath the black cuffs, but there was no help for that now. Dirt-streaked lace—not something she wanted to explain to Matilda.

"This trash stinks, but I think this will work." Gretta shoved one last barrel into place and checked her own pocket watch. "We've almost a quarter hour before they show. Right?"

Addison pulled a dirt-smudged notebook from his navy wool coat and thumbed a couple of pages. He'd cut the fingers out of his gloves to assure the dexterity he needed for his calculations. "Aye. We're right on time."

"And they think they're so smart, hiding the gold in shipments of coal. Didn't take Addi long to figure out how they moved the loot." Gretta shook her head. "Now if you can just figure out how the Makers Guild actually turns the lead into gold. That would be a real coup."

Addison rolled his eyes at his sister. "I've told you before. Several hundredweight of lead are required to get just a couple of ounces of gold. Let them do the work for us."

Marion snapped the filtering lens onto the goggles attached to her helmet and pulled them over her eyes. Murky darkness rearranged itself into a scene as clear as day. "William's done it again." She saw Addison and Gretta as clearly as if they were standing outside in the noon sun. "The polish on these turns dark into light. Just like he promised."

"Humph." Gretta frowned. "If he was half the genius you claim, he'd have had goggles for all of us, not just you."

Addison rounded on his sister. "You know Will spent most of the night getting the polish just right. He only had time for this one pair."

"Hush now." Marion darted behind the barrels and pulled her friends down out of sight. "Did you see that?" She pointed to a section of ceiling where—to them—the pipes were in shadow. "There's something—or someone—moving around. Right where that other tunnel intersects this one. We aren't only ones here."

"Those could hold the weight of several men." Gretta squinted at the pipes, her voice low. "Or it might be a trick of the lenses. You're the one most likely to be able to tell."

Marion turned toward Addison. "How easy would it be for someone else to put together the clues about this shipment of gold?"

"Not impossible." He frowned, keeping his voice low and almost inaudible. "I put it together."

Marion was so proud of this young man. As excited as he got, he was always self-effacing about his own abilities.

"In other words, highly unlikely." As much as Gretta gave her brother fits, Marion knew how proud his intellect made her. Even at his age, Addison was seldom wrong—about anything. "Do you think they saw us?"

Marion turned her gaze back to the pipes, chewing at her lower lip. "I don't think so. We should know soon." There was that slight movement again. She continued to study the area as the furtive movements finally arranged themselves into recognizable shapes. "Unless I've begun hallucinating, there two or more crouched up there. They've made no move in our direction. I think we're safe."

Addison nodded. "They must have just arrived. Otherwise they'd have heard us, what with you kicking open the grate and us shifting these barrels."

"Well, whenever they got here, you can bet they're up to no good." Gretta pulled a coil of rope from her bag. "They're after our gold."

"Technically, it's not yet our gold." Addison readied his slingshot. He'd proved to have a deadly accuracy with what Marion had considered nothing more than a toy. Bringing him along had been the right move.

"Not that." Marion revised the plan in her mind and frowned at his weapon. "Get the other rope instead. My pistol will blind them and give us time to incapacitate them." She ran her fingers along the leather corset cinching her waist, locating the lightning revolver snug in its holster before raising her hand to her bow and full quiver slung across her chest. Although the bow was always her weapon of choice, the lightning arrows hadn't been ready yet. But now, perhaps that was just as well.

Gretta studied the ceiling. "I take it there's been a change in plan?"

"Actually, we're going to let them do the work for us. I think there're no more than three up there. We'll let them take out the automatons and pack up the gold. While they're preoccupied, we'll relieve them of their burdens." She unsnapped the revolver, thumbed on the power, and a low hum met her ears. Her fingers felt a slight tingle, but she couldn't be sure if from the gun or just nerves. This gun had proved to be another of Will's useful inventions. The lightning bolts that erupted from the barrel of the altered revolver permanently disrupted an automaton's system, but wouldn't do more than temporarily blind a full organic. Exactly the weapon she needed.

A distant rumble caught her attention. She raised her head for a moment. The string of figures came closer, human-inspired metallic forms interspersed with wheeled bins piled high with coal. Clever of the Makers Guild, using old coal bins and automatons to move the gold after the transformation. What they used the gold for was anyone's guess. Thirty paces more, and they'd be within range.

Gretta fidgeted again. Marion held up a gloved hand, counting down with her fingers. As she reached one, silent chaos erupted as three men leapt from the shadowed ceiling. Their black leather garb gave them a sense of sameness, only differentiated by colored silk scarves worn around their necks. Even their heads were covered with modified aviator helmets, complete with protective goggles. Could these outlaws be those from the Pilots Guild who'd been branded traitors along with the former Guildmaster?

The automatons had no chance against these silent men wielding a variety of small arms. The deadly accuracy of their attack suggested they had lenses similar to hers that allowed them to see better in the dark. The aerial attack *had* given them a distinct advantage. Marion filed that fact away to consider later.

The attack was over in less than a minute. As the three men surveyed the now still scene, the one with a bright green scarf toed one of the automatons with his boot. Assured, he pulled his helmet from his head. "Quickly, men." He joined them as he gave orders. "Dump the bins. The gold will be in a small leather pouch beneath the coal in one of the containers."

She craned her neck to get a better view as the men moved in and emptied the bins of coal.

"The gold's here. Just like we were promised." An impossibly large man held a small pouch over his head. "Three cheers for Robin." He kept his voice low, but the sound rumbled through the tunnels.

Instead of answering with an audible sound, the other two men raised their fisted right hands above their heads as they faced the man in the green scarf. In response, Robin took a deep bow, grinning widely before turning back to the coal.

Marion frowned as she watched their antics. The leader seemed familiar somehow. His movements, combined with that wide grin, tugged at a memory. Had she met him somewhere before?

"What is it?" Gretta leaned forward. "Is there something wrong?"

There was, but now wasn't the time to figure out what. The leader was tucking the pouch into the belt at his waist. She gave a curt shake of her head. "Keep your eyes covered until you hear the pistol. They'll be blind long enough for you to incapacitate them."

She rose and sighted on the leader.

He turned at the sound of her movement, and his eyes widened. "Marion? Marion Ravenswood?" Light arced from her revolver, hitting him full in the chest. He staggered into the large man beside him, and they both went down in a heap. The smaller man was a few paces to the left, but he too stumbled, obviously blinded by the light. *Leave it to Will. His inventions never failed.*

"Quick now." Marion motioned them forward.

Gretta and Addison leapt into action, quickly tying the struggling men.

They tried to fight back, but were no match for Marion and her small band.

"Marion, is that you?" Robin sat, legs outstretched and hands tied behind his back. He moved his head from side to side, obviously unable to see. "What have you done?"

"She's blinded us, that's what she's done." The third man repeatedly opened and closed his eyes.

As Marion opened her mouth to answer, she caught Gretta's glare.

"We don't know no Marion." Gretta pitched her voice well below her normal pleasing contralto. "And the effect is temporary and will wear off in just a bit."

"Gretta Handleson, I'd know your voice anywhere." Robin cocked his head. "And where you are, Marion's not far behind. What have you two done? Let us go." He struggled against the ropes that bound his hands and feet.

"Do you know these ruffians?" The large man was menacing even trussed up like a Christmas goose.

"Ruffians?" Marion put her hand on her hip. She knew the leader now, no doubt. "You're one to talk, Robin of Loxley."

"So it is you." Even sightless, Robin's eyes found hers and bored straight to her heart. "I'd say little Marion is no longer just pestering me to take tea with her and her dolls."

Even if he couldn't see what was happening, the noise around Robin proved the little minx was making good her threat to steal his gold. Bested in front of his men—by a girl no less. Well, no longer a girl. The glimpse he'd had was of a striking young woman. As he struggled with his bonds, they began to loosen. Beautiful or not, perhaps he'd turn the tables on her yet.

"You know we'll be long gone before you wiggle free." Marion's voice was low and close.

Robin squeezed his eyes open and shut. Her tiny figure began to separate itself from the blurry blackness as she bent down and stared at him. Fuzzy outlines were definitely replacing the pitch dark. *Drat that female.* He squinted again. They hadn't lied. The blindness wasn't permanent. He forced himself to relax, to draw her attention elsewhere. "That pistol you carry. I've never seen anything like it before."

"And it's likely you never will." The gleeful voice of a young man came from somewhere behind Robin. "There's none like William with the inventions."

"Hush, you fool," said Gretta. She must have clouted him, because he yelped.

"The gun is an amazing thing." The more Robin could keep them talking, the more he'd learn. "Are there any other side-effects I should know about? Besides the blindness, that is."

"Not really." Marion's tone was curt, almost preoccupied. "You may have a lingering headache, but the dizziness you felt was a direct result of the blindness. As long as you're not an automaton, you'll be fine."

Robin's stomach lurched, and he tried to flex his right hand. Nothing, not a joint moved. The ache in his head was nothing compared to this. "So, the lightning—electricity perhaps—

disrupts an automaton's system?" He was fishing, and they both knew it. The blue light and sharp smell of hot acid made the electric component obvious. But how had this William reduced the size of a dynamo to fit in a pistol? Had he found another method to produce the electricity?

"I think I'll let you figure that out yourself." She folded her arms, her features clearer each moment. "You have all the information you need." She turned back to Gretta. "Are we close?"

"Just a bit more tidying, and we'll be off." Gretta's words were accompanied with banging.

What were they doing, cleaning up from his attack? Weren't they planning to make them the scapegoats? "So where do we go from here?" If his calculations were correct, and they usually were, they only had a few more minutes before the shipment missed the next checkpoint, and the Makers began a search. He really didn't want to be caught here when they arrived. John grunted beside him, urging him to take action. She was close enough to overpower, even with the ropes that bound his hands and feet. But without the use of his right hand, the force of his attack might injure her. That alone made him hesitate.

"*We* don't go anywhere," Marion told him. "You aren't part of the plan I have for this gold.

This gold? Recent events ran through his mind. Today's wasn't the first shipment he'd missed. He'd assumed the routes had been changed. Although he'd heard rumblings of a newcomer, he had brushed them off as rumors. He tried to remember what had been said. There was talk of a woman, what had they called her? Maiden ... that was it. Maiden of Iron. Surely this wasn't her? Not the Marion he'd grown up with?

As Marion grinned down at him, he realized her face was fully in focus. "Have we interfered with your plans before?"

She must have read his thoughts in his expression. He'd have to be more careful. No, actually she'd have to be more careful. It was his turn to grin. "Perhaps I got your name wrong, Marion. I think I might know you better as the Maiden of Iron."

She quirked an eyebrow at him. "Perhaps. What do you care?"

She had spunk, always had.

"I think I'll let you figure that out for yourself." He turned her words back at her. "You have all the information you need."

John shifted beside him, tensing to attack. "No," Robin hissed under his breath, and John stilled. The instinct to protect her was still strong.

"Back into the tunnel." Marion had turned away from him and appeared to have missed the exchange. "Get started." She ordered the other two. "And I'll catch up."

He frowned, the blurry outlines getting sharper by the moment. His vision was almost normal. "Do you intend to just leave us here? You know the Makers Guild will send troops when the shipment is late at the next check point."

"No, I'm not as heartless as you." She leaned down, and he could see her face without squinting. The goggles she'd been wearing were pushed up on her head, tangled in the dark curls. A knife glinted in her hand as she turned to Duncan. "You'll be free in a moment."

"Hey, now, Little Miss." Duncan voice squealed as he caught a glimpse of the knife. "We didn't do you no harm."

Robin almost groaned aloud. Leave it to Marion to focus on the weak link. Duncan had a good heart, but ...

"I'm just going to give the rope a bit of help." Marion chuckled, a nice change from the giggling women he'd grown used to. She sliced through almost all the strands that bound Duncan. "Can't make things too easy for the powers that be, can I?"

"I'd have thought we'd make nice scapegoats." Robin couldn't resist goading her. Old habits died hard. "You know we'll follow. That gold is ours."

"No, you won't follow. You'll be too busy getting away." Marion cocked her head. "You should learn your lesson and stay far away from me—and what's mine."

He watched her dart away. His mind conjured up a picture of Marion as a little girl, hands on hips, forbidding him to follow her to her secret place. He'd let her go then, and he'd let her go now. But just like when they were young, he'd eventually find her. He knew where to look. Their paths would cross again.

"I'm free—and I can see." Duncan's shout turned Robin's attention back to his men.

"Then untie us." John had been silent until now, but Robin knew he'd have a lot to say later. "We've work to do."

Free from the ropes, they stood and surveyed the scene. The automatons were piled to one side and the coal bins—with the coal inside—back upright. No clues remained to point to Marion, or even to him, as the culprit.

John lumbered over to inspect the entrance to the smaller tunnel Marion and her band used for their escape. "Won't take us long to catch up with them." He pulled the grate free and stuck his head and shoulders inside. "Bit of a tight fit, but Duncan can run it and give us their exit point." His words echoed back, distorted.

"Not today, gentlemen." Robin again tried to flex his right hand. "We've other things to attend to."

"But we can't just let them swoop in and best us." Now that the danger had passed, Duncan was once again all fuss and feathers.

John pulled back and glowered at Duncan. "Aye, and you're a fine one to talk." He eyed Robin's useless hand. "The lightning took it out?"

"Hopefully, not for long." Robin ignored Duncan and focused on John. "I'll need a house call from Dr. Tuck. Can you arrange that?"

John grinned. "Of course. For all his complaints, he always enjoys a visit."

Robin cocked his head, listening. "I'd say our time is up. I hear them coming." He motioned them toward the pipes. "Up we go."

CHAPTER TWO

Marion reined in her black mare, ducking as she guided her under the limbs of the huge fir tree. First again. She swung her leg out of the saddle and dropped to the ground.

Delilah nosed her shoulder, whiffling into her rider's ear.

"Enjoyed our morning out, didn't you?" Marion stroked the black's soft nose and laid her cheek against the warm neck. "I did too. And I would never replace you—or any of our guild horses—with one of those new hybrid steeds."

Delilah snorted and shook the bit as if in offense.

"I know. They say, they're more efficient, but I don't see how steel and steam can replace the heart."

At the sound of hooves in the distance, she pulled Delilah closer to the trunk. It wouldn't do to be seen by some random passerby. Although who would be on the guild grounds this early she couldn't imagine. As the horse slowed, she heard the familiar three-note whistle they used to identify each other.

Gretta ducked under the canopy of branches, leading her horse. "Any sign of Addi yet?" Her blonde hair had come free from its pins, probably from an extended gallop. If she hadn't been their decoy, her breakneck speed would have ensured she'd have been at the rendezvous before anyone else.

"Right here, Sis." Addison led his horse from behind the trunk of a nearby tree. His cheeks were flushed from the chill October morning. He'd probably been galloping as well.

Marion tamped down her irritation. "I thought we'd agreed not to take any unnecessary chances or call attention to ourselves." Was she the only one who understood how precarious their situation or how important the work? One wrong move and they would be finished. She bit her lip. Being recognized this morning could have been just such an occurrence.

"Relax." Gretta laughed. "A morning gallop is not taking chances."

There was no humor in the glare Addi turned to Marion. "You act like I can't handle a horse." He untied the black leather pouch from his saddle and hurled it at her. "Here's mine, safe and sound."

Marion caught the pouch before it hit her in the face. She hefted the bag before adding it to the one already in her pocket. Gretta strolled over and handed her a third pouch. Splitting up what they took, even if the amount was tiny, made sense. So little return for such a great risk. "Thank you both." She *was* grateful for their help. They were the only ones she could trust ... now that David was gone.

Gretta gave her a quick hug. "Like we'd let you shoulder this burden alone?"

"We're in this together." Addison bobbed his head, his still-maturing face serious but no longer angry. "Will this buy the supplies Doc needs to keep working on the cure?"

"Not enough." Marion considered the guild children who sickened each day. "It's never enough."

Addison sighed as he took the reins of their mounts. "I'll get them back." His young face was grave. "No one will suspect a thing."

Marion exchanged a look with Gretta as he led the horses away. He'd get them back in the stables with a plausible lie that would more than likely have the grooms and stable boys wide-eyed and unsuspecting.

"We all work to our strengths. Remember what your grandfather taught us." Gretta took her arm, and they ducked under the tree limbs. "Quit making up things to worry about. Addi will be fine."

"I'm not making things up. Every day this gets more convoluted." Tears flooded her eyes, and she dashed them away with a gloved hand. "And I drag you and Addi in deeper."

"Stop it." Gretta faced her, hands on hips. "You're panicking because Robin recognized you."

"I can't believe I was careless." Marion fisted her hands and began to pace. "That we were identified by the likes of him makes our job doubly dangerous."

"The fact that it *was* him minimizes any danger of our secret getting out." She grabbed Marion by the arm. "Just think. Who could he tell? No one would believe him even if he could get someone to listen. The price on his own head is too high for him to risk getting caught. Or is there something else here?" Gretta cocked her head. "Do you still have feelings for the man?"

"Of course not." Marion snorted and jerked away as her cheeks grew hot. "I just don't trust him. I've watched him nurse a grudge and wait years to get even. We can't afford to underestimate him."

"Agreed." Gretta turned toward the crumbling gazebo. "We pay attention. But we don't let him get in our way." She mounted the stone steps and waited just inside for Marion to join her. "Our task is too important. We can't lose any more children."

Marion joined her on the steps. She'd come up with a plan after she had time to think. For now, they had to get changed and back home. This would not be the day to get caught and face embarrassing questions from Matilda. She'd like nothing more than to carry tales about Marion and her escapades to her father.

Gretta had positioned herself in front of the leftmost pillar, hand on a small cherub carved into the stone. Marion matched her position with the cherub embedded into the rightmost pillar. In perfect synchronicity, they pushed against the stones. The rock floor in the center of the gazebo parted with a groan, exposing wooden stairs leading into darkness.

Marion went down several steps and felt for the small electric torch they kept hanging on the wall. She thumbed on the light and felt the small buzz that preceded the flickering light. This torch had been one of William's first.

She waited while Gretta scuffed up any footprints they might have left. When Gretta joined her, Marion turned to the wall on the left and pushed another cherub carved into the stonework. This closed the passage above them, leaving them in musty darkness, cut only by the small glow of the torch. The gloom didn't really matter. This place held no fear for Marion. Each passageway was carved into her heart.

"I still remember the first time you brought me here when we were kids," Gretta said as they walked further down the corridor, the light dancing off the rich mahogany paneling. "I really didn't believe there was a full-size airship buried here."

"I know you didn't." Marion chuckled. "The look on your face was priceless."

"I can't believe your father had this place closed off."

"He got rid of everything he could when Mother died." Marion's face hardened. "He tried to deny she'd ever even existed. And this place reminded him he was Guildmaster only because of her."

"I keep forgetting that." Gretta ran a light hand on the intricately carved paneling lining the hallway. "It's difficult to imagine that he wasn't born to be a Guildmaster. I wonder if that really makes a difference?" She put her hands on her hips. "I still don't understand why a woman can't be a Guildmaster."

Marion cocked an eyebrow at her. "You and me both." She pushed open the magnificent door and turned to the small bureau on the left, handing Gretta the torch. Marion removed the glass chimney from the brass lamp she kept there, struck a match, and lit the wick.

"But why would your father board up the entrances to this place? I'd think in these unsettling times he'd want to keep a place like this for refuge." Gretta turned off the torch.

"The place is not much of a refuge, at least from our own people. Everyone in the guild knows. The ship is part of Grandfather's legend." She shrugged. "Sad that we now have to worry about our own people."

"It wasn't that way? Before your father took over, I mean?" Gretta lit another lamp.

"All I know are the stories mother and Grandfather used to tell." Her heart lifted as she remembered the hours she'd spent here with her grandfather, listening to him spin tales. He'd been almost as bad as Addison about making things up. But no. She refused to think about the times here with Mother ... or with David. "No matter what. This is the perfect place for us now."

She shrugged out of the heavy leather duster and hung the coat on a hook. "Just look at this." Pointing at the mud ground into the back of the garment, she wrinkled her nose.

Gretta bent down to get a closer look. "Let it dry, then brush the leather clean." She shrugged. "You don't have to wear it out anywhere."

"True." Marion began to loosen the laces on her outer corset. The front lacing made possible changing costumes without the help of a lady's maid.

"I remember you also brought *him* here." Gretta turned away to change. "Do you think he'll remember."

No doubt Gretta was referring to Robin. He'd pestered her for almost a year before she'd given in and shown him her secret place. Oh, yes. He'd remember. No chance he wouldn't. She bit her lip. But it wouldn't do to worry Gretta. "I'm sure he has other things on his mind just now."

"Really?" Gretta turned back, now clad only in her chemise, arms crossed. "That's what you truly believe?"

Marion picked up the traditional corset she'd laid out on the bed and held it to her waist, turning her back to Gretta. "Come help me with this. Matilda will be the one helping me dress this evening. She'll ask too many questions if I'm not laced up tight."

Gretta snorted and crossed the room and began the intricate lacing. "You know I'm not going to stop until I get an answer."

"No, it's not what I believe." Marion grabbed a bedpost to steady herself as Gretta tugged at the strings of the corset. "But it's what I *choose* to believe."

They finished changing and set the room in order. Gretta grabbed a stiff brush and attacked the mud splatters on Marion's coat. "You go on ahead. I'll finish this and join you." She made a shooing motion with her hand. "Matilda will be less suspicious if just you show up."

"That's true. Thank you." Marion took one of the electric torches. "I'll leave the other one for you."

Instead of retracing her steps to the gazebo, Marion wound her way further along the stateroom passage until she came to the steps that led upward to what used to be the observation lounge. She lifted the skirts of her gray silk morning dress out of the accumulated dust that lay heavy on the dark stairway. The neglect since her mother's death tugged at her heart. That was when her father had ordered the ship off limits to the staff and his children.

The large expanse of the lounge still held the heavy, dark furniture that had graced it during the glory years of travel. The deep burgundy velvet on the chairs and settees was offset by patterned pillows in soft greens and blues. Only the thought of the dust that would linger on her clothing kept Marion moving through the room. She paused at the one grouping with two chairs and a tufted leather hassock. Hours of her childhood had been spent on that hassock, wide-eyed at the conversations of her mother and grandfather.

She huffed and turned away, but not before her mother's voice rang in her mind. "Remember this well. *If only* is a pit that's almost impossible to escape."

Robin strode through the hall of his underground headquarters, his boots ringing on the stones as he headed toward the old kitchen. What had possessed him to react to her like that? He hadn't allowed emotion to blind him since—

"Robin, watch out." John caught up with him just as they rounded a corner. He inserted his girth between Robin and an elderly woman. Grabbing the tray she carried with one hand and her arm with the other, John barely kept her on her feet.

"Annie, I'm sorry. I wasn't paying attention." Robin reached out to steady the woman, leaving John free to juggle the tray into submission. He had to get a leash on his wandering mind. "Are you all right?"

"It's fine I am, my darling boy." Annie cocked her head, fixing her eyes on his. "But I'd say you're in a bit of a fix."

There was no fooling Annie. She'd known him longer than anyone. "That I am." He bent down and bussed a kiss on the top of her mobcap.

"You stop that." She batted at him, but her harsh tone didn't match the expression on her face. "I was just bringing your tea."

"You wanted to check up on us." John chuckled. "To make sure no one was hurt."

Annie harrumphed. "It's dangerous work you've set for yourselves. Someone's got to look after you." She reached for the tray in John's hand.

"No, I'll carry the tray. You lead the way." John winked at her and pointed his chin at Robin. "You'll have your hands full with him."

"Whatever the problem is will go down better with a bit of tea." She bustled back down the shadowy passage, toward Robin's study.

Robin gave John a hard look as they fell into step behind her. "You just had to say that." He took off after her.

"She'd have known without my saying anything." John followed close behind.

"Too true."

Annie stopped in the doorway of Robin's study to survey the mess, then began to clear the tea table so John could have a place to set the tray. "It's not like you don't expect me to bring you your tea. You'd think a smart man would realize I need this space free." She stopped and held up a glass cylinder, one end stoppered with a large round marble, the other sprouting moveable lenses of differing colors. "And what would you be needing this for? Aren't you just a wee bit beyond toys?"

Robin took the kaleidoscope from her. He put the lens end of the device to his eye, turning toward one of the flickering gaslights on the chandelier. "The world looks different through these various colors. Sometimes the scope makes things clearer and other times not."

"If you're needing something to see the world a bit clearer, I could make a suggestion or two." Annie motioned to John to set down the tray, although she continued to remove bits and pieces from the table, transferring them to the jumbled bookcase covering the wall. Robin followed her, picking up what she'd set down and assigning each item to its rightful place.

Annie put her hands on her hips and turned to face him. "I really can't see any rhyme or reason to the way you have things in here."

"Ah, but I do." He pointed a playful finger at her. "And that's what counts—considering it's *my* study."

"Annie, this is one argument you'll never win." John chuckled as he lowered his bulk onto the old velvet sofa. "He knows where every single thing in this room is. Your tidying just upsets his system."

"Thank you." Robin bowed to friend. "All support is greatly appreciated."

Annie harrumphed again and turned to pour the tea.

Robin settled into a worn leather chair and straightened his long legs in front of him. "But we still have this morning's fiasco to contend with."

"Duncan said you'd had a bit of bad luck." Annie handed Robin his tea.

"Duncan says entirely too much." Robin leaned forward to take the cup and frowned at John. "We're going to need to do something about that."

"He's still young." John's big hands cradled the delicate china Annie passed him with ease. "I'll have a talk with him."

Annie took a cup as well and perched on the edge of the sofa. Robin raised an eyebrow. She didn't often take tea with them.

"Let's have it." He leaned forward and set his saucer on the low table. "What is it you two have to say that I'm not going to like?"

John fixed Robin with an unblinking stare. "Almost four years have gone by since the Master was framed."

Robin made an effort not to clench his hands into fists. "So?"

Annie cleared her throat. "It's getting to be time to move on."

"Move on?" Robin kept his voice low and even. "I'm not sure what exactly you mean."

"We mean this need you have for revenge. There's no purpose in it." John looked at his hands then back at Robin. "There's no purpose in you."

"You could do so much good." Annie's cup rattled in its saucer. "You're not using any of the money you've stolen. Why don't you consider trying to clear your father's name?"

"And how would you suggest I do that?" He could see his icy words cut his old nurse, but he couldn't stop. "Do you think I should just waltz into the solicitor's office and demand an investigation?" He shot to his feet and began to pace. "Or maybe I should request an audience with the Queen. Her friendship certainly helped my father as he swung from the end of the hangman's noose." He turned to John. "How about you? Is this what you want, too?"

"What I want is what your father would have wanted. He wanted you to have a purpose. For your life to count for something." John heaved himself to his feet. "You know as well as me that he didn't hold with revenge."

"Yeah. Look where that got him." Robin turned away, studying the books that lined the mahogany shelves. He turned at the gentle touch on his arm and gazed down into Annie's concerned eyes.

"What happened wasn't right. But that doesn't make living this way right either." She dabbed her eye with the edge of her apron. "The way you're attacking life is handing the victory to them that killed the Master."

Robin looked from one to the other, then threw up his hands and plopped back into his chair. "Okay. Give me the rest. You wouldn't risk this much if you didn't have a proposition to make."

John and Annie exchanged looks.

"I think you should quit trying to be a nuisance in Stanton's backside and start looking for evidence." He held up a hand when Robin tried to interrupt. "What we do with the evidence will depend on what we find."

"Hmm." Robin fingered the cleft in his chin. "Not a bad thought. We can think of that as phase two in the get-rid-of-Stanton plan. We can get started right away." He slapped his thighs. "Right after we make one more unannounced visit to the Honorable—temporary—Guildmaster Stanton and his ever-irritating son, Edward. He's having a masquerade day after tomorrow, and I'm sure he'd be bitterly disappointed if I didn't put in an appearance."

CHAPTER THREE

Marion paused just inside the door, listening for any movement. This passageway from the old airship led to a little-used corridor near the main kitchen. The servants were accustomed to her wandering, so unless she ran into Matilda, no one should remark on her presence. Marion took a deep breath and slipped through the massive door. She turned back, to make sure no could tell she'd been there before dashing to the back stairway.

Her light tread was silent on the narrow stairs, and she came out into the main house just off the blue salon. She walked past the open door where sun puddled on the room's blue silk furnishings. The salon had been her mother's favorite room to spend mornings.

"Good morning, ma'am." Betsy, one of the downstairs parlor maids, stopped to bob a curtsy as she came around the corner and caught sight of Marion.

"Good morning." Marion paused, one hand on the grand staircase balustrade. "How is your baby sister? Any change?"

"Mum says there's not much improvement." Betsy's usual cheerful demeanor faded. "If she don't get better soon, we'll be sending her to the country to one of them sick farms."

Marion motioned the parlor maid closer. "I should have some medicine this afternoon that might help. Come find me after tea."

"Oh, thank you." Her bright eyes filled with tears. "I don't know what any of us would do without you." Her face paled as her eyes locked on something—or someone behind Marion. Betsy gulped, bobbed another quick curtsy and scuttled away.

Marion turned, not bothering to look up. "Yes, Matilda?" Her lady's maid was a study in why a person couldn't judge a book by its cover. Her rosy cheeks, twinkling blue eyes, and motherly figure hid the heart of a cannibal.

"I had your costume for this morning's activities laid out." Her eyes flicked up and down the gray silk. "I seem to have missed that particular dress when choosing."

Did nothing get by this woman? Marion mounted the stairs and swept past her, refusing to engage. She'd learned long ago that there was no winning this battle. "We can go over my day's plans in my sitting room. Please ring for my morning pot of chocolate."

Matilda sniffed. "Yes, my lady."

Once inside her suite, Marion settled at her dressing table. She avoided staring at her reflection in the mirror by turning slightly toward the open draperies at the window. She could hear the call of a wren perched somewhere within the towering oak, hidden by the deep red of the turning leaves. Its sweet song reminded her of her mother. Every spring they'd spied on that particular bird as she readied her nest, protected her eggs, and raised a family.

Matilda took up a brush and began to work through Marion's long, unruly curls. Marion hated her hair. Well, to be truthful, not her hair exactly. Rather the length. She had her mother's hair. But that elegant lady had worn hers in a short mass of curls that fit under an aviator's helmet. She'd promised Marion they'd cut her hair together, when she turned sixteen. She blinked back tears, not from the roughness of her lady's maid, but from the promises left unfulfilled when her mother had died.

"Did you enjoy your early morning ride with the Lady Gretta?" Matilda jerked at a particularly stubborn knot.

"Of course." Marion stiffened her neck against the rough treatment. "The morning was lovely and the sunrise spectacular."

"I'll be informing your father."

"As you wish." Marion had long ago learned Matilda's real duty as her maid was to keep tabs on her whereabouts and tattle to her father. Not that he really cared. As long as she stayed away from him and out of trouble, he ignored her.

He'd refused her request to have her mother's maid assigned to her. In one of their few conversations during the week immediately following her mother's accident, he'd informed her Elise was too gentle for a strong-willed daughter like her. No amount of tears or tantrums had swayed him. Elise had been returned back to guild duties and now served as headmistress of the guild headquarters. Matilda had been brought in to care for Marion.

Matilda put down the brush, having wrangled the curls into some semblance of calm, and began the next stage of torture. "Where will you be taking luncheon today?"

"Keep my hair simple. I'll be dining with guild members. I have much to see to this day." That was certainly true. She needed to meet with Dr. Tuck, as well as William. The inventor would be anxious to know how the goggles had performed.

"As soon as I finish, I'll help you into the green wool skirt." Matilda began arranging her hair, ramming in hairpins to hold the curls in place. She stood back and studied her half-finished handiwork. "This should hold up to almost anything you get into on the grounds. Although my hope is you won't be seen by anyone important."

Marion could feel her maid's glare and worked to keep her face neutral. Getting the best of Matilda was one of the few pleasures she could still find in this house.

As voices raised outside her room, Marion and Matilda both turned. Gretta opened the door, at her most imperious. She dismissed the maid who held the tray of chocolate and had obviously tried to announce her. "Are you still about your toilette? You know we have a meeting this morning." She set the tray on the table by the window, her lips forming a pretty frown, and turned to Matilda. "I'll finish her hair while you lay out something suitable. How you keep her in line is more than I can imagine."

Matilda practically cooed at Gretta's conspiratorial tone and bustled into the dressing room.

"You are my hero." Marion whispered as Gretta brought her a cup of steaming chocolate and began to arrange her curls.

Gretta twisted an errant curl and was about to insert a hairpin when she made a small exclamation and bent close over Marion's scalp. "She's rammed in the pins so hard, you're actually bleeding."

"I'm used to it." Marion shrugged. "Complaining only makes her worse."

"I'd like to use some hairpins on that old harridan." Gretta's stormy face showed her true feelings about Marion's maid.

"I thought the green wool skirt with this navy sailor blouse would be appropriate for today." Matilda reappeared with the forest green skirt in her arms. "Don't you agree, Miss Gretta?" The tone she took had none of the edge that accompanied every remark made to Marion.

Gretta patted the last curl into place and turned to the maid, smiling. "That will be perfect, as your choices usually are."

Marion resisted rolling her eyes at Gretta's subterfuge.

Matilda shot a cold look at Marion. "Whenever you're ready, my lady."

Marion strode across the lawn that separated the house from the brick path to the official guild headquarters.

Gretta hurried to catch up and touched her elbow. "We'll be out of sight soon. Slow down and take a deep breath."

"Like that's an option in these stays." Marion fought the urge to tug at her bodice.

"I did not re-lace you that tightly." Gretta gave a little giggle. "It's all in your mind. Imagine how you'd feel if you'd had to endure Matilda's lacing."

"You're right. I'm strung so tight because of the situation, not your lacing." The tension retreated as they rounded the giant boxwood hedge separating the house from the path to the guild headquarters. The pungent scent of the ancient shrub would forever be linked with freedom in her mind. "Some days, I think she will be the death of me."

The short walk to the working offices of the guild was overhung with the branches of giant oak trees. The time gave Marion a chance to regain her temper. They paused at the massive gates and Marion dipped her head to the tiny, ancient gatekeeper, stiff and ramrod straight in his dark uniform complete with gold-fringed epaulets. He dipped his head past an impossibly high collar and then fixed them with a stern expression. When his eyes met Marion's, he allowed the barest of winks. She grinned as he turned and went back inside the small stone guard house. She heard him pull the lever to open the massive brass and copper gates. A hiss of steam escaped as the gates slowly swung open.

"Hey, Gret." Addi exploded out of the doors from the building on the other side of the courtyard and ran down the marble steps. "I thought you two would never get here."

Gretta held up a hand to her brother. "Addison Handleson, how many times do I have to remind you about the necessity of being civil in public?"

Addison skidded to a halt in front of Marion and scanned the walled-in yard. "There's no one here but us." He turned a dark look on his sister. "You could suck the fun out of a hot air balloon."

Gretta drew his attention to the open windows in the building that framed one side of the courtyard. "Just because you don't see anyone around does not mean you're not in public."

"Well, we're here now." Marion laughed and linked her arm with Addison, drawing him back to the building he'd so recently vacated. "Why do you need us?"

Addison wriggled his arm free and grabbed her hand, half-pulling her up the steps. "Will has finished the lightning arrows, and we were just waiting for you to give them a try."

"You have got to quit encouraging him." Gretta fell in beside Marion. "I'm trying to civilize him."

Marion paused inside the marble entry of the guild hall, turning to Gretta. "He's still a boy, with a boy's enthusiasm. Don't let's destroy his youth just yet."

"Boy or not. This world isn't a safe place for those who won't look life full in the face." Gretta's eyes took on a faraway look. "But I'll try to moderate my sisterly instincts."

"Come on." Addison was already at the end of the hall, waiting at the top of stairs that led to the basement laboratory of his mentor and friend.

"All right." Marion hurried to join him. "Never let it be said I kept genius waiting."

They followed Addison as he clattered down the dark stairwell, which opened into a room illuminated by a forest of glowing glass bulbs suspended from the ceiling. The bulbs were of every shape, size, and color. A tall, thin figure, wrapped in a dirty canvas apron and sporting large black gloves, bent over a work bench, peering at a clear liquid bubbling over a single-flame burner.

"William, what on earth is that smell?" Gretta covered her mouth and nose with a gloved hand as a sulphurous odor engulfed them.

At her voice, Will, his eyes covered by brass goggles and a clip holding his nose closed, jumped and turned. "So sorry." He turned the off the flame under the liquid and rushed to the tiny basement windows, motioning to Addison. "Quick, give me a hand." Once the windows were open, he shifted his goggles to his head, pushing his red hair into disorderly spikes and tufts. He grabbed a handful of papers from the table and began fanning the air.

"We didn't mean to surprise you." Marion gazed up again at the mass of bulbs sprouting from the ceiling. They were so beautiful she wanted to reach out and cup one in her hand, but knew from previous visits that doing so would result in a rather painful burn. "Every time we're here, you've added more of these bulbs. It's almost as bright as day in here now." She wiped a bead of perspiration from her brow. "And rather warm."

"I've been trying to find a balance between the heat and the light." William continued to wave his makeshift fan. "These incandescent bulbs of Mr. Edison provide a steady, bright light, but they do give off a good bit of heat."

Marion wandered around the large room, her shoe heels echoing on the stone floor. As she examined the various oddities jumbled on the counters and tables, she kept her hands clasped behind her back. Some of Will's experiments could be dangerous to touch. "Did you have something specific you wanted to show me?"

"It's not me as much as Dr. Tuck who has something. He should be here shortly." He handed his papers to Addison, walked to the counter that held a microscope and a tray of glass slides lined up with military precision. "How did the goggles work this morning?"

"Just like you said they would, of course. You never let me down." Marion grinned. "How soon can you get enough for all of us?"

Will blushed and the freckles on his nose stood out in stark relief. His self-effacing ways and boyish features made it hard for Marion to remember that he was a few years her senior—in age. "By the end of the week."

"Good morning." They turned toward the doorway as Dr. Tuck stooped to enter the laboratory. "I'm glad to see everyone's here."

"I got them here as quick as I could." Addison returned the papers to their place on the work bench.

"Addi." Gretta rolled her eyes at her brother's borderline disrespect.

"I'm sure you did, my young friend. And no small feat it was." Dr. Tuck winked at Gretta and patted Addison on the back as he crossed the room to join Marion and Will at the microscope.

Marion pulled the small leather pouch with the morning's gold from her belt. "It's little enough, I know." She hefted the bag once in her palm, the weight no more than a few ounces, before passing the pouch to Dr. Tuck.

"We are getting closer." He took the gold and his hand clasped hers. "And your ... ah ... donations are making the solution possible."

"Does this mean you've found the source of the illness?" Gretta's grey eyes filled with hope and she moved to stand beside Marion. "Can we offer a course of treatment, or even share how to prevent infection?"

Dr. Tuck clucked his tongue. He stuffed the pouch in a pocket of his vest and removed his frock coat, handing it to Will to hang on a peg driven into the brick wall. "I only wish it were so simple." He held out his arms as Will helped him into a stained canvas coat. He chose a slide and held it up to the light. "These bulbs are a welcome addition." He turned to grin at William before squinting again at the slide. He returned that one to the tray, chose another and repeated his inspection. This one appeared to please him, so he inserted the slide under the lens of the scope and bent almost double to gaze through the tiny tube at the top of the microscope. His large hands managed the finicky work with an unexpected delicacy. "This germ doesn't behave correctly." He made a sound of irritation and he motioned to Marion to take a look.

"What am I looking for?" She bent to peer into the scope.

"Notice the rigid conformity of the germs. They move with a clock-like precision that one doesn't normally find in the natural world."

As her eyes adjusted, she gasped. A miniature world lay before her, populated by gray and pink ovoids, fanning out from the center in a perfect spiral. They seemed to pulse in unison, as if nodding to an unseen drummer. Every other time she'd peered into this miniature world, the shapes had moved independent of each other. These appeared to operate as if driven by a single entity.

She raised her eyes to meet Dr. Tuck's worried frown. "What does this mean?"

"We think they've been engineered." William jostled Marion aside and bent to take a look. "Someone has found a way to manufacture germs." He lifted his head and his face glowed with awe and curiosity. "Do you know what this means?"

"Nothing good, I would say." Gretta glared at Will and inserted herself in place to take a look. "Considering it's our children who are suffering at the hands of this evil invention."

"But if one person can invent something like this, doesn't it mean we can reverse the symptoms and provide a cure through the same manner?" Marion posed her question to both Dr. Tuck and William.

"Perhaps." Dr. Tuck removed his spectacles and pinched the bridge of his nose. "But we don't have the first notion of how to begin. It's—"

"The miniaturization is what has us flummoxed," Will broke in. "I could manufacture small machines and make them behave in a similar fashion." He squinted at the tray of slides. "They'd be tiny to us, but we'd still be able to see them with just our eyes. I don't know of anyone who could work this far into the unseen."

"This is all well and good, I suppose." Gretta put her hands on her hips. "But what do these ..." She waved a hand in the direction of the microscope as she stumbled for a word. "... things do?"

"Ah, that we do know." Dr. Tuck replaced his spectacles and moved to a chalk board attached to the wall opposite the pegs. He studied the numbers and symbols that covered the board before he erased a corner. He drew what Marion recognized as a pair of human lungs. Beside them he added one of the spirals she'd seen under the scope. "These little buggers come in through the blood and begin by attacking the lining of a host's lungs—in effect puncturing and inhabiting the millions of tiny sacs that make it possible for us to breath."

"Begin?" Marion felt a spiral of fear unwind in her stomach. "It doesn't end with the breathing trouble?"

"No." Tuck set down the chalk. "We believe they also inhabit other organs—heart, liver, even the skin. They change the very stuff that makes us human." His eyes took on a faraway look. "I've seen something similar, but we've got to do more testing to be sure."

Before Marion could ask him more, Gretta jumped in, "Why just the children? Why isn't everyone getting sick?"

"These tiny machines are powered by something within our bodies." Will's eyes pleaded with the doctor, who nodded his permission for Will to continue. "There is something within the bloodstream of children that enables them to grow. This substance also appears to provides the power for these invaders."

"Can you isolate and block this substance somehow?" Addison studied the chalk board, then frowned. "Of course not. It would mean the children would stop growing."

Dr. Tuck beamed at Addison's understanding. "You see our dilemma now." He turned back to the board. "It's also why taking children to the country appears to help—in the earliest stages. The fresh air makes breathing easier."

"But being in the country hastens the progression of the disease, doesn't it?" Marion could follow the logic he'd begun. "By providing the children with an environment that promotes health and growth, we're providing the attackers with more of what makes them strong."

"Very good, Lady Marion." Dr. Tuck fairly beamed at her quick grasp.

"And that's why we don't see any children returning from the country farms." Gretta frowned. "But why do those who run the farms continue to transport wagon loads of children if none survive?"

Dr. Tuck touched his nose with a knobby finger. "Excellent question. That is just one more piece of the puzzle we're facing."

"And one that's much more likely to be solved on full stomachs than on empty ones." A stately woman stood in the doorway of the basement room, her arms folded across a snowy white shirtwaist. Her once golden hair had been swept into a practical chignon. One eyebrow quirked above her snapping green eyes. "Miss Marion, I do hope you'll be joining the staff for luncheon."

Warmth suffused Marion's heart at the sight of Elise. Her mother's former maid had been her comforter in those dark days following Lady Ravenswood's fatal accident. "I'm pleased to say I will." She crossed the room and kissed the older woman on the cheek.

Elise patted Marion and studied her face. "You're not getting enough sleep. I can always tell."

"You needn't worry. I'm in perfect health, as always." Marion turned back to the others and away from the close scrutiny. "Are you all coming?"

Dr. Tuck cleared his throat and exchanged a look with William. "Our time will be much better spent here. But perhaps a tray could be sent down?"

"I'll see to it." Elise turned a questioning look at the others. "Miss Gretta? Addison?"

"I'll stay here with Will." Addison caught Gretta's frown and caught her arm. "I'm not in the way, I promise."

"It's true." Will bobbed his head. "He brings a fresh way of looking at things when the doctor and I get stuck."

Gretta studied Will and her brother for a moment. "Very well. It will just be myself and Marion imposing on the guild's hospitality today." She joined them as they climbed the stairs. "It's just as well because there's something Elise and I have been meaning to discuss with you."

Chapter Four

Lord Edward Stanton, the heir-apparent of the temporary Guildmaster, leaned against the doorway of his main stables, one booted foot elevated on the stonework foundation just so. What was keeping that dratted groom? He tapped the riding crop he carried against his boot. Old Durstin should know better than to keep his master waiting.

"We're on our way, yer lordship." The voice of the groom floated out to Edward from the depths of the massive stone structure, as if anticipating his displeasure. "Man O' War had a wee bit of internal upset. Took a mite longer to get him ready." A hiss of steam accompanied the metallic ring of hooves on stone, and the groom continued to natter away at the equine. "Now don't you get excited. It's in top condition you are now. Pride of the master's stables, I say."

"Oh, shut up." Lord Stanton stepped away from the doorway to examine the stallion as the groom led him into the bright sun of the stone-cobbled yard. Edward's chest expanded as he gazed on his latest creation. Easily eighteen hands, but not just the size distinguished this equine. Man O' War was the perfect union between horse and machine. The technology he used integrated the latest steam devices grafted on and within a living, breathing animal. The massive hindquarters were a miracle of intricate cogs, pistons, and flesh.

Edward completed a circuit around the horse, studying him from every angle. Aesthetically speaking, the equine was as much of a masterpiece as any painting gracing the walls of his manor house. The original black of the horse's coat was now set off by the glint of steel and copper. The intricately carved and tastefully adorned saddle was now a permanent part of the animal, relegating the tiresome task of saddling and unsaddling one's mount a thing of the past.

This innovation had been carried onto the horse's head, which now sported a refashioned bit, with shiny brass rings for the reins to snap onto. These additions also aided the comfort of the horse. No more saddle sores or irritated mouth from an ill-fitting bit. Although the comfort of the horse had never been one of his prime considerations, he couldn't argue that a horse performed better without the impediment of pain.

And performance was what mattered most.

The horse whinnied and tossed his head, jerking the old groom off balance. Durstin stumbled into the horse and fell when the animal shied away.

"Here now, that's a good fellow. Nothing to fear." Edward grabbed at the dangling reins and ran a hand along the restive horse's neck. He followed the line of the neck down to the front leg, checking for any damage. He finished quieting the horse before he turned on the groom. "How dare you endanger my horse with your clumsiness? I'll have you whipped within an inch of your miserable life if you cost me so much as a penny more."

"Tis sorry I am, yer lordship." The groom rose unsteadily to his feet and pulled his cap from his head. "These old bones don't respond the way I need these days. I'll make sure it don't happen again."

Edward huffed and turned back to the horse. "See that it doesn't."

"See that what doesn't happen again?" An older man strode into the yard from the gateway that led to the house, took in the scene and began to laugh. "Are you bullying the staff again?"

"Very funny, Father." Edward's glare quieted his father's guffaw.

"Tis my fault, Lord Stanton." The groom stole a quick look at Edward. "I'll just be gettin' back to my work, with yer permission."

"That dolt nearly undid seven years' work with a bit of clumsiness." Edward watched the groom disappear into the stables before turning to his father. "Come see my magnificent creation."

"You have managed a feat no one else ever imagined." Lord Stanton pulled his monocle from a vest pocket and peered at the equine. "I'll say it to any who'll listen. There's none who can match the brilliance of my boy."

Edward grimaced. "What news from the Queen? Has she officially designated you as Guildmaster? Can we make the announcement at the Pilots Guild Masquerade as planned?"

"I have had word." Lord Stanton fumbled with an official-looking paper, now wadded up in his hand. "It's not the news for which we'd hoped."

"Let me see that." Edward jerked the parchment from his father, still holding the reins. He scanned the contents. "What is that stupid woman thinking?" He balled up the paper and threw it on the ground.

"Hush now." Lord Stanton put a hand on Edward's arm and looked around the vacant yard. "That's the Queen you're speaking of. We can't have anyone carrying tales of disrespect to her—especially right now."

"What is she waiting for? She's been *investigating* for four long years." Edward shook off his father's arm and turned back to the stables. "Durstin, get out here."

"Yes, yer lordship?" The man appeared in an instant. He must have been lurking just inside the door. There truly were ears and eyes everywhere.

"Turn Man O' War out in the south pasture for some exercise. I won't be riding today. Plans have changed." He squinted up at the blue sky, dotted with clouds. "And keep an eye on the weather. We had the deuce of a time getting him in last time it rained."

"Of course, sir. I'll see to it." The groom took the horse's lead and bobbed his head as he led the horse toward the field gate.

Edward softened his expression and then turned back to his father. "I'm frustrated for you. You've done so much for the guild since that traitorous excuse of a Guildmaster was hanged. I won't stand idly by to see you insulted like this." They both knew that wasn't exactly the truth of what had occurred but they never discussed the situation.

Lord Stanton winked at him. "You're a good son." He reached down and picked up the paper that lay on the ground, smoothing it against his paunch. "But you know it's not for my sake that I agreed to the position of Guildmaster. The Pilots Guild, so much more than any of the others, needs a strong leader." He poked a pudgy finger into his son's chest. "They need you. And they can only get *you* through me."

"So where do we go from here?" Edward motioned for his father to accompany him back to the house.

"I suppose we're back to waiting on Her Majesty's pleasure. I promised I'd do my best for you." Lord Stanton heaved a sigh and frowned. "But it appears we must wait a while longer before it's official."

"But you're already carrying out the duties of the station. You've regained order and quelled the plot on the Queen's life." Edward slapped his crop against his boot. Did she suspect their machinations? She must, and was stalling for time as she hunted for proof. Well he was tired of waiting, and he had a trick up his sleeve that she didn't suspect. He turned and faced his father. "I think you've waited long enough."

"What do you have in mind?" His father frowned at him.

"Several things. But first, we need to prepare to announce you as the new Guildmaster." He held up a hand as Lord Stanton began to sputter. "With or without the Queen's consent."

"Are you mad?" His father looked around, searching for someone near enough to overhear. No one was in sight.

"Hear me out." Edward rubbed his hands and walked toward the house. "She's not in so strong a position herself. With the might of the strongest guild in the realm fully behind you it won't be easy for her to level charges—no matter what she finds."

"It might work at that." Lord Stanton fell in step with his son. "But it's a risk. We've waited so long, I'd hate to fail now."

"Then let's stack the deck." Edward gave him a tight grin.

"What are you planning, my boy?"

"Wouldn't you say it's high time for me to find a wife?" He covered his heart with his hand. "Now that I've helped you with guild business, I can once again turn my ear to the siren call of love."

Lord Stanton stared at him in open-mouthed surprise, then closed his mouth and swallowed hard. "The siren call of love?"

Edward threw back his head and laughed. "And here I thought you knew me so well. Of course, I have a wife picked out." He clapped his father on the shoulder. "And I'm certain when I tell you who she is, you'll see the wisdom in my choice."

They had reached the portico off the west side of the house. Edward knocked his boots free of stable mud, and they made their way to the study. He plopped into one of the leather chairs that flanked the massive fireplace.

Lord Stanton closed the door firmly and joined him. "Do I get to know the name of the young lady you've chosen to honor?"

Edward laced his fingers behind his head and leaned back. "The woman I've chosen is Lady Marion Ravenswood."

Elise led the two girls back up the stairs. "I took the liberty of ordering luncheon served in your private dining room for the three of us."

Marion shot her a glance. "It's not really mine. It's Father's."

"You've spent more time there in recent years than he has," Gretta said with some heat.

Elise gave Gretta a stern look before turning to Marion. "You and your family both suffered tragedy, but you put the guild above your own hurt. Therefore, I chose to name the room yours, no matter what convention dictates."

Marion swallowed hard against the lump that rose in her throat—the good opinion of Elise mattered so much to her. They came out into the marble lobby of the main floor and crossed to the brass cage that held the elevator.

"Good day, mistress." Antonio, the lift operator tipped his gold-trimmed cap to her. His red uniform was as perfectly pressed as always—the only wrinkles visible were in his ancient but grinning face. He held open the polished gate and waited for the three women to enter before joining them in the elevator. He'd been conveying those on guild business up the six stories for as long as Marion could remember. He carefully latched the door and twisted the brass knob. A hiss of steam escaped as they began their ascent to the Guildmaster's suite of offices at the top of the building.

Marion stood close to the brass bars enclosing the elevator and counted the floors as they zipped past, a habit she'd learned as a child while riding with her grandfather. Antonio twisted the knob slowly, and the lift seemed to float to a smooth stop lined up perfectly with the entry to the Guildmaster offices. He unlatched the gate and stood to one side, gesturing them into the spacious foyer of the suite. "All safe and sound among the clouds."

Gretta gave a delicate sniff, but she rushed ahead of Marion. "It seems they've delivered our lunch."

Marion strode to a doorway that branched off the left of the foyer, her mouth watering. She stopped just inside the dining room, gazing at the plentiful offering resting on the sideboard. There was a heaping platter of neatly sliced roast fowl as well as several steaming bowls with vegetables floating in different sauces.

Along with these were rolls, jams, and myriad other tantalizing tidbits obviously orchestrated to tempt a lady's appetite.

James, the young man Marion had recently promoted to the position of guild butler, stood just inside the door. He fidgeted, tugging at his coat. "I hope lunch meets with your approval."

She put a reassuring hand on his arm. "The food looks perfect. You're doing a grand job." She turned to Elise, knowing quite well who had planned the menu. "Quite a bit of food, don't you think, for three ladies taking luncheon?"

Elise lifted her chin. "I told you I was worried you weren't getting enough to eat."

"Well, I don't care *why* you did it. I'm just glad you did." Gretta brushed past them and picked up a china plate, which she proceeded to fill, picking and choosing with dainty fingers.

Marion laughed and joined her at the sideboard. Elise had included many of Marion's favorite dishes. Her stomach gave a quick rumble as the enticing odors reminded her she'd skipped breakfast in exchange for the early morning raid.

One end of the formal mahogany table was covered in a snowy linen cloth and the women gathered there for their repast. A maid appeared from the nearby butler's pantry with a fresh pot of tea.

"James, I think that will be all. I can see to things here." Elise motioned the maid to leave the tea on the table.

"As you wish, ma'am."

Elise watched the two servants leave, then turned to Gretta. "You said you had something you needed to discuss with me."

"Indeed we do." Gretta jumped in, even as Marion tried to glare her into silence. "We ran into an old friend on this morning's foray."

Marion groaned inwardly as Elise deliberately set down her fork and stared at them. "You were recognized?"

"It's not as bad as you might think." Marion kept her tone matter-of-fact. "It was Robin ... Robin Loxley."

"I see." Elise's tone was unreadable. "Go on."

"He just caught me by surprise." Marion took a sip of tea.

"Actually, it was Marion who caught him by surprise." Gretta clapped her hands together. "She was brilliant. She let him ambush the automatons, and then we ambushed him."

Elise leaned forward. "Something like this is exactly what Dr. Tuck and I have been worried about. Now you must see the need to give up on this ridiculous notion."

"Give up? I'll never give up." Heat suffused Marion's face and she pushed back from the table. "There are children out there dying."

"Let's not jump to anything drastic." Gretta extended a hand to Marion, even as she made eye contact with Elise. "He's as much of an outlaw as the Maiden of Iron. So we know he won't go to the authorities. This was a good learning experience."

"The fact is, you've been recognized. The stakes are just too high for you to continue this charade." Elise used her napkin to dab at the corners of her mouth. "I was never comfortable with this method of obtaining funds to support the work for a cure."

"The choice isn't yours to make." Marion's heart was in her voice. "I love you and value your opinion." She got up and walked to the window. "But the choice is mine to make. I will continue to do what I think is best for the guild ... until my father returns to his duties." She stared out at the jagged outline of London, willing herself to see beyond the physical. Somewhere the answer lurked, and her destiny was to find the solution.

"And if I choose to tell your father?" Elise moved to stand behind Marion. She laid a hand on her shoulder and turned Marion to face her. "I want to support you, I have supported you. But I won't allow you to risk yourself needlessly."

"You wouldn't dare." Tears burned hot with the need to fall, but Marion stood ramrod straight. "We discussed this. You agreed to keep my secret."

Elise held up a finger. "I agreed on the one condition that you weren't in any more danger than absolutely necessary."

"Nothing has changed. I'm in no more danger now than I was before." Marion turned back to the window.

"I disagree." Elise returned to her seat at the table. "I've been uneasy about your role as the Maiden of Iron for the past few weeks. Her existence is being whispered about everywhere. Your alter ego is just too well known."

"But what of the children?" Gretta moved to stand with Marion. "We cannot give up our search when the cure is so close."

"I'm not suggesting we give up. I believe there's a better way to continue." She motioned them back to the table. "I think it's time for you to return to the search for a husband."

"A husband?" Marion bit back a laugh. "How could that possibly help. A betrothal was exactly what got me *into* this situation."

"Hear me out." Elise picked up the teapot and refilled her cup before continuing. "I know you may disagree, but I truly believe your father's retreat from the world is fueled by guilt, not anger. Seeing you safely on the way to the alter would assuage some of his self-loathing."

Try as she might, Marion couldn't force words past her seething thoughts as fragments of conversations and confrontations flashed through her mind. The attack of Lord Maylon, the duel, her father's blame as her brother's body was laid to rest. Most of all, the cutting words he wielded like a blade after the funeral, slashing at her until her soul lay bare and exposed.

The touch of Gretta's arm around her as she forced a handkerchief into Marion's hand brought her back to the present. Only then did Marion notice she was now seated with silent tears streaming down her cheeks.

Elise had kneeled on her other side, stroking her hair. "I know what he did and what he said when David was killed. Your father was a man tormented by poor decisions, and you were the only one left. You bore the brunt of his self-loathing."

Gretta turned on Elise. "Then how could you possible suggest she open herself back up to this?"

"Because I know she's strong enough." Elise rose and looked down at Marion. "I know doing so will be hard. But there'll be no going forward till you can make peace with the past."

CHAPTER FIVE

At the knock on the study door, Robin looked over the papers on his desk at John, who avoided his eyes. "Yes?" Robin called as he slid the papers they'd been studying into a drawer as the door opened.

"You sent for me?" Dr. Tuck's large form filled the doorway.

"Not me." Robin glared at John.

He returned Robin's glare with one of his own. "I asked Duncan to find you. We ran into a spot of trouble earlier and Robin could use your assistance."

Robin glanced at his useless arm. "I was going to send for him ... eventually."

"Hmmm." Dr. Tuck set down his dark leather bag and advanced on Robin and took hold of his arm. "Push up the sleeve past the elbow and let me have a look. What exactly happened?"

"I was caught by an unexpected jolt of electricity." When John opened his mouth to add something to the explanation, Robin cut him off with a gesture before rolling up his sleeve. Tuck had his back to John and missed the interaction.

"I've warned you that electricity can interfere with the arm's performance." The doctor felt around the elbow with his thumb and forefinger, finally finding the spot he wanted and applying pressure. After only a moment, the arm jerked, and Robin's eyes widened.

"You fixed my arm." He flexed his arm, rotated the wrist, and wiggled his fingers. "What did you do?"

"There's actually a reset button just under the skin of your inner elbow." He shook his finger at Robin. "Resetting's not always enough though, so stay away from live current."

"The arm feels good to me." He grinned at Tuck. "I should have known you'd have added a trick or two to your design." Robin continued to move his arm, testing mobility. "Can I offer you a cup of tea—in addition to my heartfelt thanks?"

"Save your thanks for John. Waiting much longer could have meant opening you up again." Tuck gathered up his bag. "I've got to get back to work. I've a project that's urgent right now."

Duncan opened the door a crack and peered in. "Holden and Marcus are here with the report your requested."

"I'll leave you to your business." Dr. Tuck left as Duncan ushered the two men inside.

"Good, I've been waiting." Robin took a seat behind his desk, and John eased his bulk into the leather chair in front of it.

"Have you managed to earn your keep?" Robin studied the two burly men. He saw their hungry looks take in the littered tea table, and he waved them toward the food. "By all means help yourselves."

They grinned at him and attacked the remaining scones.

Robin lifted an eyebrow at Duncan. "Didn't you think to feed them before you brought them to me?"

"They said their information couldn't wait." Duncan glared at the men. "It appears they were wrong."

"Well, Holden, do you have something to report?" Robin directed his question to the shorter of the two men gobbling the leftovers.

Holden's mouth was too full to answer. He poured a cup of the tea, took a quick swig and noisily cleared his throat. "That I do."

Robin exchanged a look with John before he turned to Duncan. "I'll not get a coherent word till they've eaten. Go ask Annie to bring another tray."

"Thank you, sir." The taller man had also poured a cup of tea, draining the pot. He frowned and held up the cup. "You wouldn't have something to sweeten this brew would you?"

Robin laughed and opened one of the desk drawers. He took out a silver flask and tossed it to the man. "This should loosen your tongue."

Marcus opened the flask and poured a bit of amber liquid into his cup before passing the flask to Holden.

"We've been following Lord Edward like you asked." Holden added some to his cup before walking the flask back to Robin. "He's a wily one, and not easy to track."

"How so?" Robin's look was intent.

"He never travels the same way twice. It's not just the routes he takes either. One time he'll be in a carriage. The next, he'll be astride one of those demon horses of his." Marcus gave a shudder. "It's not right, doing that to a living thing."

"Them things can run for hours." Holden grinned. "But the smell of 'em makes light work of tracking."

"Smell?" John's eyebrows rose. "Have you somehow managed to become a bloodhound?"

"Don't have to," said Marcus. "Those mechanical mounts give off a powerful odor."

"You mean like an engine?" Robin leaned forward. "Be specific, the details could be important."

"Not just like an engine." He closed his eyes for a moment and paused. "It smelled almost like a machine that's died."

"Hmmm. Perhaps his creations aren't quite as complete as he's led the world to believe." Robin fingered his chin, then pulled out the papers he'd shoved in the drawer and began making notes.

Annie bustled into the room, followed by Duncan carrying a loaded tea tray. She cleared off the remains of the previous tray and turned to the two men still standing. "It's not good for the digestion to eat while you stand. Sit, and I'll pour you a fresh cuppa." She narrowed her eyes. "But I'll not be adding anything extra to your brew."

Robin laughed as the men took their seats. "Is that all you have for me? The smell of a dead machine, and he's hard to track?" He quirked an eyebrow. "I think that's hardly worth the trouble of having Annie bring you tea." He watched as she handed Duncan the tray and closed the door behind him.

The men exchanged looks, and Holden cleared his throat before he began. "We also have all the information you asked for about the big party his lordship is throwing day after tomorrow."

"Robin?" John folded his arms across his chest. "What are you planning?"

Robin waved him to silence, then gestured for Holden to continue.

"I was talking to a ... a ..." He gestured to Marcus.

Marcus winked. "We knows someone on the inside, as it were. Turns out the Queen has put off naming that scoundrel as permanent Guildmaster." He held up a hand when Robin made a move to speak. "But those scalawags are going ahead with the announcement."

"They wouldn't dare." John shot to his feet and began to pace. "Your contact must be mistaken. Even Edward wouldn't risk the ire of the Queen with a stunt like this."

"Don't be too sure." Robin leaned back, put his boots on his desk, and stared at the ceiling. "It does make sense. The Queen's popularity is at an all-time low, what with all the children in the country suddenly falling ill. If Edward and his father play this right, they could come out smelling like roses."

Holden's Adam's apple kept time with his vigorous nod. "That's exactly what our contact said. He also told us that there would be another announcement, but hadn't been able to find out exactly what. Seems it was more of a personal sort of thing, probably not important."

"You're actually going to break in on the masquerade?" John moved to stand in front of Robin's desk, placed both hands on the surface and leaned forward. "You cannot be serious."

"What? I can't imagine what you're talking about." Robin feigned innocence.

"He'll be expecting you." John lumbered back to his chair and dropped into it, shaking his head.

"And we wouldn't want to disappoint our old friend, would we?" Robin turned to Annie. "You raised me with better manners than that, didn't you?"

Annie made an exasperated noise and pointed a finger at him. "You'll not be using me to justify your shenanigans." She held his eyes for a long moment, then left the room, closing the door behind her softly.

Marcus shifted in his seat. "They *are* expecting you to make an appearance. Part of Edward's plan is to present you to the authorities and use that to wring concessions from the crown."

"That will never happen." Robin jumped up from his chair and went to the large chalkboard affixed to the old brick. "But we must make plans to guarantee a smooth entrance and exit."

Marion let out a deep breath as she closed her bedroom door behind her. She'd made it to her room without encountering Matilda. She laid the notebooks she'd gathered from the guild office on the writing desk nestled in her bay window, and checked her reflection in the mirror. The green skirt and navy sailor blouse were still in good condition, but her tartan tie had tilted crazily to the left. Retying took only a moment and then, she turned her attention to her hair. Ringlets had begun to escape and now framed her face. Oh, well, no help for it. She'd rather die than ring for Matilda and endure another torture session.

Now that passing inspection from her imperious lady's maid was no longer a worry, she settled at the desk to organize the notes she had from the day. The sheaf of papers Dr. Tuck had given her interested her the most, so she started with those.

A knock at the door made her jump. "Yes, who is it?" She pulled a book over the top of the notes just as Matilda entered the room.

"You have a gentleman caller, my lady. It's Lord Edward." Matilda stared at the scattered papers on Marion's desk. "If you'd like to go down, I can tidy this up for you."

"I can see to this. Make sure our guest is served tea, and I'll be down directly." There was no way she'd let Matilda get her hands on these notes.

Matilda bobbed her head, even as she glared at Marion. "As you wish."

What on earth could Lord Edward want with her? They'd known each other all their lives, but she couldn't remember the last time they'd actually exchanged pleasantries, much less taken tea together. He'd been a spiteful little boy, always making mischief and then blaming someone else. Perhaps he'd changed. He deserved the benefit of the doubt.

She took only a moment to gather her papers. With a quick look at the door, she entered her dressing room and crossed to the south wall. Pushing aside the garments hanging there, she pried open a small door hidden behind the molding. With difficulty, she managed to add the papers to the stack already inside the small cubby. She'd soon have to transfer this lot to the big safe in the underground airship.

Back in her main room, she smoothed her dress once more and slipped out of her room.

Marion paused at the door of the main salon. A silver tea service sat on the table, teapot steaming, while Edward stood at the huge picture window, his profile sharply outlined by the strong afternoon sun.

He caught sight of her and moved to join her, extending his hand. "I hope you don't mind the intrusion, Lady Marion."

"It's no intrusion at all." She allowed him to seat her behind the teapot. "Your name just caught me off guard."

"As well it might." He took a seat across from her. "I've been remiss in calling on you since my father took over as Guildmaster."

She poured a cup and passed it to him. "I must be behind the times as buried as we are here. I hadn't heard of the Queen's confirmation."

His face hardened for a brief second before he waved a hand. "I'm certain that's only a matter of time. Father has done a magnificent job piecing the guild back together after that nasty unpleasantness with Guildmaster Loxley."

Marion poured herself a cup and took a sip. "Is that why you're here? Guild business? If so, you'd best arrange an appointment with my father."

Edward set his cup down on the table and leaned forward. "Lady Marion, may I be frank with you?"

The hair on the back of Marion's neck prickled. "Of course. How may I be of service?"

"I'm hoping we can help each other." He cleared his throat. "I'm not unaware of your treatment at the hands of that vile cad, Maylon."

Warmth suffused her face, and Marion held up a hand to stop him. "I'd rather not discuss that topic."

He grabbed her hand. "I would never in a million years offer you insult. Your treatment since that incident has been shameful." He brought her palm to his lips for the lightest brush of his lips. "What I'd like to do is help you erase the memory completely."

"Are you mad?" She pulled her hand away, and he freed her instantly. "I'm sure you know what aligning yourself with me would mean." She took another sip of tea before answering. "In the eyes of the guilds, I'm damaged goods, not fit as the wife of a Guildmaster."

"And yet that's what your birth has destined you to become." He clicked his tongue. "Only a fool would hold what happened against you."

"Please do not call my father a fool."

"I didn't intend to insult your father. I cannot begin to understand the loss he must feel." He got up and began to pace. "I can see I've handled this poorly. Let me begin again."

"Of course." She set her tea aside and met his eyes.

"What I'm proposing is a partnership. Of course, we would marry. But the partnership would go beyond being husband and wife. We would jointly manage both the Pilots Guild and the Engineers Guild. Our alliance could usher in a new age of cooperation and advancement." He took a seat beside her on the settee. "I know it's been your genius that's kept the Engineers Guild running while your father has been indisposed. You're the partner I've dreamed of my entire life. A woman who shares my passion and my intellect."

Marion's mind churned. Could he be the answer she'd been waiting for? She'd long ago given up the dream of marrying for love. But a partnership of equals? Without emotion to cloud things, this possibility held promise. Could she trust him? She got up and walked to the bookcase, running her fingers across the spines. Her father would have to approve the match, but she doubted he cared anymore who she married.

Edward came up behind her and touched her lightly on the arm. "I'm not asking for a love match."

"You must have read my mind." She turned to face him. "Love is a useless emotion and can only get a person in trouble." She swallowed. Never again would she make the mistake of looking at marriage as anything except a business arrangement.

He clapped his hands. "That's my girl. I knew you'd be the perfect partner for me."

"Don't celebrate yet." She wanted to roll her eyes at his boyish outburst. "There's still my father to convince."

"Never fear my powers of persuasion." He put his hand on his heart. "Is he here now? Will he see me?"

Marion walked over to a small square box, set into the wall next to the door. She pushed one of the buttons. "I've summoned his man. He'll know if Father is available."

Edward peered at the box. "Leave it to the engineers to have a contraption that saves running up and down the stairs. You must have the laziest servants in the country."

"Hardly." She gestured toward the tea table. "I'll pour you a fresh cup while we wait."

Edward had barely settled into the gray tufted chair when an elderly man entered. "You rang for me, my lady?"

"Thank you, Nathaniel." Her heart warmed at the sight of the faithful retainer. "Lord Edward would like to see my father. Is he available?"

"His Lordship has left word he is not to be disturbed." The servant frowned as he looked from Marion to Edward.

Marion knew the reason for his hesitation. Over the last year, her father had taken more and more to using spirits to dull his tragedy. He was probably passed out across his bed. He usually managed to make his way to dinner, though. Her eyes narrowed. "Very well. Inform the cook there'll be a guest for dinner." There was more than one way to get past her father's self-imposed seclusion.

CHAPTER SIX

After Edward had left, promising to return for dinner, Marion scribbled a note for Gretta and handed the envelope to a footman. "Deliver this immediately." She rang once again for Nathaniel, pacing around the salon until he arrived.

"Was there something else, my lady?"

She crossed the room to face him. "Whatever you have to do, I need you to make certain my father is at dinner tonight."

"He was in his cups early today. So he should ... uh ... be presentable by this evening." Nathaniel frowned. "But sometimes he takes things into his head and won't budge."

"I know he can be difficult, but you of all people can manage him." Marion put a hand on his arm. "I've had a proposal."

A broad grin cut across his lines face. "That's very good to hear. From the young man who was here earlier? And he'll be wanting to speak to your father after dinner?"

A smile tugged at the corners of her mouth as he lapsed into his native brogue. "Yes, to both questions."

"We've all been so worried about you." He took her hand in his for just a moment. "If it's in my power, I'll make sure His Lordship is there for dinner."

"Thank you." Marion gave him a brief peck on the cheek.

His face flushed, but the grin widened even more. "You shouldn't be a doin' that, Miss Marion. Isn't proper. I'll see to your father. You go on, and don't worry about it."

"I knew I could count on you." She resisted the urge to plant another kiss on his cheek and just patted it as she slipped past and hurried to her room.

Marion closed the door of her suite and leaned against it, letting out a deep breath. Despite this positive turn of events, she still had work to do with her notes. She looked at the china timepiece on her bureau. There'd be at least an hour to work before Gretta arrived and began to help her with her toilette for the evening.

She didn't take long to retrieve her notes and settle at her desk. Keeping up to date allowed her to sow hope among the guild members whose children were suffering. Hope *was* important, as long as it was served along with a healthy helping of realism.

The knock at Marion's chamber door made her jump. She rubbed her stiff neck as Gretta waltzed in.

Her friend skidded to a stop as she took in the papers strewn across the desk. "This is the big news? Your urgent cry for help was about paperwork?"

"Of course not." Marion gathered the papers. "I know you better than that."

"Well, I should hope so." Gretta eyed her, hands on her hips.

"I need your fashion expertise."

Gretta clapped her hands. "Now that's more like it. What do you have in mind?"

"Just a moment, and I'll give you the details." Marion disappeared into her dressing room to return the papers to the hidey-hole.

"This just gets better and better."

Gretta had settled herself on the chaise lounge, her yellow skirt arranged prettily, when Marion returned to the main room.

Marion took a seat opposite her and then hesitated.

"Well, what?" Gretta leaned forward. "Spit it out."

Marion took a deep breath before beginning. "I had a caller this afternoon—Lord Edward Stanton."

"The traitor's son?"

Heat rose in Marion's cheeks. "As I recall, the traitor was the old Guildmaster, Robin's father."

"That was the official story, but I never believed that report for a moment." She arched an eyebrow. "And as I recall, you didn't either."

Marion avoided her friend's eyes. "I've learned there's always more to the story than appears." She gave in and looked at Gretta. "Anyway, I didn't meet with the father. I met with Edward."

"And ..." Gretta made a motion with her hand.

Marion blew out air. This wasn't going as she'd hoped. "He proposed an alliance—between the two of us."

"Marriage?" Gretta's eyes widened. "He proposed marriage to you?"

"And why would that be so hard to believe?" Marion didn't know whether to be hurt or angry at her friend's reaction.

Gretta reached a conciliatory hand toward her. "I'm not shocked that any man would want you for a wife. I'm shocked that Edward is crawling out of the woodwork to pursue you. Don't you remember what a nasty little boy he was? Always telling tales and stirring up trouble so he could come to the rescue?"

"People change." Marion raised an eyebrow. "I certainly have. Anyway, it's the right time for him to be looking for a bride. I believe his father is, or is about to be, confirmed as Guildmaster of the Pilots Guild."

Gretta clicked her tongue. "That's not what I've heard."

"What have you heard?" Marion knew that Gretta's coquettish manner elicited more confidences and gossip than anyone else in their circle.

"That the Queen isn't convinced." Gretta settled back against the cushion. "She wasn't satisfied with the investigation and has enlisted her own men to look deeper into the matter."

Marion considered her friend's words for a moment. "I don't care. I liked what he had to say. He made sense."

"Convince me." Gretta folded her arms. "What did the esteemed Lord Edward have to say?"

Marion took a moment to focus her thoughts and then shared what Edward proposed. She finished, and her stomach began to twist when Gretta just gazed at her, an inscrutable look in her eye.

"Well?" Marion shifted, waiting for Gretta to comment.

"You're seriously considering this idea? Even after all Elise had to say?"

"Especially after all Elise had to say." Marion rose and began to pace.

"What about love?"

Marion rounded on her, fists clenched. "I cannot—will not—ever make the mistake of looking for love in a business relationship again."

Gretta studied her for a long moment, then came to her feet. "Then we shan't speak of such again. How can I help you?"

Marion expelled the breath she hadn't realized she'd been holding. "I need to look the part tonight. He's coming back to dine, then he'll ask to speak to Father alone."

"Look the part?" Gretta frowned. "I don't even know what that means."

"I don't want anything to deter Edward from pressing his suit or give Father a reason to turn him down. I must be the embodiment of a Guildmaster's daughter—ready for those duties."

Gretta slowly walked around Marion, viewing her from every angle before she spoke again. "I'm still not sure if what you're asking for is possible."

Tears began to blur Marion's vision. "I know I don't have much to work with. I'm not tall like you or blonde. I'm short and my hair never behaves."

"It's not you that's deficient—but the vision of you that you carry in your mind that needs fixing." Gretta took hold of Marion's chin and forced her to meet her eyes. "You don't *look* the part. You *are* the part. You've just been so busy filling the role, you haven't noticed the transformation."

"I'm not certain of that. But it's encouraging to hear you say it." Marion brushed away the moisture that threatened to overflow her eyes. "But can you still help me get dressed?"

Marion took a deep breath and paused at the top of the staircase. Gretta had done wonders with her rebellious curls, smoothing her hair to one side and securing it with an emerald clip below her left ear. The curls cascaded down her shoulder in demur ringlets. She caught Edward watching her, something she couldn't quite read on his impassable face. Oh well, no turning back now. She remembered Gretta's advice and slowed her pace as she descended.

He met her and reached for hand, bowing low, his lips just brushing her fingers. "You look like a vision—the embodiment of a Guildmaster's wife."

"Thank you, my lord." The tension in her back eased at his words. Perhaps she could fulfill the destiny she'd once thought would be forever beyond her reach. That left only her father to convince.

They walked into the parlor, where she found her father standing at the sideboard, holding a decanter and a glass. He turned as they entered and frowned. "I hadn't been informed we'd be entertaining tonight." He directed his ire at Marion.

"My apologies, Father." Heat rose in her cheeks as she crossed the room to him. Why hadn't she remember to remind the servants to remove the decanters? "This was rather a …" How could she explain the last-minute situation without making Edward look bad?

Before she could decide what to say, Edward joined them and bowed to her father. "It's all my fault, Lord Richard."

Her father set down the decanter and studied him. "I'm afraid I don't have the memory I used to. Have we met before?"

"We have indeed." Edward grinned at him. "But years ago, when I was still in short pants. I'm Edward Stanton. My father is Lord Henry Stanford, acting Guildmaster of the Pilots Guild."

"Ah, yes." Lord Richard motioned to the tray that held the whisky canister and glasses. "Would you care for a glass before we go in to dinner?"

Marion fought back a groan and willed Edward to decline. Her father needed food to balance what spirits he'd already imbibed, not an excuse to linger.

"I believe I'll pass, but thank you." Edward pulled out his pocket watch. "I always prefer to relax with a glass of port after, but not before."

Marion could feel her father's eyes on her, but she kept her expression neutral.

"Dinner is served." Ambrose, their personal butler, in his formal evening uniform, entered the parlor. Nathaniel had primed the staff and made sure they were ready, even if he hadn't been able to control her father.

"About time." Her father stomped past her without offering his arm. Surely another purposeful slight. Oh, well, she hoped the gaffe wouldn't prejudice Lord Edward against her. He obviously knew of her difficulties since he'd alluded to them earlier. She raised her head and took a step toward the door. Just one more example of how alone she was.

Edward touched her elbow lightly. "May I escort you in to dinner?" He offered her his arm.

Marion hoped she didn't appear too relieved. "Thank you."

The grand mahogany table in the dining room was set for a formal dinner, with the crystal and silver both sparkling in the light. Several elaborate candelabra gleamed down the center of the table, while the gas-lit wall sconces flickered in their polished brass fixtures. The effect was warm and welcoming, completely at odds with her father's icy demeanor. He'd already seated himself at the head of the table, leaving the places on either side of him vacant. Marion chose the chair on his left, making sure Edward could have the seat of honor to his host's right. Ambrose took his position, supervising the automatons, also dressed in formal attire. She really despised the mechanical replacements her father insisted on. Using them instead of organics had added prestige, but left less room for the faithful servants she loved. Many had been sent to the poorhouse. As long as she was running the guild in her father's name, she refused to allow them near her.

Edward took care to seat her before taking his own place. Lord Richard watched them with narrowed eyes, and Marion's stomach began tying itself into knots. Her father gestured to Ambrose, who in turn signaled the automatons to begin service.

As a creamy butternut squash soup was ladled into her bowl, Marion's mouth watered. The smell of the nutmeg and other spices Cook used to season this dish brought back memories of happier times. She wanted to send her compliments to the cook but knew her father would jump on the impropriety of his daughter opening the conversation, so she kept silent.

They were well into the second course when her father cleared his throat and set down his fork. "I'm curious as to why the son of acting Guildmaster Stanton would grace us with his presence at dinner."

Marion had been in the process of swallowing, and the bite lodged in her throat. She couldn't have answered if the question had been focused toward her. As it was, her father's gaze was locked with Edward's. She coughed and reached for her goblet, sipping the cool water to force the food down.

Edward met Lord Richard's gaze. "I had hoped to meet with you after dinner to discuss that very thing."

"I'm not certain I'll be up to a private discussion after dinner." Lord Richard took a large gulp of wine and gestured to an automaton to refill the glass. "Why don't we dispense with the formality and have our discussion right now?"

"Father, I really believe it would be better to wait." Marion tried to keep her voice low and relaxed. As his bushy brows drew together, she hurried on. "Or I could retire now and give you gentlemen your privacy." She began to rise. There was no way her staying could do anything but hurt Edward's suite.

Her father reached out and gripped her arm, forcing her back into her seat. "You stay right where you are, missy. I'm certain Lord Edward's topic for discussion won't contain anything you don't already know."

Edward half rose, and she tried to give him a look that said everything was fine. She refrained from rubbing her arm, knowing there'd be bruises where her father had grabbed her.

"Go ahead, Lord Edward, share what's on your mind." Lord Richard once again picked up his fork and returned to his meal.

"As you may or may not be aware, I'm now of age, and it's time for me to choose a wife." His eyes drifted across the table to Marion. "It would be an honor to win the hand of your daughter, Lady Marion."

"An honor to have my daughter as your wife ..." Lord Edward sat back in his chair, motioning for the mechanicals to serve the next course. "There aren't many who feel that way these days."

Marion felt the impact of his words like a slap. Tears smarted in her eyes at the thought of how much this man must hate her.

Edward's face hardened. "Then they are extremely shortsighted."

"And what makes you so much more ... uh ... astute?" Richard attacked the roasted pheasant placed before him.

Marion moved the food around her plate. There'd be no way she could swallow anything past the lump in her throat.

"She's certainly rumored to be much more than a figure-head here in the Engineers Guild. A woman like Lady Marion would be an asset to any Guildmaster."

"But you're not a Guildmaster." Richard gave Edward an evil grin. "And your father's only the acting Guildmaster. I've heard the Queen has no intention of bestowing that rank on him either."

Edward took a deep breath. "Then you've heard wrong. We're merely awaiting Her Majesty's formal announcement."

"Interesting." Richard returned his attention to the pheasant.

Edward cleared his throat. "I would like your permission to marry your daughter."

The silence around the table hung like mist on a foggy night. Marion was acutely aware of the servants' hungry interest. A shudder ran down her spine at the thought of the rumors that would result from this night's dinner conversation.

"Do you love her?" asked her father.

Marion stared open-mouthed at Lord Richard.

Edward chuckled at the question. "Surely as men of the world, we know love is an emotion for boys and weaklings."

The flutter in Marion's heart retreated. He was right, of course. Love was for children. More than that, marrying for love was an infantile dream.

"Perhaps." Richard dabbed his lips with his napkin. "Or perhaps only a strong man would attempt the risk that love opens up. So I'll ask again. Do you love her?"

"I don't really understand what love has to do with my proposal." Edward shifted in his seat. "This is a business arrangement." He turned a warm look toward Marion. "And the Lady Marion and I are eminently suited for each other."

"Then this conversation is at an end." Lord Richard threw his napkin on the table and rose. "I will never approve a match for my daughter with a man who does not love her."

"But, Father. How can you do this? When will you quit punishing me?" Marion reached a hand to her father but recoiled at the expression on his face.

"I did wrong by you once before." His voice was hoarse, and he stumbled as he turned to leave the room. "I'll not make the same mistake again."

"Lord Richard." Edward rushed to catch up to her father, Marion close behind. "I don't understand. The match is suitable. I can protect your daughter and help her reach her full potential."

"Poppycock," Lord Richard roared as he turned back to Edward, his face red. "Do *not* presume upon your supposed station and my supposed incompetence. This discussion is closed and your presence is no longer welcome in this house." He turned to Ambrose, who had come to assist Lord Richard upstairs. "See that Lord Edward is shown to the door." His eyes narrowed. "Immediately."

"There's no need for that." Edward eyed her father with an expression of contempt. "I'll take my leave of you both." He gave Lord Richard a curt bow and then turned to her. He took her hand, and as he bent low, he whispered, "Meet me in the park tomorrow."

CHAPTER SEVEN

Edward strode into the manor house on the grounds of the
Pilots Guild, flinging his coat at Jeremiah, his valet. "Have a tray
sent to my study. I didn't get to finish dinner." He started toward
the study and then turned back. "Where's my father this evening?"

"He's out, sir."

"Just as well." He continued on down the hall.

"But, sir." Jeremiah hurried to follow him, catching him at
the door of the study. "You do have a visitor."

"That will be all." A woman's voice floated out of the room,
followed by the solid form of Matilda, clad in an deep aubergine
evening frock. "See to the tray. Then you won't be needed
downstairs any more this evening. "

Jeremiah bowed his way out.

"Good evening, Mother." Edward relaxed and leaned down
to kiss her on the cheek. "Your timing is, as always, impeccable."

"I assume you've had a difficult evening." She settled into one
of the leather chairs flanking the fireplace and picked up a half-

empty teacup from the inlaid table. "Pour yourself a brandy and catch me up while you wait for dinner."

Edward did as she suggested and joined her. "How much did you hear before you left?"

"Enough to know the old man wasn't going to allow his precious daughter to marry you." She took a sip. "Whatever possessed you to follow the advice of that woman?"

"That woman—as you term her—is the one I've chosen as my wife." He drained his glass. "I'll thank you to remember that."

"I'm not criticizing your choice." She set her cup back on the table with a click. "Only the precedent you're setting by allowing her to dictate your actions."

A footman, followed by several automatons also carrying trays, entered. He set his tray on the table adjoining the massive desk. The mechanicals followed suit and soon there were several appetizing dishes, piping hot and sending out tantalizing aromas. The footman poured a small bit of deep red wine into a glass and presented it to Edward.

Edward took a sip and inclined his head. The footman filled the glass and left the bottle open on the table. "Will there be anything else?"

"That will be all. You may go." Edward waved a hand toward the door, already perusing the steaming dishes.

Matilda joined her son. "What is your next step?"

"I told her to meet me in the park tomorrow." He finished filling a plate and took a seat by the fire.

"You'll have to do something a little stronger to break through his resistance." Matilda took a sip of tea. "That old man is stubborn to the point of idiocy."

Edward gave a disgusted snort. "Well obviously. Only a fool would abdicate the position of Guildmaster as he has done."

"By doing so, he has also given the daughter dangerous ideas." She frowned. "Because his defection has allowed her taste that power, however briefly, he may have awakened something that can't be contained."

"Oh, please, Mother." He waved a negligent hand. "You imply I'm not capable of curing her of bad habits after we're married."

"I know you think you are." Matilda pursed her lips. "But that girl has way too much of her mother in her. You may have chosen a difficult woman to work with."

"I didn't really have a choice. Anyway, it's her very tendency to think too much of herself that has her playing right into my hands." Edward gave her a smirk. "She's tasted the power and now will jump at my offer to share with her after we marry."

"Possibly."

Edward got up and grabbed the brass poker, stabbing at the glowing embers of the fire. "That difficult streak in her is what makes my plan so workable.

"Actually, the plan was ours."

"What?" He turned to stare at her.

"You heard me." Matilda folded her hands in her lap and met his eyes. "I don't want you to forget what you owe me."

"Yes, yes. I remember." He turned back to the fire.

"Your father is a liability to your ultimate goal." She moved to stand beside him and put a hand on his arm. "And I owe him for all those years of neglect."

He shook off her hand. "You weren't even married. He didn't owe you a thing."

"I gave him you. That should have counted for something." She returned to her seat, face serene.

"So it did." He winked at her. "I gave you my word. You'll have your chance for revenge."

"Thank you."

He clapped his hands together and began to pace. "Now, let me tell you what I'm thinking."

"Please do." She twitched her skirt into place, covering her tiny feet.

"You know we're hosting that masquerade day after tomorrow?" He raised a questioning eyebrow.

"Isn't the party to announce your father's official appointment as Guildmaster?" She frowned. "Have you heard from the Queen?"

"We have, and she's put us off again." He held up a finger when she started to speak. "But we are going to go ahead with the announcement. We're gambling that she knows she's not in a secure enough position to fight."

"A calculated risk, but one that seems reasonable." She cocked her head. "And?"

"I will use that night to profess my undying love to Marion." He put a dramatic hand to his heart and sunk to one knee. "I'll do so in front of the entire assembly. Her father won't dare do anything to stop us then." He made a face. "The old man wants love in her future, so I'll give him a love he can't deny."

"Hmm." She put a finger to her chin. "Have you told the bride-to-be of this plan yet?"

"No. I'll convince her tomorrow." He took his seat again. "After her father's reaction tonight, I'm confident she'll see the reason for this."

"Perhaps." She sighed. "But with that one, you just cannot predict how she'll react."

Marion stretched and pushed back from the desk as the view out the window caught her eye. She'd arrived at the Guildmaster's office early this morning to get a jump on the never-ending stack of papers that guild personnel seemed to generate. This view from the penthouse suite of offices was one of her favorites anywhere on the grounds. She pushed back her chair, smoothing her navy and green plaid taffeta skirt into place as she walked to the middle of the three floor-to-ceiling windows.

The sun was high enough to have burned off most of the fog, leaving the verdant green landing field glistening with dew beneath several swaying airships moored there. Two had their balloons fully inflated and the bright sunlight glinted off the golden cables anchoring the ships to the oval balloons. These were smaller, private models, some owned by guild personnel. This field was far too small to house the magnificent commercial liners her guild kept in perfect order. The main skyports were located for the ease of the passengers in major metropolitan centers, like London.

Several small figures of various personnel—ground crew in bright green and flight crew in pristine white—scurried about from the ships to the immense stone and steel hanger on the opposite side of the field. Her eyes strained to see into the dark maw of the open hanger door, knowing her mother's tiny sport would be tucked into the southwest corner. There was no way she could spot the ship from here, but in her mind's eye, she saw the rich mahogany basket trimmed with copper, aged with a patina no craftsman could recreate. How she longed for another trip in that magical ship. Her last had been a moonlit flight, just she and her mother with two crewmen. Her mother had ordered the canopy left behind, and she'd helped her mother steer the small ship with the night breeze ruffling her hair. A brisk knock at the door brought her back to the present. "Yes?"

The door flew open and William bounded in, his wiry frame preceding the white-coated Dr. Tuck. "We've news and it's good."

Dr. Tuck clicked his tongue and frowned at William. "It's good, but we're not there yet." He carried several papers and gestured to the large conference table near the ornate fireplace. "Perhaps you'd have the time to see what we've found?"

"Of course." Marion hurried to move a few stacks of paper, so he could spread his out for them all to see.

Elise arrived with a fresh tray. "I thought you'd want some tea for this impromptu meeting."

"Please stay." Marion put a hand on Elise's arm when she started to leave. "I'm sure you're as interested in this as I am."

"Interested, yes." Elise turned back, ready to stay. "But probably not able to comprehend what you'll be talking about."

"Nonsense. You're an intelligent woman." Dr. Tuck peered at her over his glasses. "I forbid you to demean yourself, even in your own eyes."

Elise's cheeks colored and she busied herself pouring tea. Marion and William exchanged glances. *Interesting.*

Dr. Tuck finished arranging his papers as Elise returned with cups for each of them. He cleared his throat and then pointed to the first paper, covered with a diagram. "You will remember these manufactured germs we discovered?"

Marion recognized the spiral of the germs she'd seen under the microscope the day before. "You hadn't found anything to kill them. Has that changed?"

"They don't like the cold." Will gulped and his Adam's apple bobbed as he stepped back at Dr. Tuck's frown.

"Yes." He continued to stare at William. "They are susceptible to the cold—extreme cold. Not at a temperature a person could survive for very long."

"But that's more than you had before, correct?" Marion took a sip of tea to cover the leap of joy she felt. "If just cold can kill them, then maybe they're susceptible to something else as well."

"They aren't destroyed by the cold, but it definitely disrupts their ... ah ... cooperation with each other." Dr. Tuck pulled another paper close for her to see, this one covered with the same spirals, but less dense and less perfectly aligned. "They can't communicate and act as a united front, so that allows the body's own defenses to swarm in and begin attacking."

"Do you think this a promising path to a cure?" Marion couldn't quiet the hopeful note in voice.

Dr. Tuck held up a hand. "It's the best lead we've had." He took off his glasses and began polishing them with his handkerchief. "But we need a way to lower the temperatures more than with just ice."

"The freezers in the kitchen." Elise snapped her fingers. "We have several large walk-in units. Would those help?"

"Oh, those would be perfect." William grinned in spite of Dr. Tuck's frown. "We hoped you'd offer the use of them."

"We could build our own units." Dr. Tuck thought for a moment. "But more money would be required to get the parts we need. I thought such a long time has elapsed since all the units were in use ..."

Marion swallowed past a lump in her throat. There had been no guild celebrations since her engagement to the odious Lord Maylon. And wouldn't likely be either, not with the guild coffers in such disarray. "Of course, you shall have them. I'll authorize their use immediately." She went back to her father's desk, searching for the requisite forms.

"No need." Elise touched her shoulder. "I oversee the kitchen. I'll take care of it."

"Excellent, most excellent." Dr. Tuck clapped his hands together as Will gathered up the papers. "I think we're on the right track and will soon know for sure."

Marion returned to the table. "Is there anything else you need?" She put a finger to her chin. "Do you need to dismantle the units and move them to your lab? Or can you work with them in the kitchen?"

Dr. Tuck paused for a moment. "I think it will save time to keep them where they are." He turned to Elise. "Can you help devise a way to keep the kitchen staff from wandering into the wrong freezers?"

"Of course." She paused as she considered the problem. "I'll assign you the two closest to the stairs. That should make them easier for you and your staff to reach and further from the bustle of the kitchen."

As Tuck and William left, Elise began to clear up the remains of the tea.

"Sit with me a moment." Marion plopped into a chair at the now empty table. "I'd like your advice on what went on last night."

"Oh?" Elise picked up her own teacup and took a seat close by. "How can I help?"

Before she could answer, another knock at the door interrupted them. "Yes," Marion called. "Come in."

The footman entered, bearing a note on a silver tray. "This was just delivered for you, my lady."

Marion rose and took the proffered card with only her name scribbled across the front of the envelope. "Who delivered this?"

"A messenger from the Pilots Guild."

"Very well." She waved a hand at the footman. "I'll ring if I need to send a reply."

"The Pilots Guild?" Elise raised an eyebrow. "That wouldn't be from Edward would it?"

"I should have known you'd have heard about last night." Marion went to her desk and used a letter opener to get beneath the wax seal. "Did Gretta tattle?"

Elise laughed. "I think you girls are beyond tattling." Her face sobered. "She's worried about you. She knows what sort of man he is."

"No." Marion set the letter opener on the desk with a deliberate click. "She knows what kind of boy he *was*. There's a big difference."

"What does he have to say?" Her tone was conciliatory.

Marion skimmed the short note. "He'd like to meet me in the park for a ride after lunch." She met Elise's questioning gaze. "To discuss how to get around my father."

Elise's gaze met hers. "You've heard the whispered rumors as much as we have."

"Yes, I have." Marion tucked the card back into the envelope and turned back to her desk and sat down. "Just as I'm certain he's heard the rumors about me."

CHAPTER EIGHT

Marion took one last look in the mirrored door of the tall wardrobe in her room. She adjusted her riding hat with its large bow and long veil over her velvet-clad shoulder. Her appearance shouldn't embarrass Edward.

She grabbed her riding crop and skipped down the stairs and out the door to the stable. It had been ages since she'd been riding in the park. Riding in public was one of the things she'd avoided after her brother's death. Appearances in polite society just left her open to glares and snide remarks. Chewing at her lower lip, she considered the past public slights from those of her class. Perhaps going out wasn't the best idea after all.

As she rounded the corner, her doubts vanished. Her dainty mare awaited her in the stone courtyard of the stables, tacked in her formal sidesaddle. The young groomsman holding her reins gave a quick bob of his head. "She's excited about getting out today, my lady. The weather is just about perfect, cool and clear but without too much wind." At least they hadn't designed automatons able to work with horses. Equines refused to respond to any hand but a human's.

"It is a perfect day." The horse snuffled at her skirt, and Marion pulled the purloined apple from her pocket, and offered it from her gloved hand. "Oh, Delilah. You're as incorrigible as your namesake. You always know I come with a treat." The black mare took the apple with a dainty nip and tossed her head.

Marion ducked under her neck and checked the bridle and martingale to be certain the mare had enough freedom to move her head. She tugged at the supple leather straps, then grinned at Justin. "Well done. Exactly what I'd expect from you." She led Delilah to the stone mounting steps and leapt lightly into the saddle.

She adjusted her hat and veil once more, then urged the mare forward with a tap of her booted heel. This would be a beautiful day. She wouldn't allow her outing to be anything less.

The short ride to the park passed quickly, as fall leaves cascaded down from the oak trees lining the path. As she approached, she could only see Edward's head and shoulders above the wall of onlookers and grooms.

When Edward caught her eye, he barked a command, and his grooms began pushing back the crowd. Her breath caught in her throat as she gazed at the horse-like contraption on which he sat. Of course, she was familiar with mechanical horses, but they were mere automatons compared with this beauty. She'd heard of his experiments, but had no idea that he'd managed to bring them to fruition.

Edward's face wore a superior look as he guided the—here her mind failed, could this thing really be called a horse?—toward her. Delilah snorted and tossed her head, taking a step back from the man and machine who approached. "Easy girl." Marion stroked her trembling mount. "I know just how you feel."

At a quick motion from Edward, one of his grooms broke off herding onlookers and ran to take a firm hold on Delilah's bridle. She acknowledged the young man who'd come to her aid with a duck of her head.

While still several yards away, Edward dismounted and handed the reins to the oldest groom. He closed the distance between them in long strides and gazed up at her. "What do you think of my creation?"

"It ... he ... is amazing." Delilah continued to dance, even with the assistance of the groom.

"Why don't we walk our mounts and give them time to get accustomed to one another." Edward reached up and easily swung her slight form from the saddle.

As he steadied her, he held her briefly, and she felt the strength in the man he'd become. "Thank you."

Edward offered her his arm. "Let Thompson see to your horse, and you can get acquainted with Man O' War."

The grooms had managed to get most of the crowd to move away and pretend they were going about their own business. Marion didn't feel quite as much the center of attention as she studied the huge black stallion before her. "He's truly a magnificent creation." She stared at Edward as she began to realize the ramifications of what he'd achieved. "May I?" She gestured her intent to examine the horse more closely.

"Of course." He took the place of the groom and led her within inches of the calm beast. "I've kept a lot of the horse's behavior, even with the modifications. Give him a minute to get to know you."

The horse's big brown eyes were alive with personality so Marion approached Man O' War as she would any other horse. His snort at the new person approaching him carried a metallic odor with the escaping steam, instead of a grassy one. But the stallion's reactions were well within the normal equine parameters. She stroked his soft neck and began cataloguing the things Edward had accomplished. The seamless transition between living and machine was beyond belief.

She ducked below the horse's neck as she followed the integration of the bridle into living flesh. "With this, you've completely removed the possibility of ill-fitting equipment interfering with the horse's comfort." The horse's neck rippled with living muscles and was soft to her exploring fingers. The saddle caught her eye next. Every part of this beast was a work of art. And a work of heart. She turned shining eyes back to Edward. Only a man who cared for an animal's well-being could have incorporated so much for its benefit. Her heart settled into a strong rhythm, even as her scientist's soul began to soar. This would be the man who could help her save the children and cement the future of her guild and of Britannia.

Edward quirked an eyebrow at her. "And your thoughts?"

"The things you have accomplished are beyond anything I've ever imagined." She clasped her hands together. "Of course I love him, but I've so many questions. Would you be willing to show me your designs?"

"I'm so glad you approve and can see my vision so clearly." He expelled a deep breath. "There have been more than a few who name what I'm attempting a crime."

Marion put a hand on his arm. "That's always the way, isn't it?"

His expression was warm. "As my wife, I'd expect you to be my partner in my endeavors."

Her heart fluttered as she gazed again at the marvel of animal and machine. Could they find a way to pull off such a union? Her father would fight them around every corner, she could feel his opposition in her bones. "I would like that more than anything." She thought back to her father's behavior the previous night. "But I'm not certain how we can succeed. I know my father when he's bent on one course of action."

"I think I have a solution to our dilemma." He guided Man O' War back to where the groom held Delilah. "Let's walk them together as we talk." He frowned at the crowd still on the periphery. "Perhaps that will afford us a bit more privacy."

She took her horse's reins as they began to stroll deeper into the interior of the park. "I'm open to suggestions."

"Of course, you're aware that tomorrow night is the annual Pilots Guild Masquerade. And not even your father would think of missing such an event."

"Oh, we'll be there." She snorted. He might neglect the day-to-day business of the guild, but he still kept up outside appearances. And the rumor mill knew it.

He leaned in closer. "My father has an important announcement to make, one that will affect the future direction of the Pilots Guild. As the excitement builds and plans are solidified, I'll take that time to propose to you publicly."

Marion gasped, but before she could speak he hurried on.

"Let me finish. In front of all those present, peers of the realm, Guildmasters from every guild, even your father will have to think twice about forbidding such a match. He'll be seen as a fool and could even be accused of undermining the foundation of the Engineers Guild."

She tugged at Delilah's reins as the horse bent to crop the tender shoots of grass from between the fall leaves. "It could work. Although he'll become less manageable as the night goes on."

"I'll help you manage him." Edward reached for her hand. "You won't have to cope with his mercurial moods and addictions much longer."

Robin and John stood with their horses on the edge of a copse of trees, observing Marion and Edward. Robin's fists clenched as Edward took her hand. "It's all true—everything we've heard about him and his experiments."

"Yes, and I'll wager there's a lot we haven't heard." John reached up to soothe his horse. "And somehow his plans include that little lady."

"Not if I have anything to say about it."

"Really?" John blew out air. "I thought you didn't care about her."

"I don't." Robin clenched his teeth as he saw Edward hand off the reins of his mount to a nearby groom and help Marion into her saddle. "But I intend to take him down, and she could be central to my plans."

"I'm sure." John's tone was unreadable.

They continued to watch the pair as Edward swung into the saddle. His beast gave a short cough accompanied by a burst of steam, and before anyone could react, Marion's mount shied and took off at a dead run.

Robin watched for only an instant. When Edward seemed to have difficulty making his mount obey, Robin swung up into the saddle of his own horse and raced to intercept Marion's fleeing form.

Marion crouched low over her spooked horse's neck as branches tugged the hat from her head. "Easy girl." Marion tried to keep her voice level and calm as she reached for the closest of the dangling reins. Delilah's sudden bolt had jerked the reins from her hands. "Slow down. There's no need to be afraid."

The panicked horse was having none of it. She continued to race through the park as though Satan himself was at her back. Given time, Marion knew she could regain control, but time wasn't on her side. Delilah's path had them streaking toward the busy roadway that bordered the park on the east. Marion bit down on her lip, refusing to consider what could happen if Delilah suddenly ran into that major thoroughfare. Oh, what she wouldn't give to be riding astride.

Behind her she heard the pounding hooves of another horse and prayed it was Edward. Surely that stallion he'd created could overtake a mere horse. Although if the rider was him, it explained Delilah's refusal to halt.

Robin gave Windmere his head, urging him to greater speed. He didn't have much time before they rocketed into the busy thoroughfare. He had to get to them before they reached it. Inch by torturous inch, Windmere gained on Delilah. Robin was close enough to see the white-knuckled grip Marion had on the saddle horn. How she'd managed to stay in the saddle this long was a mystery. But she'd always been an excellent horsewoman. He gritted his teeth. And far too stubborn to fail at anything she tried.

"Just a little further, boy." He directed his voice to Windmere's ear and it gave a twitch as if in agreement. From somewhere, the horse pulled more speed, and Robin drew even with Marion. They locked eyes, and he could see the terror in them. Not a sight he'd ever expected to witness.

"We don't have much time," he told her. The low rock wall was fast approaching. Jumping the wall wouldn't slow down her horse and would put them both in the middle of the crowded road. "I'm going to force Windmere into your horse and at the same time, grab you from the saddle. When that happens, you'll have to let go, or we'll all end up in a tangled mess."

Her eyes no longer held that flash of terror. Perhaps he'd imagined it. "I'm ready." She kicked one booted foot free from the hanging stirrup.

Robin dug his heels into Windmere's sides and used one hand to turn the horse directly into hers. At the same time, he reached out and grabbed her outstretched arm.

The collision rocked them both as the horses cried out. Unable to keep his balance as the horses tumbled, he kept a firm grip on Marion and somehow shifted her onto his lap. Before they could be caught beneath the falling horses, he rolled them both off the back of his horse. They landed hard on the leaf-strewn ground. She came to rest on top of him, and her weight caused him to lose what breath he had.

He started to lift his head, but stopped when the world moved in crazy circles.

"Robin?" She moved off him and took his face between her hands. "Are you okay? Say something."

"Mffff." He groaned, then moved his head again. Much better, the world was slowing. "I'm fine. Just give me a moment to catch my breath." He heard another horse gallop up and recognized the bulk of John, who began to see to their horses.

Marion looked in the direction of their still-tangled mounts, and he could tell she was torn between staying with him and going to see about them.

"Stay a minute," he whispered, his voice low. "John will take care of them. I need you to know something."

He tried to rise into a sitting position, but she pushed him flat. "Don't you move. Give yourself some time to recover."

"There isn't any time." He glared at her. "As long as you're with Edward, you're in grave danger. Whatever you think you know about him is wrong. The things he's doing are wrong." He forced himself up, in spite of her protests. "You need to stay far away from him."

"You are crazy." Sounds of Edward's stallion echoed closer distance. "You've had a bump and don't know what you're saying."

"I do know." How could he convince her of what he knew in his gut. He still lacked the proof she'd demand. Ah, well. Useless to argue. He rose, staggered a little, then joined John. "How are they?"

John set down Delilah's right front leg. "A few bumps, but both horses are sound. None the worse for wear." He grinned at Marion. "Thanks to Robin, of course."

"Of course you have my thanks." She blushed. "But now you have to go. If anyone finds you here ..." She looked around again as the sounds of other riders came closer.

John led Robin's horse to a nearby thicket while Robin turned back to her. "You just never listen."

Marion crossed her arms. "And you never make any sense."

Robin hadn't followed a whim in years, but he did just then. He grabbed her by the shoulders and kissed her startled mouth. It had begun as a way to have the last word, but the electric shock that ran through him caused him to draw back. Her expression told him she'd felt it as well. While she was still speechless, he darted into the trees and disappeared.

CHAPTER NINE

Edward galloped up as Marion staggered toward Delilah. "My dear, I'm so sorry." He threw himself off his horse and reached out to steady her. "Are you hurt?"

"No, I'm fine." What had he seen? She searched the faces of the gathering onlookers—would her humiliations always occur in front of a crowd? Had one of them witnessed Robin's rescue? She shook her head as her mind whirled. Now was not the time to go fuzzy from the effects of one scoundrel's kiss. She reached up and felt at the mess that was left of her hair. "I seem to have lost my hat."

"You are fortunate." He ran his hands over her shoulders and arms, obviously checking for injuries. "You could have lost so much more. I'm impressed with your skills. I didn't think you'd be able to gain control of your mount before disaster happened. However did you manage?"

Marion busied herself brushing off her skirt, fingers catching in a long rip. So he hadn't seen Robin's pursuit and rescue. "Pure luck. I was able to reach one of Delilah's reins at the last moment."

She gave her torn skirt a shake. "Although, the results would have been better if I'd been able to snag them both. I could have perhaps kept us both upright and off the ground."

"Still. That was a magnificent bit of horsemanship." He touched his hat to her. "I will be proud to have such a rider to help me with further innovations."

Just then one of his grooms trotted up, her hat and veil in his hand. Edward snatched the hat from the groom's outstretched hand and smoothed at the torn veil before handing it to her. "I will of course replace your chapeau."

Marion examined the mangled mess that was left of her hat. At least the return of the torn headpiece had interrupted Edward's line of inquiry. "Out of the question. The tumble was entirely my fault. We'll speak no more about it."

"Ah, but you'll soon learn I always pay my debts." He gestured for his groom to take Delilah's reins. She stood cropping the late fall grass as calm as if in her own field. "I've sent for my steam-carriage. I'll see you home in grand style."

Marion quirked an eyebrow at him. "More steam? I'm not sure either my horse nor I are up to any more modern conveniences."

Edward's face reddened, and he scowled. "I assure you it will be a smooth ride. This slight hiccup with Man O' War was an aberration, I assure you."

Slight hiccup? My, but he was touchy. Perhaps he was just worried. "I meant no disrespect. I have every confidence in your abilities and inventions. I'm not sure I can stand any more of the attention your conveyance is sure to attract. And I know my father will not take kindly hearing about this morning's escapade."

"My carriage isn't flashy and will get you safely home in the quickest way. Leave the transport to me."

Marion let a small sigh escape her lips. It would be good not to have to be the one with the final say about everything, even for a few short minutes. Unbidden, a vision of Robin danced before her mind's eye. That rogue had left her to fend for herself—why was it his face that intruded on her thoughts? "Thank you." She took sterner hold of her emotions. Her heart had no part in this decision. Only Edward could help achieve her goals.

He took her by the arm and led her away from the audience and toward the closest gate. "Rest assured we'll have you out from under his hard hand soon. I truly believe he'll be unable to object to our match after tomorrow night's proposal."

"Oh, he's always able to object." She bit her lip. "But perhaps tomorrow night will persuade him."

Edward's heavy silence accompanied them as they made their way to the park's south entrance. He pulled her to one side, stopping them in the shade of the massive iron portal, partially shielding her from the crowd. "I am not one to be thwarted. Now that I have your consent, I *will* make this happen."

Before she could answer, the sound of an approaching steam carriage replaced the noise of the street. The vehicle gleamed in the sun, the brass providing a bright counterpoint to the black lacquered wood. The driver was swathed in a dark touring coat, goggles, and leather cap. Everything this man owned was top drawer.

He handed her into the open-air leather seats. "I know you might have preferred a more discreet delivery home, but I wouldn't risk your reputation with a closed conveyance."

"I do appreciate your thoughtfulness." Thankfully, one of them was thinking clearly. At this point, all she wanted was the quiet of her room and a hot bath. Her muscles were beginning to protest her morning's exertions.

"Will you tell me what you'll be wearing to our masquerade?" He took a seat opposite her in the carriage. "I'm certain your beauty will be recognizable no matter what you wear. But the unmasking won't take place until midnight, and I want to make sure we have time together before."

Drat her hardheadedness. She should have listened to Gretta. Perhaps her chosen costume *had* been ill advised. But she'd chosen the costume knowing how it would irritate her father and ... well ... to tweak the noses of those who thought ill of her. Too late to change now. "I'll be going as the Maiden of Iron."

He blinked at her. "My dear ..." He cleared his throat. "What a charming idea." The expression on his face conveyed the exact opposite of his words, and if she hadn't been in such pain she might have giggled. "You shall be the hit of the ball, " he added.

She raised her chin at his tone. "I think it's high time for women to take more responsibility for plotting their own courses."

"Of course. I applaud a female with independence and strength. But I do think there is a time and place for such action." He clicked his tongue. "And perhaps an outlaw isn't quite the role model you wish to emulate?"

Gretta sat in Marion's room, perusing the latest issue of the *Times*, when Marion dragged herself up the stairs. She tossed the magazine aside and rushed to Marion. "What on earth has happened to you?"

"In a word, Robin happened to me." She lay the mangled remnants of her hat on the dressing table.

"Robin did … this … to you?" Gretta gestured to Marion, obviously at a loss for description.

Marion paused and pursed her lips. "That's not exactly accurate. Robin didn't cause the fiasco that was my afternoon, but he certainly didn't help."

A discreet knock at the door announced the arrival of several maids and footmen, bearing pails of steaming water. Matilda followed them issuing orders. "Pull that screen from the corner and get the tub filled immediately."

"In here, my lady." Matilda gestured Marion into her adjoining dressing room. "I cannot imagine what your father will have to say about this latest escapade of yours."

"I believe you forget yourself, Matilda." Marion tried to stand still amidst her maid's jerking motions as she helped Marion disrobe. What had she ever done to make an enemy of this woman?

"Humph." Her maid's reply, while not overtly disrespectful, managed to convey a world of venom and disapproval. She wrapped Marion in a dressing gown and went back to check the progress of the bath.

Marion wandered back into her room, and Gretta handed her a cup of tea. "You look like you can use this."

"Indeed I can." Marion took the cup. Whatever would she do without her friend?

The door closed behind the bevy of servants, and Matilda turned toward her. "Your bath is ready."

Marion stepped behind the screen and eased her bruised body into the warm water. She took a deep breath, inhaling the soothing aroma of mint and lavender. Unexpected tears pricked her eyes as she remembered former times. Her mother had always ordered this combination of herbs for sore muscles. She blinked and turned to Matilda, who had picked up a brush for Marion's hair. "I'll soak for thirty minutes, then you may return and help me finish."

"But time is—" Matilda began.

"Don't worry." Gretta took the brush from Matilda's hand. "I'll see to her. She's had a difficult day. Tell Cook to send her up a tray. She needs to rest before the event tomorrow night."

"Yes, ma'am."

Gretta stayed silent until they heard the click of the door, then she settled onto the nearby stool. "Okay. Tell me what happened."

Marion took another deep breath, letting the calming herbs clear her mind. What had happened? "Delilah got spooked and I took a tumble."

Gretta narrowed her eyes. "Oh, no, you don't. I want details. Start at the beginning and tell me exactly what happened."

Marion took almost a quarter-hour to fill Gretta in on the details about her afternoon in the park, although she was careful to omit the part about Robin's kiss. "Satisfied?"

Gretta tapped her chin with a long finger. "So Robin rescued you."

"He did *not* rescue me. I would have managed somehow."

Gretta rolled her eyes. "Of course, you would have."

Marion flushed. "Well, I might have. Besides, out of everything I told you, Robin is what you want to discuss? Really?"

"Oh, I agree the other *is* interesting." She giggled. "But so is how you're avoiding your feelings for Robin."

Marion lurched upright in the tub, causing a wave of scented water to cascade on the floor. "I do *not* have feelings for Robin."

She glared at Gretta before settling back. "Certainly not positive ones."

Gretta stepped behind Marion pulling the remaining hairpins from her curls. "So tell me more about this horse monster that Lord Edward has created."

"Man O' War isn't a monster. He's a work of art." Marion closed her eyes, picturing the stallion in her mind. "The integration of flesh and machine was as much art as mechanics. The man is a genius."

"Evil genius." Gretta ran a brush through Marion's hair with long, slow strokes.

Marion decided to ignore that as she nestled lower into the tub, letting her hair cascade over the edge. "I'm more convinced than ever that Edward is the one to help me find a cure for the children."

"And have you discussed this with him specifically?"

Marion frowned. "There really hasn't been an opportunity. But given his abilities with machine and flesh integration, I'm certain he'll be the ally I've been seeking."

Gretta was silent for a few moments. "Do you think your father will go along with the proposal?"

"I really don't know." Marion bit her lip. "I haven't been able to anticipate Father's whims since Mother's accident. Only my brother was able to talk sense into him when he was in one of his moods. Now that David is gone, there's no talking to him." She gave a shrug. "I'll just have to let tomorrow evening run its course."

"I'm certain your costume isn't going to help matters." Gretta paused her brushing. "Does Edward know what you're wearing?"

"Yes. I told him." She tried to keep her tone light.

"Didn't go over well, did it? I can imagine the oh-so-proper Lord Edward didn't like that at all." Gretta folded her arms. "How did he react?"

"Better than you might imagine. But still, I could tell he wasn't thrilled." She met her friend's eyes. "But his support didn't waver."

Gretta snorted. "Of course it didn't. He has big plans, and somehow you are central to them. He won't do anything to jeopardize that. So how are you going to keep your father from finding out what you're wearing in advance of the evening?"

"Didn't I tell you?" Marion turned a grin on her friend. "You've insisted I ride with you, so you're not unescorted in a closed carriage."

CHAPTER TEN

The next morning, Robin halted just inside the long alleyway, John close behind him. His men had told him about these collection stops, and he wanted to see them for himself. A large enclosed steam wagon being loaded with older children blocked the cross street in front of them. Medical automatons moved through the children, dispensing tin cups of what must have been medicine since the children were obviously ill. Many bent double with racking coughs, while some just stared, tears running down grimy faces. Their distraught parents gathered around a team of men in expensive frock coats and tall silk hats.

"I assure you we'll take excellent care of your children," one of the men said. "We must get them out in the fresh country air for the cure to work." He gestured with a cane. "Surely you want them to get well?"

"That we do." A rough man stepped forward. "But why would you care about the likes of us?"

Another of the high hats stepped up, as the automatons continued to dose and load their living cargo. "Sir, we know that ultimately the fate of Britannia rests with her children, whether highborn or not. As patriots, our duty is to care for those less fortunate."

The rough man spat, but a woman wrapped in a shawl pushed in front of him, holding up her infant. "Then take my baby." Sobs clogged her words. "He's sick, too. Can't you make him well?"

"All full up, guvnor." An human coachman closed the door of the now full wagon, and secured it with a chain.

"Find us on another trip, madam." He tipped his hat and followed the others to a black enclosed carriage pulled by two metal equines. Even though there was no identifying crest, Robin could see the workmanship of the fine vehicle. The man leaned out of the conveyance. "We'll be back here at the same time tomorrow." The crowd surged forward, but the wagon and the carriage roared away without trouble.

"This is the third charity pick-up I've seen this week." John stroked his chin. "I don't like it, not one bit."

Robin snorted. "I'd wager an entire wagon of gold those children are being carted off to workhouses or worse. They're not being sent somewhere in the country to regain their health."

They waited in silence for another five minutes until the worst of the crowd dispersed. Then, Robin led the way down another alley before they arrived at the warehouse district which lined the water's edge.

Robin and John surveyed the grimy Thames wending its way past the rickety boardwalk where they stood. Two almost-sober ruffians stumbled past, one of them turning to spit and just missing John's boot. Robin put a hand on his arm, but his friend growled, a low ominous sound deep in his throat. The drunk focused bleary eyes on John and almost tripped in his haste to get away. "Pardon me, guvnor."

John huffed, but didn't follow.

When the boardwalk had cleared, Robin ducked into the alley past heaps of garbage, and then into a recessed doorway. With John's bulk behind him, Robin rapped on the door three times, paused, then rapped twice, paused again and rapped once more.

A small wooden window set at eye level in the door slid back. "What?"

Robin didn't hesitate. "Mister Wood needs some coal."

The window slammed shut, and the door opened into darkness.

Robin didn't want to wait until his eyes adjusted to the darkness. "Winston, is that you? Our horses are tied up in the usual place. They're restive this morning." Robin's jaw tensed. "Get someone to relieve you, and go help Duncan. They're probably more than he can handle alone."

The old man grimaced. "That boy is all mouth and no might."

"He's still growing. We've all been there—it's not an unforgivable sin." Robin laid a hand on the man's shoulder. "Don't let him know I told you to go."

Winston huffed. "He may not be unforgivable, but he's a pain."

Robin didn't reply as he and John strode down the hall to the study. Once there, John settled into the leather arm chair fronting the fireplace while Robin leaned against the mantle staring into the smoldering fire. He thought about all they'd witnessed that morning, coupled with the day before. "That lordling has plans afoot." He tried to grin at John. "And we're going to beat him at his own game."

John raised a bushy eyebrow. "And when did we discover what exactly his game is?"

"We're close, just dancing around the edges." Robin huffed out air. "We have the pieces. We just haven't put it all together yet."

"So what do we know?"

Robin took a seat at his desk and dug through the scattered papers on top, finally pulling one out. "We know he and his father want permanent control of the Pilots Guild. And he's achieved that." When John started to protest, Robin held up a finger. "Maybe he and his father don't have the support of the Queen, but for all intents and purposes, they are in control."

He waited for John to nod before he continued. "We also know he's experimenting with implanting mechanical parts in living tissue." He unconsciously flexed his right arm. Tuck had fixed him up well. There was no lasting damage from the lightning gun.

"We saw the results of that yesterday. That equine was as impressive as it was a perversion." John frowned. "And we're certain that Dr. Tuck isn't working with him?"

"We are. But that doesn't mean that Edward wouldn't love to have his expertise on his staff." He tapped his chin. "Remember to set some men to watch Tuck—discreetly. We know he doesn't like to be meddled with, but if he comes under Edward's scrutiny, he may need our help."

"Shouldn't we warn the good doctor? Or Marion—since he works for her?" The innocent expression on John's face remained, even as Robin glared at him.

Robin returned to the paper in front of him. "We'll leave that to later. I'll wager she's in no mood to listen to what I have to say."

John's low chuckle was his only reply.

Robin ignored him and continued, "We also have the seemingly unrelated epidemic of children falling ill from a mysterious disease and being shipped to the country." He banged his fist on the desk. "I know this ties in somehow, but I need more information."

John got up and took the poker from the peg by the fireplace. He began coaxing the coals into a small flame. "Gathering information can't be hurried." He quit poking and gave the coals time to gather momentum. "Sometimes you have to poke at it, and other times you have to give it time to burst into flame." Almost on cue, the small fire took hold and leapt to life. He turned to Robin. "You've poked and prodded. Give it a day or two for the sparks to catch."

"And where exactly do you think you're going, young lady?"

Marion's back stiffened. She'd almost made the door. After a long night's sleep, she'd awakened feeling refreshed and ready for the event that night. She turned to face her father standing in the door of his study. "I'm going to Lady Gretta's to dress and ride with her to the masquerade tonight." Thank goodness, she'd sent the footman ahead to load her costume in the carriage. She might still get away with her ruse.

He swayed slightly in the doorway and reached out a hand to brace himself on the doorframe. "Did you not think it more appropriate to accompany your father?"

"I did." She kept her face neutral. "But Lady Gretta had no one to accompany her and didn't think it seemly to ride alone in a closed carriage. I agreed to go with her for appearance's sake."

"I see." He frowned and seemed to consider her words. The seconds ticking away on the grandfather clock in the hall echoed the thump of her heart. "You acted appropriately, but I would appreciate knowing in advance of such a change in plans."

"Yes, Father." She dipped her head, more to hide the relief she knew would show on her face than out of respect.

"But …" He held up a hand when she moved toward the front door. "I do expect you to ride home with me. If Miss Gretta requires an escort, we will see her home in our carriage."

"Of course." Not bloody likely. The man would be well into his cups before the evening fully began. She kept a decorous pace until she was well out of his sight, then drew in a deep breath.

Justin met her at the door. "I've loaded your costume, ma'am." He handed her up into the carriage, waiting until she tucked in her full skirts before closing the door.

"Thank you." She waved as the carriage lurched away from the door.

The ride to Gretta's didn't take long, and her friend was standing at the top of the steps. "I thought something had happened to hold you up." She rushed to open the door before the footman. "Is everything all right?"

Marion allowed the footman to help her out of the carriage and waited for Gretta's lady's maid as she took the wrapped bundle that held her costume from the coachman. "Thank you, Sarah."

"I'm happy to help, my lady." The maid curtsied, and the braids woven crown-like on her head bobbed.

Marion turned to Gretta. "My father stopped me in the hall as I was leaving."

Gretta grabbed her arm. "He was up this early? Did he suspect your plans? However did you get away?"

"He didn't suspect, and I just explained that you couldn't attend unescorted." Marion laughed and led the way up the steps and into the foyer. "It was a tricky couple of minutes, but he agreed."

"He agreed?" Gretta ran up the steps behind her, holding her skirts a tad bit too high. "I can't remember the last time he agreed with anything you said."

"I know." Marion frowned. "I wondered at first if he was playing one of his twisted games. All he required was that I agree to ride home with him tonight after the evening has ended." She glanced at her friend. "He did say that if you required an escort, you could ride with us."

Gretta rolled her eyes. "He'll be too far gone in drink to even know when it's time to leave."

"I've had them send up an early luncheon." Sarah stood at the bottom of the stairs, her petite frame almost lost beneath the large bundle. "Then it will be time to begin your toilette." A footman had followed her in, and tried to take the load from her. She swatted at him with a hand and glowered. "Get away from me, you fool. You muss this dress, and I'll add twice your work."

Marion giggled as they followed her up the stairs to Gretta's suite. There was such joy in this house, so unlike the mausoleum-like quality that dominated her own home. Her heart skipped a beat. If she and Edward married, she'd be free from the past and be able to set the tone in her own household.

Marion walked to the window and gazed out at the view, the cupola that crowned the main guild building looming over the tops of the trees. What would become of the guild if she agreed to an alliance with Edward? Would it be swallowed whole by the Pilots Guild or continue to operate in its own right?

"What has you so preoccupied?" Gretta helped Sarah unwrap Marion's costume.

"This?" Sarah pointed open-mouthed at the trousers, covered by a split overskirt. They were accompanied by a white shirtwaist and long, black-leather duster. "You think this appropriate for a lady?" She stared at first one, then the other and finally threw up her hands. "What do I care? I know there is only so much I can do. You two have been into mischief since you were babies."

Gretta ignored her and instead went to the hatbox that had accompanied Marion's costume, lifted the lid and pulled out a top hat. "Ooooh. I was hoping you'd choose this instead of the helmet." She held it up to the light.

Marion's heart swelled. The hat had been her mother's prize possession, once belonging to her father. He'd tossed the silk hat into the air after their wedding, and it had landed on her head. From then on, she'd claimed the hat as her own. The black velvet shone with the patina of age, and a faded silk ribbon in vibrant green encircled the crown. His set of handcrafted flying goggles now rested above the brim. Marion had added a veil of black tulle dipping low over the front to act as a mask and draped up the side to finally be caught up at the back with the large cameo broach her grandmother had loved. The tulle continued in a cascade down her back almost to the floor.

"Let me see how you look." Gretta held it out to her.

Marion took it and walked to the full-length mirror in the corner. She adjusted the hat to a rakish angle and faced Gretta.

"Magnificent." Gretta clapped her hands. She turned to Sarah. "You must admit it is beautiful."

"That it is." Sarah let out a deep breath. "You're the spitting image of your mother."

Marion wrapped her arms around her own waist and turned back to the mirror, searching for signs of her mother. She could see glimpses in the set of her chin, the shape of her mouth. Tears pricked her eyes but they didn't fall as she turned back to Gretta. "Let's eat before we begin to get ready."

CHAPTER ELEVEN

Edward scanned the crowd again. Swirls of color mingled with rich fabrics filled the glowing ballroom as his guests danced and sampled delicacies from silver trays offered by servants and automatons. Gaslight gleamed from sconces on the walls and the three massive chandeliers that hung over the immense space. On tables, candles flickered with the ebb and flow of the crowd. Underlying all was the pulse of the music, punctuated with the staccato voices of those in attendance. The steward still announced his guests—or more accurately, his guests' personas. But the crowd had moved on from that stale pursuit in search of new entertainment. After all, how excited could one get about yet another pirate or wood nymph?

"The Maiden of Iron." The steward's announcement had somehow fallen into a lull in the music and rang out, once again capturing the crowd's attention. Everyone turned toward the grand staircase. She stood at the top, impossibly beautiful, her slight frame commanding the room as if she were seven feet tall.

"Interesting choice for a wife, my boy." Lord Stanton stood by Edward's side. "I'll say this. Life will never be boring."

Heat suffused Edward's face. "She will be someone the people can love. Her quirks will work in my favor."

"But can you control her?" His father watched Marion's regal descent. "She's already proved more than her father can handle."

"That lush." Edward spit the words. "He's a bigger fool than Loxley was. Once we get his blessing, he'll be free to destroy himself in private."

Edward moved through the crowd and was ready with a hand as Marion reached the parquet floor of the ballroom. "Welcome, my lady." He took her black gloved hand in his and bowed. "We are honored by such a ... notorious ... guest."

"Thank you for your kind welcome." The pink bow of her lips relaxed in an almost smile, revealing the dimple in her left cheek. He imagined there was an accompanying twinkle in her hazel eyes, but they were well hidden beneath the folds of tulle covering the top half of her delicate face.

A waltz began, and he led her to the dance floor. As he took her in his arms, a warmth settled in his chest and the world seemed to retreat. "You have caused quite a stir. The exploits of that daring woman are legendary."

"The people know her concern is for the children." Her mouth thinned into a line. "If I could assist her in her endeavors I would. My heart bleeds for the plight of the littlest ones in our great city."

Was she testing him somehow? "I hope you know I feel the burden of this epidemic as well." He noticed the stares and whispers of the growing crowd. "They are dying to find out who you are. Your entrance has ensured my humble ball will be the talk of the town for years to come."

Before she could answer, a trumpet sounded announcing the Queen. The dancing stopped and Edward turned to the stairs, knowing what was to come.

"It seems I've been eclipsed." She stepped back, releasing him to his duties. "Go see to your guest."

He watched as she moved to stand by one of the open doorways leading to the balcony before he strode to the base of the grand staircase. The steward's voice again rang out just as he stopped beside his father. "Her Majesty, Queen Victoria." He had everything he could do to keep the triumph from his face. She'd fallen for the ruse, and tonight the Pilots Guild would be theirs.

Robin stood in the shadows of the open balcony watching Marion walk toward his hiding place. He knew his black pirate garb rendered him unremarkable, especially since the low-hanging clouds obscured the soon-to-rise full moon. It almost seemed she knew he was there. She stopped a few feet in front of him, no flicker of recognition in her face, and turned to watch the Queen's entrance.

He forced his attention back to the top of the stairs. *Why had the Queen decided to put in an appearance?* He'd grown up knowing he owed her allegiance, but where had she been when his father needed her loyalty?

"Unexpected." John's words issued from the monk's cowl he had pulled up as a hood. "Could be the sparks are flying sooner than expected."

Robin grunted as he watched as the Queen's personal bodyguards took up unobtrusive stations around the room's perimeter.

"Those guards could work to our advantage." John hadn't missed the guards' appearance either. "When we enter, they'll surround the Queen and add to the general chaos."

"My thoughts exactly." Robin grinned. "And Lord Stanton's humiliation will be all the more memorable with a royal witness." His grin faded. "But we will watch and choose the right moment to make our move. I will not lose anyone else in my care to a Stanton thug."

John gestured toward the carved stone balustrade of the balcony. "The men are well hidden and will be ready when you give the signal."

Robin returned his attention to the Queen. Lord Stanton and Edward flanked her as she made her way around the room, greeting her subjects. She paused several times to speak to different people. He caught the subtle stiffening of Marion's spine as the Queen turned in her direction. Marion swept a deep curtsey, and he was struck anew by the bravery of this young woman.

"Plucky one, isn't she?" John's whisper was a low rumble in Robin's ear.

Robin cut John off with a motion of his hand. "Be quiet." He strained to catch the monarch's words as she paused in front of Marion.

"Rise, my child. Your mother was a great friend in my youth." The Queen touched a lace-gloved hand to Marion's cheek. "You have the look of her. I know she would be proud."

He saw Marion incline her head, but couldn't catch her words. Then the Queen moved on.

As Lord Stanton settled the Queen in a throne-like chair positioned in a place of prominence, Edward signaled the orchestra. They played a fanfare and an army of servants appeared with trays of champagne for each guest. "We have much to celebrate tonight." He waited for the bustle to settle before continuing. "We are honored by our Her Majesty's presence on such an evening as this." He raised his glass to her, and she dipped her head, face set in stone and unreadable. "But we have even greater news. Tonight marks the announcement of a new head of the Pilots Guild." He gestured to his father. "It is my great pleasure to introduce Guildmaster Stanton." The room erupted with cheers and clapping.

Robin watched the Queen for her response. Surely she hadn't precipitated this announcement. If she had, she'd have made the announcement herself. Would she contest it now? Her face remained impassive. She neither objected nor joined those clustered around Lord Stanton to offer their congratulations. Interesting.

Lord Stanton pulled away from the crowd and clapped his hands for quiet. "My appointment ..." His eyes cut ever so briefly in the direction of the Queen. "...isn't the only announcement worth celebrating." He gestured toward Edward who had appeared in front of Marion.

"May I?" Edward waited for Marion's ascent before he removed her hat and veil, tossing them into a nearby chair and dropped to one knee. "My dearest Lady Marion, would you do me the honor of agreeing to become my wife?"

The room once again exploded in chaos. This time the Queen was also on her feet, her face mirroring the alarm ringing in Robin's mind.

Robin turned to John as he ignored the sword hanging at his side and drew his dagger. "Now."

Men in black pirate garb materialized from every corner of the room, shouting and wreaking destruction on the furnishings. Screams and shouts added to the pandemonium and out of the corner of his eye, he saw the Queen's bodyguards surround her, swords drawn. But his focus was the petite woman only feet in front of him.

Edward spun to survey the room, and while his back was turned, Robin swooped in and grabbed her from behind, locking his arm around her waist and putting tip of his dagger at her throat. "I think we'll be taking a little trip, my lady."

"You." Her body trembled, and he recognized the rage inside her without mistaking it for fear. "You'll never get away with this."

"I'd say I already have." He inclined his head at the chaos of the room. Women screamed, men blustered, but his band was in control. They avoided the Queen, but overturned tables, tossing food at the crowd and destroying the well-crafted banquet.

Edward had turned back at Marion's outcry and reached for his own sword.

"I wouldn't." Robin kept his voice light, but knew the other man could read the resolve in his face. He began backing toward the railing on the balcony. "I will draw blood and more from your lady love if you come one step closer."

"You interfering fool." Marion's words hissed between clenched teeth. "I'll kill you myself. I don't need protection."

"Shut up, Marion." Edward's face reddened, and he spit out an additional epithet under his breath. "I'll make you pay." He focused on Robin. "In ways you could never conceive."

"How dare you?" Marion said, and Robin was unsure whether the words were aimed at him or Edward.

He felt her tense as if ready to break his hold, and he leaned forward to whisper in her ear, even as he continued toward the railing. "If you continue to squirm, I'll be forced to knock you out." He raised his head. "I am taking her with me—one way or another—and there's not a thing you, or she, can do. It's time she learned the truth about you, and I'm just the person to educate her."

"The truth?" Edward gave a bark of hard laughter even as he glared at John's sword keeping him from the focus of his fury. "You wouldn't know the truth if it walked up and introduced itself. Marion will see you for what you are, a thief and the son of a traitor. And I'll be waiting to—"

"You're wrong. The Lady Marion is many things, but a fool isn't one of them." He watched her face redden. She appeared to know he was serious about his threat. "At least she didn't used to be." He returned his gaze to Edward. "But either way, I'm not going to dignify your tirade with discussion." In one quick movement, Robin sheathed his dagger and swung her up in his arms as John stepped between Edward and him. She squirmed and hissed, almost like a cat. He tightened his grip on her. "Struggling will you do you no good."

"Let her go." Edward commanded as he surged toward them.

"Not so fast, young sir." John's sword glinted in light, forcing Edward back into the melee of the main room.

"I think you have underestimated me." Robin cocked his head toward the darkness and listened. "Ah. Right on time." And with Marion held close, he leapt over the railing. Marion screamed and buried her head in his shoulder, but he landed lightly in the basket of the small airship rising to the level of the balcony. He looked back as John feinted at Edward, and then turned and ran toward them. For a large man, he moved with deceptive speed and grace and soon joined them in the dirigible. Edward yelled and gestured to his men, but the light dirigible was already rising on the night wind. Robin's heart swelled. The taste of having bested his rival at long last sat sweet upon his tongue.

Chapter Twelve

"Put me down this instant." Marion reached a hand to scratch his face, but Robin was too quick. He opened his arms, and she landed with a hard thump on the polished floor of the small ship, all the breath whooshing from her lungs. She could do no more than glare up at him.

Robin raised an eyebrow at her. "You did ask."

Marion fought the urge to scream her frustration at the source of her problem. That was a luxury she could ill afford. Her mind was the way out of this disaster. Emotion was the enemy. She'd bested him before. She'd do so again.

John crossed the small space and helped Marion to her feet. "My apologies for his manners. You seem to bring out the worst in him."

"That is no excuse." Her hair whipped around her face as the airship gained altitude and broke through the low-hanging clouds. A crystal sky, dotted with the twinkling lights from a thousand stars pulled a gasp from her throat. It had been so long since she'd last flown at night.

She moved to the side of the ship, one hand trying to tame the mass of curls bent on obscuring her view, the other on the mahogany railing, steadying her stance.

Robin nudged her attention away from the sky and handed her a pair of goggles. "These should help."

Marion hesitated, searching for a trap.

"Oh, for heaven's sake, they're just a pair of glasses. Use them or not. I couldn't care less." He turned away and walked to the tiller in the bow that connected to the steering sail that hung below the craft. "Go see to the fire," he told the man guiding the ship. "I'll take over here."

Marion wrestled her hair into submission with the help of the goggles. With her eyes protected, the view was even more breathtaking. She couldn't let herself get sidetracked, so she turned back to Robin.

He lounged against the side of the craft, one hand on the tiller, guiding the craft with little effort. The sign of a true pilot. "Where are you taking me?"

"We're going to my headquarters. There are some things you need to know about the man offering for your hand." Only his mouth beneath his leather goggles was visible in the dark, and it was set in a hard line. "If you're still fool enough to go through with this marriage after you know everything, then it's on your head, and I'll wash my hands of you."

"I was never any concern of yours." She put her hands on her hips. "And I'll thank you to forgo the great revelation and take me straight to my guild."

He pointed a finger at her. "No. I owe you the truth—for our shared childhood if for nothing else. After that, we're done." He dusted his hands together to illustrate his meaning.

Their shared childhood. That one phrase brought the memories back in a rush. As children, the grounds of their guilds had intersected in a field not far from her grandfather's buried airship. It was only natural they'd have shared many adventures growing up. The group was fairly large, but she and Robin had been special friends, and as they'd grown, that bond had developed into something more. She shook off the memories. "We were children, there's nothing owed from time spent at play."

He opened his mouth, closed it, and cocked his head at her. "Do you still like to fly?"

She was certain that wasn't what he'd been about to say but ignored the urge to question him. She was weary of fighting. He'd destroyed her evening and the quicker they got down, the quicker she could return home and do damage control. "I do. But I haven't had the opportunity of late."

"Come on then. Let's see if you've lost your touch." He motioned toward the tiller.

"Flying is something I'd never forget." Without waiting for a second invitation, she joined him.

"Then she's all yours." He moved to give her room to squeeze in beside him, but kept his hand close in case he needed to intervene. "She's a resilient craft, sensitive to the slightest touch."

Marion could feel the thrum of the steam engine through the warm wood of the tiller. "She's a beauty." She rubbed the smooth wood. "What's her name?"

"I call her Night Maiden." He grinned and the lines of his mouth relaxed. "She's as stealthy and beautiful as the evenings that slip up unawares."

Marion clenched the tiller and made a small adjustment as the ship bucked in answer to a gust of wind. "She is a responsive lady." She patted the tiller as the ship returned to a smooth glide. "Have you had her long? I don't remember her in your father's fleet."

He didn't answer immediately, and she wanted to bite her tongue. She shouldn't have brought up his father.

"I've had her a while." The moon worked its way further into the sky. "Move us to a more westerly tack."

She adjusted their course, and they seemed to sail directly at the glowing orb.

"You're just as natural as ever."

"I told you." She relaxed into the moment.

They held their position for a few more minutes, watching clouds drift across their path before Robin took hold of the tiller. "We're almost there. I'll need to take her in."

She dropped the tiller and moved to face him. "As you wish." Marion's stomach clenched as she remembered her predicament.

"Oh, relax." Robin frowned at her movement. "I just have a few things to show you, and then you can leave."

"Of course." Not even the wind could drown out the sarcasm inherent in her words.

"Back off on the pressure," Robin called to the man at the boiler. "We'll bring her in from the east. Duncan will be watching for us."

John had grabbed the mooring line with the grappling hook at its end and stood poised at the edge of the ship's basket. Their rapid descent took them once more into the clouds, and the fog swirled around the basket almost obscuring them from each other. Marion edged toward the railing, but Robin's arm shot out.

"Oh, no, you don't." He pulled her hard against him. "I didn't go to all this trouble just have you jump over the edge."

"Let go of me." She clenched her fists. That had been her plan exactly. She should have been more subtle.

As her struggle caused the ship to buck, John strode over and took her arm in a grip of steel. "You're as reckless as him. Causing us to wreck won't get you home any faster. Settle down and behave."

"Stop it. I have to get home." She doubled up her fist and hit John as hard as she could. He just grinned at her. She'd have been better off swatting at iron.

Before she could plan her next move, John dropped the mooring line, picked up a rope and wrapped the strand around her, pinning her arms to her sides.

"How dare you?" she screeched. He fastened a handkerchief around her mouth, muffling the sound.

"I'd just as soon you not bring any attention to us." He picked up the line and with one eye still on her eased the hook over the side.

Marion studied her surroundings. During her struggles, they'd dropped into the city, probably somewhere near the wharves judging from the smell of dead fish and the smokestacks on either side of the small ship. The ship slowed as Robin guided the small ship, avoiding all obstacles with apparent ease.

John whistled and dropped the end of the mooring line. The ship jerked to a stop and Marion struggled to stay on her feet.

"Kill the engine," Robin ordered.

"Done." The boiler hissed as the red glow faded into black. "I'll sit with her until I'm certain she's cool."

"Excellent."

Somewhere below them a winch creaked, and the ship was pulled downward. Marion squinted trying to pinpoint their location. She might need to return, or lead the authorities here.

"I don't think so." Robin gathered up burlap sack from one corner of the ship and advanced on her. "We're not going any further until we're safe from your prying eyes."

Edward kicked a chair out of the way as he strode from the balcony back into the ballroom. The earlier swirl of color and pattern had disintegrated into chaos. What guests remained milled about as the servants worked to clean up the havoc wreaked by the outlaw's invasion. He sheathed his sword, along with his emotions, as his eyes swept the room. Not a single black-garbed pirate remained. That man would pay, and he would enjoy extracting the price owed, but now he had to salvage the evening. He strode toward his father, who was conferring with the captain of the Queen's personal guards.

"My apologies, sir." Lord Stanton mopped his brow with a snowy white handkerchief. "Please convey my regrets to the Queen."

"You may speak them yourself." The Queen moved into view, her gray eyes snapping. "I should have expected this level of incompetence from one I deemed unworthy."

"Your Majesty." Lord Stanton bowed from the waist. "I meant only good to come from this evening. The guild has known only strife of late, and I sought to alleviate that."

"So I noted." The Queen managed to convey the impression of looking down her nose at him, even though he stood a good head taller. "And usurping my prerogative doesn't seemed to have worked out so well, does it?"

Lord Stanton's face reddened. "This guild has too long been in contention. Someone had to act. With your reticence on the subject, I began to think it a test."

"A test?" Her eyebrow raised.

"Yes." He nodded and his neck wobbled a counterpart. "I thought to prove my worth by stepping in and acting as a Guildmaster should. My only motivation is the good of the guild."

"Of course." Her face remained hard and unyielding. "What's done is done and I'll not undo it." She fixed him with stare. "But we're not finished. If you're wise, you'll take that as a warning. However, now is not the time for that. How could you allow such entrance into the grounds?"

He stepped back, a hand to his heart. "That outlaw grew up here and knows this place better than any other." It was his turn to glare at her. "Besides, this outlaw has run amuck all across our fair city. If you couldn't contain him, how could I be expected to on his home ground."

"You dare to insult Her Majesty?" The guard half drew his sword.

"No." The Queen put her hand on his sword arm. "Let the imbecile speak."

Lord Stanton's red face had gone pale. "I meant no disrespect, Your Majesty. I only wanted to point out ... that is ...." His shoulders drooped. "Never mind."

Edward stepped up beside his father. "We are only grateful that no one was harmed."

"No one harmed?" Marion's father, carrying himself like the Lord Ravenswood of the past, joined them. He stood erect and coldly furious. "My daughter has been taken. I demand action."

"As do I." The Queen gestured to one of her men, and he strode from the room. She turned to Lord Stanton. "What do you intend to do about it?"

"I'll be leaving immediately to track her." Edward answered for his father. No point in waiting for him to hem and haw an answer. "That outlaw is reputed to have a haven somewhere near the wharves. I should be able to ferret him out."

Lord Ravenswood turned to Edward. "You will have my gratitude if you return my daughter to me unharmed."

"That is my intent, no matter what." Edward kept his face calm. Perhaps he could turn this situation to his benefit yet. "I would rather die than see one hair on your daughter's head harmed."

Lord Ravenswood stroked his chin, not an ounce of intoxication apparent in his actions. "Perhaps I've misjudged you after all." He gave Edward a searching look. "A man who could protect my daughter would definitely be one I would deem a good match."

"I am grateful for your consideration, my lord." Edward inclined his head. "But with or without that promise, I will see her safely home before the night is through."

The Queen paused for a moment. "My men will also begin a search."

The guard motioned her to precede him from the room. But she stopped a step or two away and turned back. "I will not forget what happened here tonight."

Her words could have referred to Loxley's raid, but Edward doubted it. He and his father had been marked openly as an enemy of the crown, and he'd have to move fast before she could bring her power to bear against them.

"Of course, Your Majesty." Lord Stanton bowed again. "Please accept the guild's humblest apologies."

Her only answer was a sniff as she quit the room.

CHAPTER THIRTEEN

Edward turned back to where his father had been standing. Guildmaster Stanton had followed the commander of the Queen's guard and now blocked his exit. Edward bit back another oath. He crossed the littered remains of the banquet to intervene between Lord Stanton and the obviously irritated military man.

"Make sure Her Majesty knows this wasn't my fault." Lord Stanton mopped his red face with a starched handkerchief.

"And whose fault was it?" A sneer curled the commander's lip. "Any Guildmaster worth his salt would have been prepared for such contingencies."

"Now see here …"

"I believe your duty is to the Queen's safety." Edward stopped beside his father and eyed the guardsman. "We have the matter here well in hand."

The commander didn't reply, instead he turned on his heel and left the ballroom.

"The effrontery of that man." Lord Stanton continued to mop at his face. "Why didn't he and his men help?"

Edward closed his eyes for a moment and took a deep breath before he answered. "It's our job to police the guild, not the Queen's. If we allowed her interference with that, she'd have a precedence for other meddling."

"Well, what do we do?"

"I will assemble some men and retrieve the Lady Marion, and hopefully, that outlaw as well." He gestured to the ballroom. "As Guildmaster, your place is here, of course."

"Excellent. My thought exactly." His father's coloring began to return to normal.

Edward turned away, unwilling to trust himself not to speak the hot words that burned on the back of his tongue. How had such a fool sired a man of his intellect? His gaze met that of the steward and the man hurried over.

"How may I help, sir?"

"Send word to my men and have my horse saddled. I'll not let that fiend get away with my future wife." He kept his face neutral and dragged his eyes from the spectacle of his father. It wouldn't do for the servants to see too clearly what he really thought of that man. "See that you keep the Guildmaster safe."

The steward inclined his head, but not before Edward saw the derision on his face.

As he made his way to the outer door, Marion's father stepped in front of him. "I hold you solely responsible for the safety of my daughter." The man standing in front of him swayed slightly, but his eyes had none of the bleary look of before. He once again held himself like the Guildmaster he was.

"Only a man who's betrothed can claim responsibility for another man's daughter." Edward narrowed his eyes. This was working to his advantage. "When I return Lady Marion to you unharmed, you will acknowledge my right to wed her?"

Lord Ravenswood swallowed, then inclined his head once in an almost regal gesture. "When you bring her back to me unharmed, I will formally announce your betrothal."

"Very good."

Before he could move, the Guildmaster gripped his upper arm, swinging Edward to face him. "If she's not returned unharmed, I will use every ounce of my power to destroy what you're trying to build."

Edward stared at Marion's father until he released his arm. Edward brushed the wrinkles from his sleeve before meeting his gaze. "I'm a man of my word and will return the Lady Marion unharmed, but I'd think it over carefully before you choose to irritate me unduly. I'm a dangerous enemy."

"So am I." Lord Ravenswood's leaned forward, the alcohol on his breath evident. "So am I."

Robin tugged the sack over Marion's head. and then pulled her goggles back down to secure it. "When we get inside, I'll loosen your hood."

His hands were warm on either side of her head, and the blood rushed to her cheeks. She swallowed hard. Surely it was the stench of the nearby wharves that made her stomach roil, not his touch.

The rope around her dropped away and each man took an arm—Robin on her right and John her left. "You can trust us to be your eyes," Robin said. "We'll make certain you come to no harm."

She gritted her teeth and let them guide her out of the swaying craft. She felt the tar of the roof beneath her booted feet as they walked.

"Small step here." Robin slowed and gave her time to feel the single stone step. Her other senses seemed to have heightened with the blindfold, and she heard the latch of a door click before whining open on rusted hinges. If they weren't careful, the entire kingdom would rust shut.

"I've got you." John tightened his grip as Robin dropped her arm and moved away. "He's just securing the door."

Even without the sounds, she'd known they were indoors from the musty odor and lack of wind. If she had to guess, she'd say they were in a large building, perhaps even a warehouse. Robin's footsteps echoed back to the doorway where they'd entered, then away. Another door opened, and then his footsteps brought him back to her.

"Here we go." Robin once again took her other arm. "Just down these stairs."

This time the steps were wooden, creaking with each footfall although they felt sturdy enough. They must be narrow. Robin moved to a position slightly ahead of her and John kept his hand on her arm from behind her. She kept count in her head, twenty-three steps, with two turns. Perhaps two flights?

"Last step, my lady," Robin said.

Marion's boot left the wooden step and came to rest on a solid surface. She dragged her foot, feeling for more information.

Yes, definitely stone, but not polished. They could be on the main floor of one of the warehouses. Robin and John once again took up positions on either side of her. Listening to the echoes of their footfalls, the space was big. Just how big, she couldn't tell.

"Hang on a moment." John moved away to fiddle with another door—this one just as creaky.

"There's a small sill here." Robin guided her foot to the obstacle. "Then more stairs."

Once inside this doorway, Robin reached up and pulled the gag from her mouth. "I am sorry for the necessity, but I really didn't want the world to know we're here."

Marion worked her jaws. The gag hadn't been painful, but she'd strained against it so much her jaw had cramped. "No doubt." Sarcasm wasn't much, but it was the only weapon she had at her disposal right now.

"You wound me." Robin's merriment curled around his words.

"How dare you laugh at me." She jerked her arm from his and lost her balance. Only John kept her from pitching forward down who knew how many stairs.

"Easy there, my lady." John set her back on her feet. "There'll be time later for recriminations. For now, let's get safely down."

She didn't jerk away when Robin took her arm, but she refused to give him the satisfaction of conversation. Besides, counting stairs took concentration. She was at fifty-eight when her foot reached solid stone. They must be in the basement of one of the warehouses. Before she could gather more clues about her surroundings, the men hurried her onward down a hallway. They traveled for several minutes, turning multiple times until her sense of direction began to cloud.

"Duck down." Robin's hand forced her head down. "It's a bit tight here."

If she had to duck, John must be bent almost double. "Is it much farther?"

"We'll be there soon." He kept her moving. The texture beneath her feet didn't change, but the odors did. At first a rusty damp—overlaid with the smoke from sputtering gaslight fixtures. These morphed into the more domestic smell of bread baking and meat roasting.

Was it this far to his lair or a ruse to confuse her? Only time would tell.

"And we're here." Robin's words announced a halt to their travels as he pulled the bag from her head.

She blinked to adjust her eyes to the light. They stood in front of an open door that led into a masculine study. There was too much clutter in the room to catalogue quickly, but there seemed to be a sort of tangled order, as if its owner had a subtle method for the madness.

"Please." Robin gestured for her to precede him. "Be my guest. I'll send for some tea, if you like."

"I won't be staying that long." She flounced into the room, followed by John and reached her icy hands toward the warmth of the fireplace. "Just get on with your revelations, so I may return home. I'm certain my disappearance is causing a quite a stir."

At Robin's glare, John covered his bark of laughter with a cough. "I'll go see to the tea." He beat a hasty retreat.

"As you wish." Robin shrugged and took a seat behind the desk. "But you should know we're working on my timetable, not yours." The words were said in a pleasant enough tone, but she could sense the steel behind them. It wouldn't do to underestimate him.

However, it would help if he continued to underestimate her. "As you wish." She perched on the edge of a leather chair, still close to the heat of the fire. "I'm all ears."

"Not hardly." Robin let his eyes roam over her black-garbed form.

"Indeed." Marion, face flushing, got up and began to pace. "I'm doing my best to be civil and that is your response?"

"My apologies," Robin said. "Please return to your seat. I'll try to behave."

Her eyes fell on a heavy brass cylinder on a bookshelf. She positioned herself between it and Robin and tucked the cylinder into the folds of her skirt before she turned back to him. "Perhaps we bring out the worst in each other." She took a seat in the chair she had vacated.

"Perhaps we do at that." Robin ran a hand through his hair. "But these are perilous times and we need to be allies, not enemies."

Marion bit down on the inside of her cheek to keep the words she wanted to speak from escaping. *Allies indeed.* "Why don't you tell me what you know."

Robin searched her face. "What I've discovered takes some explanation, so promise you'll not interrupt until I'm finished."

"You have my word." She folded her hands in her lap, covering the brass cylinder clutched in her hand.

"Two years ago, my men began to pick up whispers of someone experimenting with the integration of flesh and machine." He flexed his right arm.

Marion frowned, there was something in the movement of his arm that didn't look quite right. She filed that anomaly away for further consideration later. "But that kind of experimentation has been going on for years. What was different about what you're hearing now?"

Robin took a deep breath. "These experiments involved weapons. And beyond that, the experiments were being done on children."

"On children?" Her mind whirled. "When?" She leaned forward. "When exactly did this supposedly start? This could be the missing link we've been searching for."

"Missing link you've been searching for?" Robin's face reflected his puzzled tone. "What are you talking about?"

"The epidemic with the children." She closed her eyes to try to align dates in her mind. "We've determined the virus isn't natural."

"Wait a minute." Robin held up a hand. "We've determined? You already knew about this?" Comprehension dawned on his face. "That's why you've been gallivanting around in this ridiculous persona, stealing gold. You're not just bored, you're financing a cure."

"Of all the insulting—" Marion balled her hands into fists, letting her nails bite into the soft flesh of her palms. She truly didn't know which accusation to address first.

"Now, Marion." Robin was on his feet in a flash, pacing. "I didn't mean to anger you. But it appears we've been working at cross purposes—coming at the same problem from different directions."

"What else have you discovered?" She bit out the words between clenched teeth.

He leaned on the mantle. "You may not want to hear this, but we believe Edward Stanton is behind this."

"Believe?" She fixed him with a level look. "Do you have proof?"

Robin turned away from her toward the fire. "Not as yet. But we have a trail of suspicious activity."

"Of course there's no proof." She blew out breath and threw up her hands, careful not to dislodge the cylinder in her lap. So much for getting something helpful from this man. "Does your antipathy for the man have no bounds? You've found actual information, but instead of pursuing it, you're clinging to an old feud."

"That old feud, as you put it, began with the death of my father." His voice was low, but the anger in his eyes caused her to recoil slightly.

"Nonetheless." She rose, grasping her weapon securely, but still hidden by her skirt. "Is there anything else I should know?"

Robin glared for a moment then turned away. "No. Not a thing."

"Very well." She raised a ladylike hand and brought the cylinder crashing down on his head.

CHAPTER FOURTEEN

His head pounded as he swam toward consciousness and a familiar voice. The furnishings of his study coalesced as his mind processed where he was and what had happened.

"Robin?" John's grave face was at odds with the grin tugging at his friend's mouth. "Did you let that girl get the better of you again?"

"Yes." Robin gritted his teeth as he struggled into a sitting position. "And I'm getting just a bit tired of it. How long have I been out?"

"I'd say no more than ten minutes." John rose, poured a goblet of liquid, and offered it. "This will be good for what ails you."

Robin squinted at the bubbling liquid in the glass. "May I know what the elixir is before I accept? Recent experience has made me wary."

"Some of Dr. Tuck's new restorative," John said. "There are no ingredients that will harm you. And they should help with the headache you're fighting."

He sipped at the glass and wrinkled his nose. "Could be worse. And I need my wits about me. I'm not about to let her get away with this again." He upended the glass, swallowing every drop. "Make ready. We're going after her."

"That's the spirit." John clapped him on the back and Robin struggled to stay upright. "She may still be down here. This place is maze if a person isn't familiar."

"I wouldn't count on that." Robin bit back his frustration and rose. "That girl has more than her fair share of luck."

"Too true." John turned back to the desk.

"We had her blindfolded when we brought her down here, but she could tell our general direction." Robin stroked his chin. "She'll be looking for the stairs. If luck is with us, she'll head to the north passage and be stopped by the cave in."

"With our luck—and hers—she'll head west." John heaved a sigh. "If she takes the first set of stairs, she'll go straight to the street. She won't have any trouble finding her way home from there."

They hurried into the main hall where several men lounged around scarred wooden tables. The fire reflected the tarnished glare of the gaslights inset at regular intervals along the stone walls. They stilled when Robin and John entered.

"We've got an intruder loose." Robin strode to the cabinet against one wall and removed his bow and sheaf.

The men scrambled to their feet and began to arm themselves.

"Relax. It's just a wee girl." John grinned. "But don't underestimate her."

"And don't hurt her." Robin glared at John. "I want her back, but back unharmed."

"Not her again." Duncan had ducked his head, but the words were still audible.

In two steps, Robin had him pinned against the wall. "I'll thank you to keep a civil tongue in your mouth."

Duncan's face reddened and he avoided Robin's intent gaze. "I meant no disrespect."

"I'd hope not." John's chuckle was more of a rumble than a laugh. "She bested you as much as the rest of us."

"All right then." Robin turned to face the rest of the room. "John will come with me out the west exit. Duncan, you take Holden and Marcus and search the north. I don't think she'll have gone that way, but remember what I said. She's not to be harmed, just held."

"Yes, sir." Duncan was obviously pleased Robin had put him back in charge after the reprimand. "You can count on me."

"I know I can," Robin said. "Let's be off. Too much time has passed as is." Robin dashed into the stone corridor, his mind turning over recent events. If Marion would only trust him, they'd get further working together. He snorted. If he was perfectly honest, he'd have to admit she wasn't the only one with trust issues. Oh, well, they'd cross those barriers later. He returned his attention to the path searching for any clue she'd come this way.

"There's no sign she's been here." John's voice was hopeful as they continued up the stairs, nearing the top.

"No." Robin held out a hand to stop John's progress. "Listen. I thought I heard something."

John cocked his head, but only silence surrounded them. "I don't hear a thing. But it could have been the door at the top you heard."

"Maybe." Robin resumed the climb, but kept his pace slow enough so he could listen closer. They rounded the last landing and faced the closed door. He pointed at the latch. "She came this way. The bolt isn't latched." Finally, luck was on his side.

"We should be gaining on her too." John took a deep breath, only slightly winded after the steep climb. He turned on a battery torch he took from his vest pocket, keeping the beam shielded with his hand.

Robin put his finger to his lips and eased open the door, peering into the dark alleyway. Far down the way, a ghostly outline of a gaslight wavered in the fog, marking the intersection with the street. No sound of hurrying footsteps reached his ears. He motioned with his head and they both slipped into the dark, one on each side of the doorway. Robin pulled an arrow out of his quiver and held it at his side, lightly notched in the bowstring and ready for trouble.

John focused the light on the ground, giving them a chance to search for clues as they made their way toward the street. Normal late night sounds drifted to them, an occasional voice—from the tavern around the corner. The river beat against the jetty and a mournful horn from a barge announced its way.

Step by step they inched their way through the inky blackness toward the light. At the edge of the alley, Robin halted, keeping within the shadows. "She's probably gone directly to the Engineers' compound." He replaced the arrow in the quiver on his back. "We still have a chance to catch up with her, if we hurry."

John followed him into the light. Robin darted across the street, but stumbled on a large bundle of rags in the gutter.

"Hey, there. Watch where you're a'going." The bundle stood and morphed into the dirty stick-figure of a child.

"Whoa." Robin rocked back on his heels and John stopped beside him. "What do we have here?"

Robin moved in a closer. Mud covered the waif, but her long hair and delicate features identified her as a girl, probably a few years older than she looked. He bent down and she flinched back, but didn't run away. "What is a little one like you doing out here this time of night?"

"I'm not little. I'm ten and plenty big enough to tend to Tom." She rubbed her nose with the back of her hand. "Had to get Tom away from them people. You gotta help us." She sniffed. "They done something to my brother."

The rags still at her feet shifted and a moan came from them. They couldn't just leave these children here. Marion would have to wait.

John joined Robin on the ground as he examined the now-still boy. He was obviously older than the girl—probably closer to thirteen, but still too young to have been subjected to this. Robin's breath caught in his throat at the sight before them.

A bloody bandage covered the boy's right shoulder, ending at the elbow joint. Instead of continuing into a normal forearm and hand, metal glinted in the light. The weapon-like appendage was somehow bonded onto his arm, obviously causing him great pain. He moaned again when Robin touched him, feeling for broken bones and other possible injuries. The boy was hot, burning up with fever. But Robin couldn't stop staring at the monstrosity attached to his body.

The girl poked Robin to get his attention. "It ain't just his arm. His head don't work right neither."

"I'll carry him." John's cold voice was at odds with the gentleness of his touch as he lifted the boy.

145

"Wait now. Where you taking him?" The girl danced around John, eluding Robin's grasp.

He finally grabbed an arm and pulled her to face him. "We're taking him someplace safe." He frowned. This would be beyond the skill of Annie. He'd have to send for Dr. Tuck. "I'll get him a doctor. I promise."

She studied him for a long moment as John stood by. "We'll go with you, but if you hurt him, I'll hunt you down."

Marion continued to look back from where she'd come, certain Robin and his henchmen would appear, swarming from the shadows any minute. Thank goodness, she still had on her "Maiden of Iron" costume. The well-worn boots, leather trousers, and long black coat rendered her almost invisible—comfortable as well. Even still, she took care to stick to the shadows and avoid the few others out this late. Those lurking about weren't up to anything good.

The sound of a horse's hooves and a metallic snort made her start as she backed against the clammy bricks of the building. She focused her gaze toward the sound. The glow from the equine's nostrils were apparent several long seconds before the shape of the horse—with the man astride—became clear. Edward had come after her. When he drew even with her hiding place, she stepped into the light.

"Marion." He threw himself from the horse and grabbed her in a tight embrace. "You're safe. Did he just let you go?"

"No." She stiffened and pulled back. "I managed to escape on my own."

Edward loosened his hold. "Of course you did. I didn't mean to imply anything else. The important thing is that you're out of his clutches."

"My father must be worried. I need to get back to him." She almost laughed, just thinking how unlikely it was that her father was concerned about her.

He studied her outfit. "It seems your costume is much more suitable than I envisioned. Can you manage my horse astride?"

"Of course." What kind of a ninny did the man think she was? "I've been riding astride all my life."

He ignored her attitude and offered his cupped hands so she could mount. He vaulted into the saddle behind her and guided the equine into a slow walk.

"I assured your father that I'd mount a rescue. So this little escapade has worked to our advantage." Edward's arms were warm and his voice low in her ear. "He was so desperate to see you safe that he gave his word he'd approve our match if I returned you unharmed."

Her father worried? That concept would take some consideration. She gave herself a mental shake. Not now though. Now she needed to concentrate on Edward. Before she'd enter into any type of permanent agreement with him, she had to be certain he wasn't the man Robin claimed. He'd promised a partnership. Was that truly what he was after?

"When *you* returned me safe and sound?" She half turned in the saddle to read his face. "You do realize I'm perfectly capable of taking care of myself, right?"

"Of course I do. That is why we make such a perfect match." He gave the mount a slight nudge, urging him into a faster gait.

"But we must work within your father's expectations until you're out from under his thumb."

"But don't you see? This is the perfect time to show him how wrong he is."

"No, my dear girl. He'll never see what he doesn't want to see." Edward's arms tightened around her. "You'll have a much better chance of convincing him once you're a married lady, with power of your own. Now he only sees you as his little girl."

Marion bit her lip. It sounded plausible, when put that way. But still, something inside resisted the thought.

"This will go much easier if you consent to playing the rescued damsel." Edward's hand brushed her cheek as he tucked a lock of hair back into its chignon.

"I am no damsel in distress." Marion spit the words between gritted teeth.

"Of course you're not." Edward threw back his head and laughed. "I pity the man who makes that mistake. I'd even pit you against that unladylike villain, the Maiden of Iron."

The knot in her chest began to loosen. Her secret was still safe. "Well, then, what exactly shall we tell my father?"

CHAPTER FIFTEEN

"Annie? Duncan?" Robin's voice echoed down the stairs of his headquarters as he and John carried the children toward help.

Annie appeared first with Duncan close on her heels. She took one look at the bundles cradled in their arms and turned to Duncan. "Go for Dr. Tuck. Make haste and don't take no for an answer."

Robin let out the breath he'd been holding. Annie and Tuck would know how best to help them. "Where should we put them?"

"They'd best be bedded down in the infirmary." She led the way past the kitchens. "There's none else in there, so I'll move in as long as needed."

Robin took in the well-ordered kitchen and again thanked his lucky stars that Annie had taken over the running of this place. Without her management these past few years, he really wouldn't have survived. He cradled the small girl in his arms. And he wouldn't be in the position to take care of those who didn't have a voice. His spirit surged. Perhaps he had a purpose after all.

"Here you are, my ducks." Annie bustled around the large room, in and out of two rows of white-clothed beds, turning up gas lamps. She pointed to two beds, side-by-side and tucked into a corner away from the door. "This will give you the most privacy and keep you from prying eyes."

"What's you gonna do with us?" The girl squirmed away as soon as Robin deposited her on one of the beds.

"We're going to make you well." Annie looked down at her as the girl stood beside the bed that now held her brother. "You're brave girl, and you've found the help your brother needs. Now it's time to let us help him."

John's eyes met Robin, and he knew they were of the same mind. Whoever did this must be stopped. At any cost.

"You two stop staring at each other and get busy. I need your help."

John lumbered over. "What do you need?"

Annie's hands were a blur as she worked on the boy, removing the filthy garments and covering him with clean sheet. "John, bring me hot soapy water. Robin begin arranging those screens." She used her head to point at the cloth screens stacked neatly in one corner. "We'll position them around the bed to keep out the chill and give them some privacy."

The small girl leapt in front of Annie, a knife pulled from somewhere in her apron. "You can't do no more 'til you tell me first."

"That's a reasonable request." Annie's expression didn't change. "But not one that needs a knife to be asking. I wouldn't think much of you as a protector if you didn't."

"There's none left but us." The girl's chin quivered. "Tom's took care of me, and now I'm watching out for him."

Annie pointed to Robin. "It's him that's in charge. He brought you here for protection. You can trust him." She met the girl's eyes and waited for a sign of acceptance. "I'm cleaning up your brother and making him comfortable, so he'll be ready when the doctor gets here."

The girl didn't move from in front of her brother. "I wants to help."

"I couldn't take care of your brother without your help." Leave it to Annie to know how to put the girl at ease. "What's your name?"

"I'm Bessie ... Elizabeth." Her small body vibrated with worry and fear. "Will he be okay?"

"Only the good Lord knows for sure, but I would say he'll pull through." Annie clucked her tongue. "Here's John with the water. You can help me get him cleaned up."

The girl eyed Annie one long moment, then slipped the knife into a hidden pocket.

Robin relaxed. He'd been poised to act if the need arose. Before he could comment, Dr. Tuck entered. He paused in the doorway with black bag in hand, taking in the scene before he advanced on the bed. "Now what do we have here?"

"They done something to Tom." Bessie sniffed. "You got to fix him."

"Hmm." Dr. Tuck began working the bandage on the mutilated arm free. The smell of putrefaction engulfed them in waves as he removed the layers of dirty wrappings. "How long ago was this done."

"I'm not for certain. I got him away from the farm three nights ago." Bessie squinted at the process. "They rounded us up on the wagons a fortnight or so before that."

"Rounded you up?" Robin forced himself closer. "Were you kidnapped."

"They promised to make us well." She kept her focus on Dr. Tuck. "Tom'd caught the nasty, and I didn't have no way to pay a doctor."

The boy moaned as Dr. Tuck removed the last layer. His eyes met Annie's, and she scurried away. They all stared in horror at the area on his shoulder where festering flesh congealed amidst the dull flash of metal.

Bessie gave a small cry and flung her body onto her brother's and sobbed.

"Doc?" Robin put a hand on the girl's shoulder.

"I've heard of such." He gestured to the fusion of flesh and metal. "And so have you. It's not dissimilar to what I did for you, replacing bones with steel." He gave Robin's arm a long look. "However, Lord Stanton's experimentation with animals has actually integrated the metal with flesh."

Before Robin could reply, Annie returned with a steaming cup of tea.

Dr. Tuck bent down and pulled Bessie away from her brother. "I'm going to give your brother some medicine to help him sleep while I get the wound cleaned up. If he was awake, it would hurt him too much. Is that okay with you?"

Bessie wiped the back of her hand across her eyes. "Yes."

Tuck pulled a small glass vial from his bag and tipped a couple drops into the tea. He put a hand on boy's flushed forehead. He counted the shallow breaths then tipped in a few more. "We need to get a third or more of this down him before I start work."

Annie put an arm around Bessie. "We can do it, can't we?"

"Yes, ma'am." Bessie knelt beside her brother's head.

John levered the boy's head up and Annie put the cup to his lips. Between Bessie's crooning encouragement and Annie's deft manipulation of the cup, the boy began to swallow.

Dr. Tuck watched for a moment before he motioned Robin to join him at the other end of the room. "I don't know what you know, but I'm almost certain the epidemic in our children is directly linked to this."

Robin stroked his chin. "You're working with Marion, aren't you?"

"I wondered how long it would take you to put it all together."

"I might have figured it out sooner if that little minx had been more forthcoming." He rubbed his head as a grim expression crossed his lips. "You're aware that the younger Lord Stanton is involved of course."

"No. I can't say that I did know that." Tuck raised an eyebrow. "Do you have proof?"

"Now you sound like Marion. I'm working on concrete proof, but just the fact that Stanton has perfected the melding of flesh and metal in that equine of his is proof enough." He pounded the wall with his fist. "And that dratted girl is bent on marrying that monster."

Tuck's face was grave as he returned his attention back to his patient. "We must work to prevent that at all cost."

Marion could see the lights from the guild compound glowing behind the trees. Her father was making a good show of caring that she'd been taken. If only his feelings were genuine. She blinked back moisture. Sparks of flame illuminated the dirigibles dotting the night sky—probably out searching for her. She shifted her weight in the saddle. The warmth from the great beast coupled with Edward's arms encircling her filled her with the urge to escape.

"Relax." Even his breath was hot on her ear, and she fought against her reaction to jerk away. "This will work to our benefit."

Marion clamped down on her urge to slip down from the saddle and run. It wouldn't be much longer, then she'd be free. "Yes, I believe you're correct." Assuming her father wasn't drunk. *Please God, don't let him have succumbed.* Dealing with her father in a drunken rage would tax her to the point of breaking. She kept her silence as the entrance to the compound came into view.

"Miss Marion, we were so worried." The guard at the gate rushed toward them. "Your father has been beside himself." He remembered his duty then and bowed to Lord Edward. "We're so grateful you've found her."

"Open the gate, man." Edward didn't even slow his horse, and the guard barely had time to fling open the portal and scramble out of the path of the huge equine. "I need to get your mistress to her father."

"Thank you." Marion twisted around Edward, hoping to catch the guard's eye. "Couldn't you have slowed?"

"Remember your station."

His cold words stung, but now wasn't the time to take issue. He also had to be feeling the effects of the night's events. Her eyes focused on the form of her father standing on the steps ... waiting. His silhouetted form seemed solid enough, no tell-tale swaying. He appeared to all the world as a competent Guildmaster. Well, looks could be deceiving.

Edward pulled up the horse and flung the reins to a servant. He swung to the ground, then lifted Marion off the horse. Keeping her hand in his, they faced the unmoving form of her father. "I've done as you requested." Edward's eyes locked on the Guildmaster. "Now it's your turn."

Lord Ravenswood didn't once turn his eyes toward his daughter. "As a token of my gratitude, I award you the hand of my daughter in marriage." He turned to the house servant who also served as his secretary. "Draw up the documents, so we may make this official and broadcast the good news."

Marion's eyes swam with tears. She should be glad, but her heart echoed with nothing but emptiness.

Edward brought her hand to his lips. "I shall take great care with your daughter. She is a prize beyond imagining."

"Indeed she is." Lord Ravenswood's eyes met his daughter's, his expression unreadable. "See that you don't forget it." He turned and disappeared inside the mansion.

"I'm so glad you're safe." Gretta came running from inside the house, enfolding her in a fierce hug. "Rescued?" She spoke into Marion's ear, her voice was almost too soft for Marion to hear. "You were rescued?"

"Later." Marion only had a moment to answer before Matilda was there too.

"Your mistress needs a long soak and a good night's sleep." Edward gestured toward the house. "See that you take good care of my affianced."

"Yes, my lord." Matilda curtsied low and urged Marion and Gretta inside. "I've already got your bath ready. I knew Lord Stanton would bring you home safe and sound."

"Stop fussing. Marion isn't a fragile thing to be coddled like this. Go on up and make sure the tea's there." Gretta planted her hands on her hips and faced Edward. "I want to know what happened. Where did you find her?"

Edward bowed low to Gretta. "I know all too well how strong our Marion is. But she has been through a great deal. I'm certain she can fill in the details adequately. I must return to the … ah … scene of the crime and assist my father in cleaning up the mess those ruffians left us with."

Gretta gaped at him. She'd obviously been hoping to goad him into a reaction. Although Marion was too tired to guess at Gretta's intent.

He turned back to Marion and reached again for her hand. "I will call on you in the morning, and we'll begin to make plans." He kissed her fingers and then turned back to his horse.

"I'd say you'd already been making plans." Gretta glared at her as he galloped away. "I think it's time we had a long talk."

Marion watched Matilda's retreating form. Gretta wouldn't leave her in peace until she shared all. "I will tell you everything, but only when we're alone." She lifted an eyebrow. "And I'd say there are some things you'll need to share with me." Such a lot had happened this evening. What she wanted was a chance to consider the events in peace. That wasn't happening, so she'd just have to make the best of it.

"Very well." Gretta linked her arm with Marion's and they followed the servant up the wide stairs. She wrinkled her nose. "Where on earth have you been? Your costume smells like you've been on a raid."

"Not quite." The grim set of her mouth relaxed at the memory of her time aboard the Night Maiden. Then the tension returned.

"But we will need to make a visit to our suppliers. Tomorrow is the next scheduled delivery. Dr. Tuck is getting too close for us to fall down on our job."

CHAPTER SIXTEEN

Edward strode past the servants into the foyer of his father's home. Some headway had been made to reclaim order from chaos. Before he could turn to the sound of his father's voice in the ballroom, a servant intercepted him. "There are two men to see you." He held out an envelope on a gold tray. "I put them in your private sitting room, my lord."

Edward tore open the envelope and gritted his teeth. This was the last thing he needed tonight. "Tell my father I'm still out if he asks. And have some food sent to my rooms."

"For just yourself?"

"Of course, just me." He glared at the man. "You don't think I'd entertain those men for long, do you?"

The servant bowed. "As you wish, sir."

Edward used the time it took to reach his sitting room to get a tighter grip on his temper. Simon and Morris knew not to bother him with anything less than a major catastrophe. This happenstance certainly met that criterion.

One hand on the doorknob, he took a final deep breath, then flung open the door. One man perched on the edge of a leather chair, the other leaned against the mantle. Both turned to him when the door opened.

"You did exactly right by coming." He waved them into chairs and took a seat behind his massive mahogany desk. "What I need is details." His eyes narrowed. "And I want to know exactly who is responsible for letting those children escape."

Morris shifted in his seat. "We're still working on that. Their escape led us to reevaluate the way they're being held."

"All right. More of that later." Edward leaned back in his chair. "Start at the beginning and tell me what happened."

Simon stood and walked to the fireplace again. "We were working with the group at Lownsdown Lake. They'd been there a fortnight or so. All well-infected, and about half had begun the alteration process."

Morris scratched his head. "It's the ones who are related that tend to be difficult. We might want to rethink how we assign them."

"Noted." Edward waved at Simon to continue.

"We noticed the count was off when they came through for the afternoon doses."

"So you weren't informed by anyone that there'd been an escape?" Edward steepled his fingers. "Interesting."

"We're also investigating that." Morris frowned. "This batch hadn't seemed difficult, but looking back they were almost too easy to manage."

Edward leaned forward. "What do you mean?"

"It's almost like they were taking orders from someone—one of their own. There wasn't the usual whining and reorientation period." Simon stroked his chin. "We may have someone on the inside."

"Get to the point, man."

Morris's face reddened. "They must have slipped out through the field right after breakfast."

"No way. The livestock is programmed to detect a threat in that field." He was certain his face communicated the malice he felt, but didn't care. "And anyone moving around in the field would be considered a threat."

"I know." Simon began to pace. "We made sure the kiddies were well aware of that fact. But we can't find another way they could have gotten out."

"Tell me about the children." Edward made a note on the paper in front of him.

Morris consulted a small notepad. "They were a brother and sister. The boy was well into the alteration process, the girl hadn't received her first graft yet. He was pretty far along. I wouldn't have thought he'd still even recognize her, much less follow her directions."

Edward stood. "So, you've lost two children. One is in an advanced state of alteration, the other is fully functional." He slammed a fist onto the desk causing the other two to jump. "So, if anyone gets hold of them, there's proof in the boy and a full explanation possible from the girl. Why are you still here? Why haven't they been found yet?"

"We tracked them to the wharves in the city, but their trail just disappeared," said Morris.

"Almost like they'd been picked up and transported somewhere." Simon appeared to wish he'd been transported somewhere.

Edward resumed his seat. "You know what has to be done. Tomorrow you'll begin the process of closing down that location, transport all to another farm."

"Yes, sir." They spoke in unison.

Edward put both hands on his desk and half-rose, his voice low. "And do whatever is necessary to find those children and get rid of the evidence. Do I make myself clear?"

"I think we have enough to information to find the farm, don't you?" John asked as he and Robin waited in the corridor for Dr. Tuck to finish giving Annie final instructions on the care of her charges.

"My thoughts exactly." Robin gritted his teeth. "We must locate the place where those children were being held as soon as possible."

"And we need Tuck along when we find it. He can identify what exactly is being done."

"What do you need me to identify?" Dr. Tuck slipped into the hallway.

"We've got to find out what's going on." Robin led them toward the stairway leading to the top of the building. "And we need your help."

Dr. Tuck fell in step with Robin. "You may need more than just my help."

"What do you mean?" Robin stopped and pinned the rotund doctor with a stare.

Tuck was silent for a long minute, then seemed to come to a decision. "You already know I've been working with Marion on the odd happenings of late." He motioned them to continue up the stairs. "You and Marion are working at cross purposes, and it's time you joined forces."

"Marion?" Robin had hesitated only a minute before blurting out his suspicions. "You're not just working with Marion, you're working *for* her."

John's rumbling chuckle filled the stairwell. "I warned you not to underestimate that girl."

"Shut up." Robin refused to be sidetracked. "Is what she told me last night about the epidemic with our children coming from you? It's not just her leaping imagination?"

"I think you have a badly skewed impression of Miss Marion. She's as level-headed a young woman ..." He glanced at Robin. "... or for that matter young man, that I've ever met. Her assessments are always grounded in logic and clear thinking. Almost to the point of her own detriment."

"Her own detriment—" Nope, he'd follow that line of thought later. Now he had to stay focused. "What exactly are her assessments?"

"Miss Marion has been convinced this epidemic wasn't natural almost from the very start. After she began funding my research, I discovered she was right."

They continued up the last flight of stairs, through the door, and into the predawn dark. John reached for the mooring ropes of the Night Maiden while Robin and Tuck boarded and made the airship ready to fly.

"It's been a while since you've had me up." Tuck took a firm hold on a deck line leading to the dirigible's balloon as the small craft bobbed.

"I wouldn't have tonight, if we'd put the old girl to bed already." Robin exchanged glances with John. "We'd had her out earlier for a little adventure."

John harrumphed, but didn't say anything.

Tuck raised an eyebrow. "Care to share?"

"I guess you'll hear about it anyway." Robin opened the steam jets and adjusted the tiller. "We paid a visit to a reception at the Pilots Guild. The honorable Lord Stanton was having himself declared Guildmaster."

"What?" Tuck stared at Robin. "I thought that type of announcement could only come from the Queen."

"Oh, she was there." Robin blew out air. "To be honest, I don't think she intended to add her congratulations, but we barged in before she had a chance."

Tuck laughed and pointed a finger at Robin. "You are a naughty boy."

"That's also where I ran into Marion." His lips thinned to a grim line. "Edward was in the process of announcing their engagement."

Tuck frowned. "That doesn't seem a bit like our level-headed Marion."

"It seems exactly like her—to me." Robin swayed as the ship lifted off. "She has a definite blind spot when it comes to Edward."

"Hmmm. I expect you're working on that part of the problem." Tuck turned toward the still-dark horizon. "Where do you think we'll find this farm?"

"From what the girl said, it's just northeast of the city, out Chelmsford way." John adjusted the line of sand-filled ballast bags and untangled the rope that kept them attached to the ship. "Not too far for them to have come, if they were desperate."

"And I know that Edward owns land out there. It's one of the places I've had my men keeping an eye on." Something like hope began to infuse Robin's outlook. Perhaps the time had finally come. "As we get close, I'll come in silent, so no talking. Sound carries from above."

They traveled in almost silence now, the hissing of the steam subsiding into shorter bursts as the little ship drifted on the wind. With one eye toward the ground, Robin found the landmark he sought. He pointed to the large pond, visible with the glittering reflection of the stars.

John lowered ballast bags over the rail of the ship, ready to cushion their landing. Robin guided the craft to a clearing at the edge of a copse of trees and set them down, leaving the engine on a low idle. He motioned the two men close. "John, stay here. It's too risky to leave her unguarded. We may have to leave quickly."

"I don't like you going alone."

"He's not alone." Tuck pulled a small pistol from his pocket. "I've been watching this young whelp's back for more years than you."

"Give us three-quarters of an hour." Robin ignored the stairs John lowered and leapt over the railing to the ground. He held out a hand to steady the doctor, who in turn glared and ignored it.

They skirted the edge of the pond and made their way toward the dark shape of the out buildings. Light flickered from several windows, but no one appeared to be moving about. They rounded a building and Robin caught the glow from a lantern carried by a watchman on rounds. He grabbed Tuck's arm and held him into place until the light faded, then they darted toward the nearest building. Guards were a good sign, proving this was no normal farm setup.

The first door they tried was locked, but the second opened with silent ease. From the outside, the structure appeared to be a barn. Once inside, they discovered a much more organized layout. They stood in an entry hall of sorts, with corridors leading off in several directions. The gaslights set high on the walls at intervals provided dim, but adequate illumination.

Tuck leaned close to Robin. "Not quite what I expected."

"I suspect that will be the theme of this visit." Robin led the way down the hallway, ignoring the closed doors they passed. The astringent bite of antiseptic lingered in the air. They were on the right track. Sure enough, the hallway ended in a viewing room. The wall in front of them was set with windows overlooking a vast dormitory. Several white-gowned figures—obviously attendants—moved among the iron beds. Robin pulled back into the shadows and turned to Tuck. "I think we've found what we were looking for."

Tuck led Robin back the way they'd come. Once in the main reception area, they took a different corridor. "What are you looking for?"

Robin's expression was grim. "Something that would prove this isn't a place for children to get better."

This hallway had a more utilitarian feel to it, and the odor of something recently burned hung in the air. He carefully tried several doors, but all were locked. The hallway ended in a set of stairs. Robin turned to Tuck. "Up or down?"

"Up is for those in charge. What we seek will be below ground."

From the set of his mouth, Robin could tell Tuck had also identified the odor. The char in the air wasn't from a fire, but from burning flesh. "Down it is, then."

CHAPTER SEVENTEEN

Marion rose before dawn. She moved with practiced silence around her room, throwing on a working dress that would have appalled her oh-so-proper maid. With her shoes in hand, she crept down the back stairs that led to the door of her hideout. Once the door closed behind her, she let out a breath she hadn't realized she'd been holding. Today's raid should net them another tidy sum to fund Dr. Tuck's research. They were so close to answers.

The light from an electric torch bounced in the hallway. Of course, Gretta would already be here. Hopefully, Addison was with her. Three was the perfect number for their forays below London. They couldn't have managed without him. He was the one who determined when the gold shipments made their way into town.

"Marion, is that you?" Gretta's dark form materialized in the doorway from the sleeping wing, only recognizable by shape since the torch pointed toward Marion's eyes.

Marion didn't need to see. She'd been in and out of these forgotten rooms since she could walk. This had been a favorite place of her mother's, and they'd spent hours here together. Some of her earliest memories involved her grandfather. They'd spent evenings here—her cuddled in his lap while he fiddled with his pipe. He'd tell her all about the times when the Lightning Bolt had been a prized dirigible in the guild's service. Now it rested here, buried and forgotten under the guild grounds—but still serving the family by giving her a much-needed place of refuge. "Who else would it be? Point that light somewhere else besides my face. The glare is blinding me."

"Oh, sorry. I'm still paranoid after last night." Gretta clicked a button on its handle, the light dimmed, and she leveled the beam at the floor. "You claimed fatigue last night. It's time to come clean. I want to know all the details."

Marion bit her lip. She should have known that Gretta wouldn't rest until she was satisfied she'd heard it all. "I told you pretty much everything."

"You barely told me anything before you pleaded a headache." Gretta led the way down the corridor toward the changing rooms. "What I want to know is what happened when you were with Robin." She stopped and turned, hands on hips. "Your father was more like himself than I've seen since your mother's accident."

"I only have time for a shortened version. We must be in place before the gold arrives." She stepped into her room. Gretta had gotten here first and lit the lamp. She began to unbutton her dress, then stopped. "Where's Addi?" That boy-child too often appeared in places he shouldn't.

"I sent him for the horses. I'm already dressed. I'll help you while you talk."

"I have to tell you that Robin has some interesting notions." Marion let her dress fall and began to wriggle into the black leather breeches. "Some of it makes sense, the rest ... well ... you know how set he is on seeing Edward as the ultimate villain."

Gretta helped Marion button the white blouse, then held out the boots. "You might be wise to take some of what he says about Edward to heart. That man just isn't trustworthy."

"Not you too?" Marion plopped onto the bed and held up first one foot, then the other as Gretta slid on the boots. "I'm going to marry Edward, and you all better get used to that fact. We need his help." She stood and stamped her feet to settle the boots. She then turned her back so Gretta could guide her arms into the full length black coat. "Especially in light of what Robin has learned." She moved to the mirror. "Help me with my hair."

"What exactly did Robin tell you?" Gretta gathered the mass of black curls and began taming it with a combination of hairpins and combs. "Does he know what's causing the illness in the children?"

"Not exactly." Marion handed her another hairpin. "But he's discovered that a couple of years ago, someone began experimenting on children—integrating flesh and machine with the end being some kind of weapon grafted in flesh." She shuddered. "If that's what the point of all this is, we could be in big trouble."

"Does he know who's behind all the experiments? Are they still going on?" Gretta gave Marion her hat.

"That's all I learned." Marion jammed two wicked-looking hatpins into the hat to keep it secure and added her night vision goggles, ready for use when needed. "At that point, he began blathering about Edward. So I knocked him out and left." She grabbed the electric torch and gloves, then doused the light and took off down the corridor.

"You did what?" Gretta ran to catch up with her. "Why did you do that—was he threatening you?"

"No. I could tell he wasn't going to give me anything else, and I knew I had to get out of there." Marion paused at the base of the staircase that led to the gazebo entrance and studied the collection of weapons hung neatly on the wall. "Do you think William has had time to make any modifications to these? Surely he'd have let us know."

Gretta's eyes were grave as she studied her friend. "Why do you fight Robin at every turn?"

Marion faced her friend. "He doesn't have anything to offer us. Edward has the power and wealth we need to get to the bottom of this." She turned back to the weapons, and pulled down the lightning gun. It had been handy last time they'd been out she shoved it into her belt. "I know it sounds mercenary, but desperate times call for desperate measures." Marion avoided Gretta's eyes and instead reached for the bow and quiver, studying the odd-looking arrows. Each one had a thin wire that ran from the arrowhead down the shaft, through the fletching, ending at the notch. "Look here. He's put in the lightning arrows he promised." She held up the bow and pointed to a tiny metal box topped with a wire ball and attached to the drawstring. Its placement corresponded to where the arrow's notch would rest. She thumbed a switch on its side and the box hummed in her hand. "I can't wait to try this electric bow out on the automatons."

Gretta swung her around, forcing Marion to meet her gaze. "Tell me this one thing. Did you let Edward know where Robin was hiding? Does he suspect you're the Maiden of Iron?"

"No. I didn't tell Edward any of that." She jerked out of Gretta's grasp. "At this point, he doesn't need that information." She laid a hand on Gretta's arm. "Can we get through this morning first? I still have a lot to process, and you know how badly Dr. Tuck needs the gold to finance the next level of research."

"Agreed." Gretta pointed a finger at Marion. "But I'm not done with this topic. We've got to talk."

"I know, I promise." Marion made an x across her chest. "Cross my heart. Now kill that light so we can go meet Addi."

Marion, Gretta, and Addison once again dropped into the dim world of underground London. Only the hazy light from street-side gas lamps punctuated the gloom. Their feeble beams filtered through the grates in the tunnel ceiling, doing little to dispel the dark. Marion shone her electric torch into the darkness. The walls oozed damp, and muck pooled around her boots with every step, releasing a despicable odor.

"Is it my imagination or does this place smell a lot worse than the last time we were down here?" Gretta held a dainty white handkerchief to her face—the only bit of white in her all-black costume.

"Gah." Addison coughed.

"Hush." Marion swallowed down her own urge to gag. "Move on toward the junction of the two tunnels. There are more grates in that area."

As they approached their usual point of ambush, the hair on the back of her neck prickled. Something wasn't right. "Hold up." She put out a hand to keep the other two in place behind her and pulled her goggles down, hoping their night-penetrating capabilities would illuminate the situation.

Gretta leaned forward and put her mouth to Marion's ear. "Listen. We're not alone."

Marion blinked once more, the scene in front of her came into view, and she gasped. Arranged in the corners and behind makeshift barriers were grotesque parodies of children. They resembled children. Instead of arms, many had what appeared to be weapons. Others wore bizarre metal headpieces that sported appendages without a function that she could decipher. Before she could verbalize what she was seeing, the group began to move. As they lurched forward into the light, she heard Addi mutter an oath. "Get back." She shoved her friends back the way they'd come, only to realize they were now surrounded.

"Saints preserve us." Gretta pulled her own lightening gun from the holster at her waist, and the three stood facing outward as the nightmare unfolded.

"Here." Marion passed her pistol to Addi and pulled her lightning bow from its place on her back, fitting it with an arrow. "All we want to do is open a path out of here."

"How can we kill children?" The sob in Gretta's voice made the words squeak.

"They're not children anymore." Addi sounded more adult that any of them. He sighted along the barrel and fired the first shot.

Marion set her mouth and began loosing arrows.

Initially, the surge pushed Marion and her band away from their objective, but slowly they gained momentum. The child-force facing them seemed to be in some sort of a trance-state. Pain didn't register and unless they were completely incapacitated, wounding didn't do more than slow them.

As she and her small band made progress toward their entry point, Marion became aware of the silence. Battles were always punctuated with noise, but not this one. Here the absence of sound was only broken by their own harsh breathing and weapons fire. Their progress was punctuated by grunts and weapon fire. Their foes remained silent.

With the tunnel where they'd entered finally in sight, Marion positioned herself slightly between her friends and the opposing force. "One at a time, make a break. Gretta you're closest, go."

With a glance at her baby brother, Gretta let go a fusillade of shots from her pistol and darted to the opening. In almost one motion, she wrenched open the cover and leapt inside. She motioned to Addi. "Come on, you're next." She knelt within the entry and kept up steady fire to cover her brother's dash toward safety. Marion continued her inexorable move toward the tunnel, keeping one eye on her friends and one on the encroaching force.

One step before Addi reached his sister, a small child-soldier rose up and drove a sharpened shaft into Addi's side.

"Nooooo." Gretta bounded down and caught her brother as he staggered, kicking his attacker out of the way.

"I'm okay." His hand gripped his side. "Keep Marion covered."

"Get inside." Marion shouted. "I'm right behind you." She let go another round of arrows that slowed the onslaught long enough for her to grab Addi's other side and help lift him into the tunnel before she joined them. She clanged the grate shut, praying it would buy them the time they needed to escape.

Marion knew Addi needed help, real help, not just rest and stitching up. "We'll go straight to Dr. Tuck."

"No." Addi grabbed Marion's sleeve. "We can't risk exposure." He coughed, a horrible gurgle of a sound. "It's almost dawn. We have to get changed."

Marion bit her lip. Exposure didn't matter, but if they were caught, he'd never get the care he needed. That left them with only one solution. "I have another option. I'm taking you both to Robin's."

CHAPTER EIGHTEEN

Robin's feet hit the floor before the first alarm bell finished sounding. All his senses flashed into high alert with any vestige of sleep instantly erased. He'd slipped into breeches and boots before the third bell ended, and hurled himself out into the hall to meet John rounding the corner.

"Report." Robin buckled his belt and adjusted his sword.

Before John could reply, the all clear bell rung. "It's not exactly a false alarm, but you better come see for yourself. She's in trouble, so I've put them in the infirmary and sent for Dr. Tuck."

Robin took off at a dead run. He didn't need clarification. Marion had come to him for help. His heart lurched, and for the first time in years, he sent up a prayer asking for her protection and the wisdom to know how to navigate this situation.

He skidded to a halt a few yards from the infirmary and took a deep breath. It wouldn't do to rush in. He could trust Annie to act on his behalf. One more breath and then he strode into the room, his eyes searching for Marion. Relief washed over him as he identified her as the small figure standing beside the bed.

Gretta knelt beside her as Annie worked with her head bent over a motionless form.

"I've got the bleeding stopped, but he's going into some kind of shock." She looked up at Robin, who'd moved to stand behind Marion. "You did send for Dr. Tuck, didn't you?"

"John did." He focused on the young man in the bed. He thrashed and moaned, but appeared unconscious. It took him a minute to place him. "Is that Addison?"

"Yes." Gretta didn't relinquish her hold on her brother's hand. "You will help us, won't you?"

"Of course, I will." He reached a hand down to grip Gretta's shoulder. "He's grown into a young man since I last saw him. How old is he now?"

"He'll turn fifteen soon." She turned back to her brother and brushed his hair back from his head. "I don't know what's wrong. It was a fairly deep stab wound but shouldn't have had this effect on him."

"He's in good hands with Annie, and Dr. Tuck will be here soon." Robin turned to face Marion, his eyes taking in her Maiden of Iron attire. "They were waiting for you, weren't they?"

"Yes."

The horror in her eyes gave him pause. He'd never seen her afraid of anything. "Automatons?"

"No, not really." She shook her head as if to clear the memory. "Maybe ... of some type. I don't know what they were. They ..." She bit her lip then tried again. "They looked like some kind of children."

"Children?" Robin's gut clenched.

"I know they couldn't have been, but that's as close as I can come to a comparison. They were waiting for us at that section where all the tunnels meet."

"Where you ambushed me?" He quirked an eyebrow. "You went to the same place twice in a row?" He had tried to keep his tone light, but winced at the accusation implied in the question.

Marion caught the nuance and glared at him. "Don't start on me. I'm not an imbecile. I work hard not to be predictable. Sometimes, I use the same place twice. Sometimes not." She folded her arms and turned back to the table. "They shouldn't have known we were coming."

"Sounds like they just got lucky." He put a hand on her arm. "Tell me exactly what happened."

The words came hesitantly, then tumbled over each other as she described what they'd been through. "The worst part was the silence. They kept coming, no matter what. And not one of them made a sound. No cries of pain, fear, or anything, just deafening silence." She passed a hand over her eyes. "They didn't move like automatons. They moved like us, like children. Some young, some older. But they acted like machines."

Children? Robin's brain began clicking facts into place. "Come on." He put a hand on her arm to lead her away. "We need to talk."

"No." She shook him off and returned her focus to the bed. "I have to stay here."

Before he could argue, Dr. Tuck rushed into the room. "I got here as quick as I could." He tossed his frock coat on a nearby chair and began rolling up his sleeves to wash in the basin Annie had nearby. "Tell me what you know."

"He's been stabbed on the right side, and I've got the bleeding controlled." Annie held a clean towel ready for when the doctor finished scrubbing. "It appeared to go in clean and miss anything major." She frowned. "But his body is reacting to something. There could have been something on the blade."

"It wasn't a blade," Gretta said. "It was some kind of a tube thing with a sharp end."

"A tube?" Tuck took the towel and gave her all his attention. "Think hard, what would you compare it to? A needle perhaps?"

Her eyes widened. "Yes, that was it exactly. It was like the biggest needle I've ever seen. A good foot in length and ..." Her eyes reflected the same horror as he'd seen in Marion's. "It was part of the child's arm."

"Child?" Robin met Tuck's eyes. "He was attacked by a child?"

"Not just one." Marion took a step forward. "There must have been two dozen of them. And we don't know if they were children, only that they looked like some kind of children/machine hybrid."

"You said part of his arm." Dr. Tuck returned his attention to Gretta. "Was it part of some body armor?"

She bit her lip. "I misspoke. It was really where the bottom part of his arm should have been." She swallowed hard. "It was truly horrible," she finished in a whisper. "Truly horrible."

Tuck resumed his examination of the patient. "You better take Marion to see my other patients while I get this young man tended to. Then we'll all need to talk."

"I'll be close if you need me." Marion patted Addison's hand, but directed her comment at Gretta.

"I know." Gretta's eyes reflected her worry, but she waved her friend away. "Go see if you can get to the bottom of this."

"The others are in here." Robin led her to another large room that was set up like a hospital ward. In the corner there were several rolling screens obviously shielding a bed. As they approached, a child slipped out to meet them."

"Wot's happenin'?" The girl was clean, but obviously from the poorer section of London. "I heard a commotion, with bells and such and decided to lie low."

"You did well." Robin bent down so he was on an equal level with the girl. "This is Lady ..." He frowned at Marion, and she knew he was seeing her in her costume. "Lady M."

The girl stuck out her hand. "I know you. You're the Maiden of Iron." Her eyes gleamed with admiration. "I'm Bessie."

Marion took the hand. "I'm glad to know you." She put a finger to her lips. "But you know mum's the word on who I am, right?"

Bessie stood straighter, her manner solemn. "I won't never tell. We know what you done for us."

Marion raised an eyebrow. "You do?"

"Sure. I know you steal gold to find a cure." She pointed to the curtained enclosure. "Even the blokes that had us talked about you."

Robin put his hands on Bessie's shoulders and turned her toward him. "What did they say? Can you remember? It's important."

"They didn't know we were awake. I heard them talking about the Maiden of Iron, and how she couldn't be allowed to continue." Bessie wrinkled her nose. "I think they said something about testing the e-fec-tiv-ity of their weapons on her." She turned back to Marion, her eyes wide. "Did they hurt you? Is that what this's about?"

"No, child, I'm fine." Marion wanted to reassure the girl, but worry about Addison made that impossible. Better to just be truthful. "But my friend was hurt. Can you help us figure out what's going on?"

Robin put a hand on Marion's elbow, guiding her to the enclosure. "I think it's time you met Tom."

"He's my brother." Bessie stayed close to Marion's side. "They're helping him."

Robin pulled aside one of the barriers and revealed the still form laying on the bed.

Marion put her hand to her mouth. "That's it. That's what we saw." She sank to her knees beside the bed, reaching a hand toward him and then pulling back. "He's so young. What kind of monsters would do this?"

The boy stirred and Bessie ran to his side. She adjusted his covers and put a finger to her lips with one hand while motioning them away with the other.

Robin helped Marion to her feet and then readjusted the screen. When they were almost to the door, he slowed. "Now you see why we have to talk."

Her mind whirled as disjointed pieces of information coalesced into answers.. Tuck here now ... the army of robotic children ... Robin as a place of refuge. Yes, now was the time to share information and join forces.

CHAPTER NINETEEN

Dr. Tuck was the last to join them in Robin's study. Marion had been unable to convince Gretta to leave Addison's bedside. She gave a mental shudder. It was probably just as well. Now their quest for a cure had turned all too personal, and the details might be too much for her friend.

Robin stood at the stone fireplace, staring into the flames. Tuck settled himself behind the desk, and Marion presided over the tea tray that Annie had assembled. Marion caught Dr. Tuck's eye. "Perhaps a cup of tea?"

Marion poured without waiting for his answer. Before she could rise to take it to him, Robin intercepted her and took the saucer from her hand. He set the beverage in front of the doctor and reached for the decanter on a nearby table. "I think this might be more of what you need." He tipped a generous portion of the libation into the cup.

"Thank you." Tuck took a restorative sip. He stared at the ceiling for a long moment before turning to Marion. "I believe your part in this story is the first place to start, my lady."

Marion set her cup in front of her and began. She held nothing back, sharing their early theories and how she and Tuck had banded together to work toward a cure.

Robin folded his arms. "So you had no idea who was behind the ... virus?" He stumbled over the unfamiliar word. "How did you discover the Makers' gold shipments?"

"Addi found out. He'd heard rumors of an influx of gold into the Makers Guild and managed to trace the source through his informants. You know Addi. He never met a stranger and has friends in the unlikeliest of places." She remembered his sharp intellect that could ferret out any secret—even hers and tears stung her eyes. "After that, it was simple for him to figure out the shipping routes. He really is a genius."

Robin paced. "And we're back to the Makers Guild. Does anyone truly know what they do?" Robin quirked an eyebrow. "Besides oversee all the other guilds, guide and distribute new technology fairly, and advise the Queen."

"I know they're identified by the black robes they wear and the fact they won't associate with anyone else." Tuck leaned forward and locked his eyes on Marion. "Except you."

Robin stopped and stared at her. "What do you have to do with the Makers Guild?"

When Marion didn't answer, Dr. Tuck continued, "She was the affianced bride of the Guildmaster's son."

"The duel, the public shame ..." Robin narrowed his eyes. "Now it finally makes sense. Your brother was killed by one of the makers. They destroyed your reputation to keep their secret."

Marion squeezed her eyes shut as the world tilted. She took a deep breath, then opened them. "That has no bearing on where we are now. Let's remain focused on the issue at hand."

Robin knelt before her and took her hand. "Marion, that's the piece we've been missing. They must have known what you were doing all along and have finally decided it was time to take steps."

Marion jerked her hand from his grasp. "Don't you think I'd have noticed black-robed guild members skulking around? We've been careful, and there's no way they could have discovered what we were about."

"I'm certain you were careful." He rose. "However, your statement proves you weren't careful enough."

Marion stared at him, open-mouthed, with her fists clinched. *How dare he?*

He folded his arms. "If the Makers are working in a clandestine fashion, of course they wouldn't go around in their usual garb. They'd either be working through agents who weren't part of the guild, or go about without their robes."

Marion gulped back her quick retort as she reviewed the past few weeks. Had they been careless?

Dr. Tuck cleared his throat. "What you say may be true. But in all the history of the guilds, they've never taken a direct hand in the management of any other guild." He leaned his elbows on the desk and steepled his fingers. "Everything about this is unprecedented. Something has changed."

"But what?" John asked. "And how can we know if the change has taken place within the Makers' secret society?"

"We do know a few things." Tuck motioned them over and began to sketch out an illustration of his words. "Here at the top of the Makers Guild we have Guildmaster Wyndom. His sons, Maylon and Perios." He turned to Marion. "Maylon was your affianced, correct?"

A shudder ran up Marion's spine and encased her heart with ice. "He was a brute. Pure evil runs through his veins."

"What makes you say that?" Robin moved closer to her, his eyes dark with concern.

"It's time." Tuck's expression was tender, but firm. "They need to know what happened that night."

Marion swallowed the lump in her throat and closed her eyes to visualize that horrible scene. "My father had told me of the offer from the Makers Guild several weeks before I actually met Maylon. Our resources had dwindled since my mother's death." Heat filled her face. Her father had so mismanaged things in his grief that the guild had been on the edge of bankruptcy. She pushed aside her anger and disgust and continued. "They promised to restore our treasury as part of my bride price. Of course, I agreed."

Robin made a sound deep in his throat, but Tuck silenced him with a look. "Continue, my lady."

"I'd always known my duty. Meeting with Maylon wasn't too bad initially. Both our fathers were present." She swallowed again and worked to relax her hands. "The Guildmaster informed my father I'd need to be examined by the physicians to verify my purity and ability to bear children." She found a place on the wall to focus her attention so she wouldn't have to meet anyone's eyes. "My father agreed."

"I was present for the examination, of course," Dr. Tuck said. "Their physician tried to insist on embedding a device just under the skin of her wrist, but I refused to allow it." He removed his spectacles and wiped them with a handkerchief. "I had no idea then how dangerous that would have been. I was operating on instinct."

184

Marion gave him a look of thanks. "They didn't care for our refusal, but backed down." Her eyes turned inward as she forced the memories in the open again. "Later, when I was alone with Maylon, he tried to inject me with some kind of hypodermic. I screamed and managed to keep him at bay until my brother arrived. He'd heard my cries and had come running." A sob escaped and she turned away from them. "They fought. David died." She turned back to them and motioned to their gathering. "The guild withdrew their offer. Father withdrew further into grief, and here we are."

The persistent knocking pulled Edward out of an already troubled sleep. "What is it?"

His manservant opened the door and bowed. "I'm sorry, sir, but there is a man who insists on seeing you."

Edward reached up and twisted the gaslight to burn more brightly. "And you couldn't deal with the nuisance yourself?"

"It's a man in a black robe." The servant backed away, his face wary. "You told me to always inform you when one such appeared."

Edward's pulse quickened. "Show him to the best parlor and bring tea. I'll be down shortly."

The servant hesitated. "Do you wish help dressing?"

"No. Go." Edward threw back the covers and had turned to his trousers by the time the servant closed the door behind him. A Maker ... here? His instinct told him this appearance didn't bode well. He finished buttoning his shirt, foregoing collar and cuffs, instead choosing to throw on a tweed jacket. The sooner he found out what was going on, the better for everyone.

He raced down the stairs, but paused in the hallway leading to the parlor. He stood long enough to control his breathing and slow his pounding heart. It wouldn't do to appear too anxious.

Striding into the room, Edward schooled his expression to one of polite concern. He bowed to the hooded figure, but kept his distance. He knew better than to approach and offer a hand. "Welcome, my lord. How may I be of assistance?"

The figure set down his cup and waved a hand at the attending servant. "Leave us."

The servant fled, closing the door with a small click.

Edward poured himself a cup of tea and took a seat opposite his guest.

"I'm aware you've been informed of the escape from one of our facilities?" He pushed back his hood, revealing a shock of white hair framing a young face.

Edward drew in a breath. He recognized the man instantly. Everyone knew the Guildmaster's son and heir. But a visit from Maylon was not what he'd been expecting. "I am. I've already begun the process of moving those at that particular installation to another. However the dismantling process will take time."

"Burn it to the ground."

"Excuse me?" Edward gritted his teeth against what he really wanted to say. "I've invested a considerable amount of my own capital on that facility."

Maylon fixed him with a stare. "And you've been amply compensated, yes?"

Edward swallowed. "Of course, but still ..."

"Do as you wish, but know that discovery could cause wide-reaching consequences." He brushed away that subject with his hand. "But my purpose here tonight is to make you aware of some additional information you now need, not manage how you handle this small contretemps."

Edward frowned at the word *now*. He'd suspected the Makers had been withholding information and this confirmed it. "I'm all ears."

"We've become aware of certain probabilities. While we were once virtually certain of our success, forces are at work that have begun to affect that outcome." When Edward began to speak, Maylon held up a hand. "Robin Loxley is the one who is currently affecting our success or failure. The escaped children are in his care, under the auspices of Dr. Tuck. That good doctor will need to be eliminated immediately."

"The doctor? Don't you mean Robin?"

"Robin is your problem. You had assured us he was out of the picture. We still expect you to follow through with your promise." Maylon's lip curled. "You are aware of the penalty failure will bring, of course."

Heat flooded Edward's face. He forced down the hot retort and inclined his head.

"Beyond the issue of Dr. Tuck, the Lady Marion has become a problem as well."

"Marion?" Edward's gaze met the Makers full on. "Are you withdrawing your promise?"

"No." Maylon picked up his cup and sipped. "But you may wish to change your mind when you learn what we've discovered."

"Go on."

"I'm sure you were surprised by her choice of costume at your recent gathering." He waited for Edward's answer.

"True." How had they known what had gone on at his private ball? Another confirmation that the Makers were manipulating events and taking an unprecedented hand in keeping track of the kingdom.

"Not the most discriminating for a woman of her station." Maylon sighed. "But since she is, in fact, the Maiden of Iron, the choice could be termed a gutsy move on her part."

Recent happenings began to assemble themselves as puzzle pieces in Edward's mind. The girl had gumption, misplaced albeit. "You of course have proof."

"Irrefutable." Maylon returned to his tea. "Do you still wish to move forward with your betrothal?"

Edward considered his options. Such a strong-willed woman would be a challenge. And she could become an asset, especially if the masses viewed her as a heroine—her martyrdom would insure the loyalty of her followers and cement his path to power—as long as no one suspected his part in her untimely death. "Yes." His lips twitched at the thought of having her as his own. "The advantages still outweigh the difficulties."

"Very well. I thought you'd be long-sighted enough to see the benefits of continuing." He placed his now-empty cup on the table and stood, pulling up his hood and draping his face in darkness. "However, if you do not get her under control, we will take steps. Do we understand each other?"

Edward also rose. "Yes. Perfectly."

"Very good."

"If you don't mind, sir?" Edward stood at the closed door. "How go the plans to encourage the Queen to approve my father's appointment."

Maylon tilted his head and fixed an eye on Edward. "It proceeds apace. You need not fear *us* holding up our side of the agreement."

Edward dipped his head. "Very good." He opened the door and was met by his servant. "My visitor will be leaving. See him out."

"Yes, sir." The servant bowed and gestured to the robed visitor to precede him.

When they were out of view, Edward walked to his study and sat behind his desk. He held his pen over the paper before beginning to write. He'd have to redouble his efforts to find Robin's lair. First, there was Tuck to deal with.

His servant appeared in the doorway. "Is there anything else, sir?"

Edward dribbled hot wax on the folded paper in front of him and affixed his seal. "Have this delivered to my men. I need them immediately. Tell them there's work to be done before the dawn."

CHAPTER TWENTY

Marion slipped into the underground safety of the buried airship just as dawn finished forcing night's retreat. The long walk from Robin's headquarters had been a calculated risk, but she'd known better than to bring the horses back. Without Addison and Gretta, it wasn't possible to get them stabled and herself back in her rooms without discovery. She blinked, refusing to allow the tears brimming her eyes to fall. She couldn't afford the luxury of grief—or even worry.

She struggled to get out of her Maiden of Iron attire and into the emergency dress she kept hanging there for the possibility of returning alone. The green wool was too loose, but made it possible for her to hide the fact she wasn't wearing a corset.

The timepiece on the bureau ticked away the precious seconds while fingers too weary for words fumbled with buttons and boots. Finally suitable attired, she walked down another corridor that led to the exit in the stables. Her grandfather had planned for every eventuality. Little had he known the use his daughter's daughter would have made of the buried airship. She cleared the memories that threatened her too emotional thoughts. Coming in from the stables would explain her attire if her lady's maid caught her entering, although Matilda was rarely about at this hour. But today of all days she couldn't risk discovery. Not when there was so much at stake.

She paused at the door leading into the main house from the buried airship. She had taken longer than she'd anticipated to redress. Her gritty eyes, remnants of the sleepless night, ached as she strained to focus in the semidarkness. Giving up, she pressed her ear to the listening panel, but heard no footsteps. She eased open the door and peered out. The tack room stood empty and she slipped out, securing the panel behind her against inadvertent discovery. She pulled an apple from the bin where cook tossed the bits and pieces unfit for human consumption, but still good enough to tempt an equine palette.

With the apple in her hand, she strode to the stall of her second favorite horse and was offering him a treat when a stable boy appeared. He started then bowed. "My lady. Can I help you this morning? Would you like me to saddle 'im for you?"

"No, I'm just out for an early morning stroll and thought I'd take a peek at Samson. I've been neglecting him lately."

"You never neglect your horses." The boy tried to hide his outrage. "Begging your pardon."

"No harm, Robbie." Marion forced a laugh through her fatigue. "I'll visit him later and see about a ride then."

She strolled toward the main house, fighting against the urge to dart through the shadows. She mustn't draw attention to herself now when she was so close. She entered the hallway near the kitchen and heard the bustle of the staff, but no one met her as she moved through the corridors and into the hallway where her suite lay. Her fingers had just closed on the doorknob of her room when Matilda bustled into sight carrying a tray.

Matilda's already dour expression went from bad to worse as she took in the state of Marion's clothes. "Words fail me, my lady."

Marion preceded her maid into the room and collapsed into the slipper chair near the bow window. "I didn't sleep well and decided an early morning walk might clear my head."

Matilda didn't answer as she set down the breakfast tray with a thump and strode into the bathing room. The sound of running water issued forth, followed by the aroma of her favorite bath salts. Perhaps a bath would help.

She took a sip of tea, but the normally appetizing roll accompanying it made her stomach turn over.

Still in a fog, Marion allowed Matilda to help her into the bath and then get her dressed for the day. She didn't even argue with her maid's choice of attire. What she wanted most was to go back to bed and awake with the night's events having been nothing but a bad dream.

Seated in front of her dressing table, with Matilda yanking a brush through her curls and pinning them viciously atop her head she wanted to weep. Not at the pain, but at the burden she faced. The plight of the guild children had become personal. They must redouble their efforts to save Addi.

"That's the best I can do with my lady's hair." Matilda stepped back to look at her charge. "You're presentable."

"Thank you." Marion rose and moved toward the door. "Tell Father not to expect me for the noon meal. There's much to do today."

"As well the Guildmaster is aware." The maid's chubby face lit triumphantly. "He's been up between times and is at guild headquarters."

Marion stopped and turned. "My father is at work?"

"Yes, my lady." The words were innocent enough, but Matilda's tone made Marion want to slap her.

Without a word Marion continued through the door and closed it with a small click. She wouldn't give Matilda the satisfaction of a slammed door.

Her thoughts raced, was her father back? Would he let her continue unsupervised in her work?

Would he have changed back to the man she'd once known?

She strode out the front of the mansion and onto the grounds. The only way to face this was head on. Worrying about what-ifs never got a person anywhere.

After a quick breakfast, Robin returned to the sick room where Dr. Tuck still worked back and forth between his two patients. "Any change?"

Tuck had shed his coat and loosened his collar. "I think they're both stable right now." He stopped to mop his brow and wipe his spectacles. "Neither young man seems to be in as much pain. But without equipment from my laboratory, I'm not going to be able to make much headway."

Before Robin could suggest a plan of action, John exploded into the room dragging a reluctant Winston with him. "We've got news and it's not good." He shoved Winston toward the other two men. "Tell them what you know."

Winston glared back at John before taking a deep breath. "I've been doing what you said. I've watched and waited to see what Sir Edward would do next. There was an awful fuss last night when a visitor came a knockin' in the wee hours." He licked his lips. "Could I have a drink, please."

Robin gestured to John. "He'll bring one, but continue. Who was the visitor?"

"Don't know. His carriage was one of them fancy black ones that the Makers use. But the one what got out didn't have the exactly right dress for me to be sure."

"What do you mean?" Tuck asked.

Winston wrinkled his nose and squinched his eyes shut. "He was in all black, but he was wearing more of a cape than a robe. And his boots were polished so bright they had to be top quality. Nothing like the pointy shoes I've seen them others in."

John returned and held out a tankard. Winston took a long drink then coughed. "What's this you give me?"

John grinned. "Water, of course. It's best when a man's got a powerful thirst."

Winston shrugged, then drained the contents before he continued. "The visitor was let straight in and all the lights started blazing. It weren't long before he came out again and took off."

Robin took the cup from the man and set it on a nearby table. "Did you follow him or stay put?"

"I was tempted to follow, but it seemed to me I'd get more information by waiting to see what his lordship did next."

"Well done." Robin slapped Winston on the back. "I knew you were the right man for the job. What happened next."

Winston threw a pointed look at John. "Well, the lights in the main house continued to shine. I moved around to the back entrance and sure enough, several of the usual thugs showed up."

"Are they men you know?" Tuck asked.

"They're more men I know of. They're not the type any of us would find pleasure in taking a sup or a nip with."

Annie came into the room and set a large tea tray down on the table in the corner that was littered with paper and books. "If you're going to be jawing the man to death, you'll all do better for some tea in you." She pushed the debris to one side and began pouring.

"Too right." Winston was the first man to grab a cup and took a seat on the far side, away from John.

"Keep talking." John took a seat across from Winston after he'd his own cup in hand.

"Sir Edward kept them inside a while, but when they came out, I followed. I worried about which one to stick with when they split up, but they never did." He scratched his head. "They all went to the same place. Your infirmary."

"What?" Tuck exploded from his chair. "Why didn't you say that right off?" He turned to Robin. "We need to get there ... find out what they're doing."

John grabbed Tuck's arm. "It's too late. Let him finish his story."

Tuck sunk into his chair.

"I'm really sorry, doc." He frowned. "They forced their way inside. I could tell they was looking for you. I could hear 'em yelling for you."

Tuck leaned forward, his eyes urgent. "My servants, what happened?"

"They didn't really hurt them. Roughed a couple of the men up a bit, but they must've been under some powerful orders, because they left the women alone. Your people were smart. They let the men search. Once they were convinced you weren't there, they left."

"That's all?" Robin leveled his gaze at Tuck, then back at Winston. "What about his equipment?"

"I don't know about what shape the place is in. I heard an awful lot of crashing and banging. But they told your people that there was a warrant out for your arrest—along with a big reward. Promised it'd be crown gold they'd be paying, but I don't believe it."

Tuck rose again. "I've got to go ... take care of my servants ... see what's salvageable ... clear up this misunderstanding. Thank goodness, I don't have any patients there right now."

"No." Robin pushed him back down. "That's exactly what you don't need to do. They'll have the place watched, hoping to catch you when you come back." He raised an eyebrow at Winston. "Right?"

"Yep, them's the exact words of one of the fellows."

Tuck took a deep breath. "Be that as it may, I still need my notes. Did you see those hooligans carry anything away with them?"

"Nary a thing."

Robin squinted at the sun just peeking above the horizon. "What time did they leave?"

"Only as long as it took me to high-tail it back here." Winston shot John another glare. "And convince Mr. High-And-Mighty that I needed to see you."

"John, round up a couple of men to go back with you and Winston. Take Duncan, he's a good one for this." Robin pulled a piece of paper from the pile and handed it to Tuck. "Tell us a way in that will attract as little attention as possible, then draw us a map to where you keep your notes hidden. We'll get what's left or die trying."

Tuck started. "I don't ... well ... how did you know?"

Robin's face held no joy. "It's perilous times we're living in. Any man with sense has a hidey-hole to keep what's important safe."

Chapter Twenty-One

Marion looked fondly at the old gatekeeper. He didn't speak but gave her an answering wink as he threw the lever that opened the massive gates with the familiar hiss of steam. She didn't pause in the beautiful courtyard but instead, mounted the marble steps leading to the imposing door of the main building. Inside she stopped, waiting for her eyes to adjust. Glancing at the steps that led to the workrooms below, she squared her shoulders and turned toward the elevator that would take her to the Guildmaster's suite of offices.

"Is he truly up there?" she asked Antonio as she entered the elevator.

"Yes, ma'am." Antonio dipped his head and the gold trim on his hat seemed to almost wink at her, a bright counterpoint to her gloomy thoughts. "He told me to bring you straight up when you arrived."

A chill settled around her heart, but she tried to school her face to an expression that conveyed pleasure at her father's return. She didn't know if she succeeded or not. "Excellent." If her father truly was returning, it was her duty to support him. Perhaps the meeting wouldn't take long, and then she could visit the laboratory and see if William had come up with anything new. They must find help for Addi.

The elevator seemed to rise quicker than usual, leaving her no time to gather her thoughts before the doors opened.

Elise stood before her in the anteroom outside the Guildmaster's suite of offices.

Marion reached for her hand as tears pricked her eyes. "Do you know? About Addi, I mean?"

Elise's expression remained grave. "Your father is in a meeting and wishes you to join him."

"With whom?" Marion's spine stiffened. She wanted time to talk with Elise, find out if she had new information about Addi ... and if her father knew of her night-time exploits.

Before Elise could answer her father's voice boomed from his office. "Is that Marion? Send her in. We've things to discuss."

Marion's mouth dropped open. He sounded sober ... and almost jovial. A shiver raced up her spine. The last time he'd used those words, the meeting had been about her betrothal to the Makers Guildmaster's son. Elise ignored her pleading eyes and motioned Marion to precede her through the reception area and into the office beyond.

Her father sat behind his desk, working spectacles perched on the end of his nose. He was once again the Guildmaster and powerful Lord Ravenswood she remembered from her childhood. Seated in one of the leather chairs facing the desk was Edward.

"Here she is, sir." Elise stopped in the doorway, but gave Marion a surreptitious push to send her further into the room.

"I'll bring tea shortly." She closed the door behind her and left Marion alone with the two men.

"My dear, I'm so glad to see you looking so well this morning." Edward came to her and took her hand. "Why don't you have a seat. Your father and I have been making preliminary plans, but we need your approval before moving forward."

The coldness inside her began to dissipate. Thankfully they weren't planning her life without her input. She glanced from her father to Edward. The Guildmaster had appeared startled that Edward had ascribed to her so much authority.

Lord Ravenswood cleared his throat. "Yes ... right. Take a chair, daughter, so we may proceed forthwith."

Edward held her chair and saw her comfortably seated before he took the seat beside her. "We've been discussing possible wedding dates and the plans that accompany an event like this."

Her father caught her eye and held it. "You're certain this is what you want."

"Yes, very." Why was he being this way? Solicitude for her desires had never been very high on his list. This new version of her father made her wary.

Edward reached across and took her hand. "Of course, we're certain. Besides being an excellent move for both guilds, Marion and I are very much in love." He brought her hand to his lips.

She resisted the urge to pull away. This was what she wanted. All her plans were falling into place and even her father appeared to be on board. Why wasn't she happier about it?

"Very well then." Her father clapped his hands together and pulled a sheet of paper toward him. "It's time to draw up the arrangement."

"I have one already drawn up. I hope you don't mind." Edward rose and pulled a folded document from the inside breast pocket of his frock coat. He handed the paper to Lord Ravenswood. "Of course, we can make any changes either of you wish."

Marion would have preferred he'd consulted her first, but satisfied she'd get a say before she signed.

Her father was still studying the document when Elise returned with the tea tray, trundled in on a wheeled table by a footman. Elise arranged the table in front of the fireplace where a grouping of chairs made a cozy seating area. There were tiny elegant cakes, buttery scones, and other morsels designed to tempt the palette. Everyone was going all out for the Guildmaster's return. She tried to keep the bitterness at bay. Of course, the people of the guild would be celebrating the return of their Guildmaster. But her heart was only for Addi and the children who were suffering so. She didn't have time for this.

"Would you like me to pour, my lord?" Elise stood by the tea table, hands clasped before her.

"No, Marion can do it." He waved a hand at them. "Go ahead, I'm still reading."

Marion took her place before the pot. She added the right amount of milk and sugar to a cup and poured for her father first.

"I'll take it." Elise was beside her, taking the cup from her hands. Her eyes conveyed support and love. She set the cup within reach of the Guildmaster and left the room.

Marion turned toward Edward. "How do you take your tea?" Odd that she didn't yet know how her future husband preferred his tea.

"Just as you pour it, thank you."

Marion added extra sugar to her own cup and took a sip. She'd need all the help she could get to make it through the day.

"This is a bit irregular, wouldn't you say?" Lord Ravenswood joined them at the tea table.

Marion frowned at her father. "The tea?"

"Of course not the tea. The arrangement." He passed over the decorated cakes, chose a blueberry scone, and took a seat.

When he didn't elaborate, Marion tried again, working hard to keep her voice level. "What about the arrangement is irregular?"

"The proposal to ultimately join our two guilds into one. I assumed you knew that." He gave her a sharp look. "And it appears the Makers have already approved that request. Now it only lacks the Queen's consent."

"It seemed the most logical thing to do." Edward brushed a crumb from his pant leg. "Eventually, I'll be Guildmaster of both and to be running back and forth would be a bit inconvenient."

Lord Ravenswood lifted an inquiring eyebrow. So that was where she'd inherited that expression. Somehow she'd thought it had come from her grandfather. "This means the Queen has approved your father's appointment as permanent Guildmaster for the Pilots?"

Edward's face was a study in confidence. "You were both at the celebration of his appointment—along with the Queen. I think there can be no doubt."

"Yes, of course." Her father took a serviette and wiped his mustache. "Then once I speak with the Queen, we'll make everything official." He handed the document to Marion. "I think you'll wish to look this over as well."

"Thank you."

The grandfather clock struck the quarter hour, and he turned to Edward. "I have much to catch up on, perhaps you'll excuse us?"

"Certainly." Edward rose. "I have things to see to as well." He took Marion's hand. "Will you dine with me this evening? With your father's approval, of course." He ignored the Guildmaster.

"Yes, yes." The curmudgeon was returning as the old man settled himself back at his desk and didn't appear to notice or care about the slight.

"I will send a carriage for you at seven this evening." Edward kissed her hand and was gone.

Marion also took a step toward the door, but her father's voice pulled her up short.

"Daughter, you will remain. There is much we must discuss."

Edward strode into the sunlight, barely acknowledging the gatekeeper or the groom who held open the carriage door for him. Arrogant old man, playing at being a Guildmaster. He didn't know who he was dealing with.

"Home, sir?" The carriage driver leaned down and peered in the window.

"Of course." Edward leaned back against the richly upholstered leather interior and took a deep breath. It wouldn't do to appear out of control at this next meeting. His mother was difficult enough as it was. But she'd been right to encourage him to approach the Makers Guild. Maylon had proved a valuable ally, but Edward didn't trust him. The Makers had their own agenda and when it veered from what Edward had planned, he'd have to take steps.

He didn't enjoy the usual commotion caused by his steam-driven equines. Instead, he went back over the events of the past few days, composing an edited version to share with his mother. He still needed her, but didn't want her to have enough information to begin manipulating things around on her own.

When they pulled up in front of his home, he leapt out before the coachman could assist him. "Where did you put her?" he asked while his butler took his coat and hat.

"Madame is in the morning room." The old man sniffed, showing his disapproval the only way Edward would allow. He wasn't sure how much the old family retainer knew about the true relationship between the lady's maid and the master's son. All Edward cared was that he knew enough to keep his mouth shut about her visits.

As he entered, he scanned the room and saw his mother seated near the fireplace, prim and plump in her black uniform, looking like a benign governess hiding sweets from her children. Amazing how much appearances could be deceiving. He forced her to speak first. Mother or not, she was still just a servant and couldn't be allowed to forget that.

Eyes narrowed at his silent stance, she rose and bobbed a curtsy. "I'm here as you requested, my lord." Her teeth snapped with her words, like a wolf devouring a helpless rabbit.

He'd pushed her far enough. He grinned, closed the distance between them, and took her hand. "And I'm grateful you did." He motioned her back to her seat and took the chair opposite her. "There's a great deal for me to share, and of course I covet your counsel."

He watched her preen at his words and inwardly sneered. She was pathetically easy to manipulate—like all the rest.

"Tell me what's happened, and we'll manage this together. I assume the situation is progressing as we planned?"

He told her about Maylon's visit and the revelation about Marion's secret persona.

"I knew she was up to something." Matilda rose and began to pace. "I should have kept closer watch on her comings and goings."

"Yes, but that can't be helped. I think she's actually helping our cause." He rubbed his hands together. "When it's time, I'll catch her as the Maiden of Iron and use that to keep her from running to the Queen."

"Yes, she'd do anything to stay in that woman's good graces. This just gives us more leverage." Matilda's angry countenance cleared. "Tell me more about this meeting with Maylon. He's a dangerous opponent. You must watch him carefully."

Edward crossed his long legs. "Yes, but that's what makes the game interesting. I'm certain he has his own agenda, and I still only know a part. A few more successes under my belt, and he'll reveal the heart of what he wants from me."

Matilda returned to her seat, studying her hands. "And your plans for your father? I assume those haven't changed ..."

"Of course not." He grinned. Her offhand question didn't fool him one bit. "But we can't move forward until I'm assured of inheriting the position of Guildmaster."

She jerked her head up. "But I thought the Queen approved it the night of the ball? You did say you had time to announce it before ... the ... uh ... commotion."

"Oh, we announced it." He frowned. "And the Queen made no public denial. But that's a far cry from setting her seal of approval on the appointment. Maylon assures me he's pushing her to do just that."

"Well, then, we must wait. I will keep a closer watch on her ladyship." The sneer was evident in her voice. "What else do you wish of me?"

"See if you can find out how she's getting in and out without your knowledge." He stood and accompanied her to the door. "I have matters of my own to tend to. Please see yourself out." No reason to give the staff any reason to suspect she was anything more than a servant.

Her face took on an expression he couldn't quite decipher. "As you wish."

Chapter Twenty-Two

Marion swallowed hard and returned to her seat in front of the Guildmaster's desk. "You wish to speak to me?"

The curmudgeon was gone and replaced by the ghost the man her father had once been. "I think we both have much to say to each other." He glared at the ledgers open on one side of his desk, then shot her a look of what seemed to be approval. "You have done well, daughter."

There it was again. The endearment she remembered from years past. She kept her eyes down. "I have done the best I could."

He slammed his open hand on his desk. "Look at me. I'm not here to discipline you." He pointed his finger at her. "I doubt David could have done better in a similar circumstance."

The mention of her brother's name hung between them.

Marion stared at her father as the room closed in around her. "I've never heard you speak his name ... since ... that night."

"I haven't done right by you—or your mother. I should have taken your part, not pushed you away." Self-recrimination rang in his tone. "And I should have been searching for a husband for you instead of wallowing in self-pity."

She wasn't ready for this. Husband indeed. Did he still see her as helpless and incompetent. For a moment she'd thought not. No matter what, there was too much for her to still do. She needed autonomy to finish what she'd started. She couldn't waste time listening to an old man share regrets. Addi needed her, and so did Gretta. She stiffened and continued to stare at him. "Well, that's been decided of now. My future husband will take care of me."

"Blast it, girl. I'm not impugning your honor. You've done well. I just said as much. However, a Guildmaster's office is no place for a woman." He pushed himself away from his desk. "Unless you care to explain how you acquired the money to keep us afloat this long. Or what's costing so much in the experimentation laboratory."

Her hands turned icy in her lap, but she kept her words calm and measured. "I'm sure I don't know to what you're referring."

"Humph. Of course you don't." He rose and gestured to the door. "Go play with your pet project. I can see you're itching to be away. But we will discuss this more in depth later after I've had time to inspect the books more closely."

"Yes, Father." Marion walked to the door, careful not to hurry, and closed it softly behind her.

She stood for a moment with her back against the wall, willing her heart to return to its normal rhythm.

"You know he'll find out."

Marion started. She hadn't noticed Elise sitting at her desk in the anteroom. "I'm sure he won't." She wished she felt as certain as she sounded. What would he do if he ever found out?

Elise rose and crossed the room. "We need to talk."

"No ... I mean yes, but not now. I have to get down to the laboratory and see if William has anything new to report." She rang the bell for the elevator. Immediately the door opened.

Elise stepped in with her, and they rode to the ground floor in silence.

"Have a good morning, my lady." The operator touched his gold-trimmed cap and she caught a glimpse of his gold front tooth before he was able to hide his smile.

"Thank you, Antonio." Marion strode from the elevator, only a modicum of decorum in her hurried steps as she headed toward the basement stairs.

"You know this changes everything." Elise kept pace without seeming to rush. How did that woman manage to convey grace and peace to every single situation?

"I know." Marion didn't even turn her head as she took the stairs two at a time. "But I can't think about that right now. My priority is Addi. Do you have any additional word from Tuck?"

"You can ask me yourself." Dr. Tuck stood unsmiling before them with William at his elbow, garbed in his usual velvet apron and stained smock.

"Is there—"

"Yes, and no." Tuck held up his hand. "Let's move into William's office and we'll discuss all." He turned to William. "With your permission, of course."

"Absolutely. Any time. Of course you may." William was always full of energy but now he was almost dithering. "It's your office now, for as long as you need it."

Tuck put a hand on William's shoulder, cutting off the flow of words. "Why don't you go make us some tea."

Marion wanted to protest. She'd had quite enough tea for the morning. But knew it would help the young man calm down to have something to do. "What has him so up in arms this morning?"

Tuck cocked his head. "You mean besides the fact that the Guildmaster has returned and you're no longer in charge?"

Marion winced. "Trust you to hit on the heart of the matter. But what I care most about is Addi. How is he?"

Tuck took a seat behind the desk and moved a couple of untidy stacks to the floor. "He's stable right now. I've given him something to keep him deeply asleep while I examine our options."

Marion let out the breath she hadn't realized she'd been holding. "I'm so glad he's no worse."

"I also brought back some of his blood to be tested." He pushed his glasses up on his nose. "But I'm almost certain he's been infected with the virus."

"It's all my fault." Marion stared hard at her hands fisted in her lap. She would *not* let the tears fall. "If I hadn't started this whole campaign, he'd never have been exposed."

"Stop that this instant." Tuck brought his hand down hard on the desk. "If you hadn't started this campaign then I wouldn't be so close to a cure. This isn't time for self-recrimination or regret. We must move forward."

"There's something else, my dear." Elise put a hand on Marion's shoulder. "There's now a reward out for the outlaw, Dr. Archibald Tuck."

Marion's eyes widened. "What? This is an outrage. Who issued the warrant? Surely not the crown." They both appeared amused by her question. "What aren't you telling me? Why doesn't this upset you?"

"It means ..." Tuck steepled his hands on the desk, his eyes twinkling. "... that our efforts have begun to alarm whomever is behind this. That means we're much closer than we'd even hoped. They've raided my dispensary and office."

"They have your notes and all your research?"

"Not at all. I had all my notes tucked away against just such a possibility. Robin sent some men early this morning to retrieve them." He pointed to several piles of notebooks and papers near the door. "I also had additional copies secreted here, in case those were unavailable or taken."

"Are the copies still here?" Marion searched the room with her eyes. Where could they hide something here?

"You bet they are." William scuttled in with a poorly arranged tray, slopping tea as he made his way to the low table in front of Elise.

Elise quietly rearranged things, mopping up the spills and pouring out cups. "Our ever-resilient Dr. Tuck was prepared well for this. However, his new status makes his presence here a danger to himself and to you."

"To me?" Marion was beginning to feel like a very uninformed parrot. Not a position she enjoyed at all. "Can you two speak in complete thoughts instead of plying me with cryptic statements and more tea?"

"So sorry. There's just so much to tell," said Dr. Tuck. "Actually William is the one who made the discovery, and in just this morning we've made amazing progress."

William's red face darkened and he dipped his head. "It wasn't really me. It's the doctor's research that gave me the idea."

"Nonsense." Dr. Tuck rose and ushered them back into the laboratory. "William can explain more easily when we're viewing his discovery through the microscope."

Robin paced his office. Ten steps up and ten steps back.

"You know that's not going to make him appear any sooner." John watched from the velvet settee as his friend wore a path in the floor.

"Easy for you to say." Robin stopped to stare into the fire. "I don't like the idea of him wandering around alone."

John rubbed his chin. "Well, he wasn't actually alone."

Robin turned. "Exactly? What *exactly* does that mean? He insisted I not send anyone with him."

"Yep. That's why I gave the order for Duncan to shadow him and make sure he arrived at Marion's in one piece."

Robin didn't know whether to thank him for his ingenuity or slug him for keeping it from him. "I do wish you'd have told me."

"And interrupt your morning constitutional?" John's lips twitched. "A fat man like you needs all the exercise he can get. Duncan would have sent word if there'd been trouble. I told him to wait and follow Tuck back here to make sure he wasn't interfered with."

Robin snorted. Only one of them carried any extra weight and John knew full well who that was. It wasn't often one of his men got the better of him. He'd let John have his fun. He frowned. The only one who seemed to get the better of him regularly was that little minx, Marion. What would she do when Tuck told her about the latest development?

"Why don't you get a little exercise and ask Winston to come here. I have an errand for him." Robin moved to his desk and bent to pen a note.

"Let me guess." John hefted his bulk from the sofa. "Sending notes to Marion now?"

Robin grimaced. "I need to make sure she doesn't go off half-cocked."

John stopped in the doorway. "She's not the one we need to worry about. That young woman has a solid head on her shoulders."

"Be that as it may, we need to coordinate our efforts. And she needs to understand how involved with all this her pet lordling is."

John's words echoed down the corridor. "She does seem to have a blind spot when it comes to men."

CHAPTER TWENTY-THREE

Marion's head swam with all the scientific facts Tuck and William were throwing back and forth. Finally, she threw up her hands. "Stop. Just stop. Give me a nonscientific explanation of what you've found and why you think it will help."

Elise was standing in one corner, and she chuckled at Marion's request. "I have to say I'm not following a thing you two say either. Please remember we don't all have the same knowledge base as yourselves."

Tuck removed his spectacles and wiped them on his handkerchief. "So sorry, ladies," he said. "In our excitement, we do quite forget who it is we're talking to."

"Please forgive me, my lady," William stammered. "I would never purposefully leave you out. I mean, I assumed you knew what I was referring too. That is …"

Marion laughed at his expression as he tried not to imply how ignorant she was. "Never mind the apology. I've become infected by your hopefulness. But now's the time to explain it in small words that someone like me can understand."

"Stop teasing him." Elise moved to stand beside the young man. "He's done a wonderful job, and we're beyond pleased with him."

"Just take a look here." Tuck gestured to the microscope in front of him. "This is the slide we've shown you before of the virus."

Marion bent to peer into the device. The familiar pattern of strange devises throbbing in unison to an unknown drummer as they coiled and uncoiled made a shiver run up her spine. Surely, no one could survive with these tiny machines living inside them. She moved to give Elise a chance to reacquaint herself with their minuscule enemies and turned back to Tuck. "I remember this tiny horrors. What do you have that's encouraging?"

"As you may remember, William discovered that these tiny machines are powered by a hormone found in preadolescent children."

William gulped. "And we've been able to modify part of that compound into something that will disrupt these machines."

"By changing the hormone's structure, it not only quits powering the machines but throws them into chaos. In their disorganized state, they turn on each other." Tuck pointed at another microscope. "You can see the result here."

Marion put her eye to the metal tube. Instead of orderliness, there was carnage. The devices appeared to be attacking each other. The liquid in which they were suspended was littered with tiny metallic bits that no longer throbbed but instead, floated as if lifeless.

She focused on the two men as a kernel of cautious hope began to expand in her heart. "Have you replicated this success?

How long does it take to make that change? How do you deliver this cure?"

Tuck frowned. "It's a long process to replicate the serum we need—"

"We're working on speeding it up," William said.

"Right now, we assume the best way is for the host to be injected. But we haven't actually tested this on anyone who's affected." He leaned against the worktop. "And there's so much we don't know. Like how long the reversal will take and how much of the metal will be left within the victim's body."

"And you suspect Addi doesn't have time to spare?" Marion faced the doctor head on. "Give me the rest of it."

"Addison is an unusual case." He mopped his brow. "Because that young man is well into the change from child to man, he shouldn't have been so susceptible. Those things you fought must have had weapons loaded with vials of that virus to spread so quickly throughout his body."

"Because he's older, the serum may not be as potent. It's not just the serum that cures, it's the fact that it changes the chemistry of the body's *own* matching compound so the body can fight the infection." William held up the now empty vial with traces of Addison's blood still clinging to it. "He will have less ammunition to fight this."

"So where do you go from here?" Elise backed away from peering at the miniature landscape.

"I go to Robin." Dr. Tuck reached back to untie his own apron. "We must move all of this to a safer place." He shot Marion a warning look when she started to speak. "No. We don't know exactly who's behind this and what reach they have. If they insist on inspecting the guild grounds, I'm done for. Finally, it's imperative that I stay close to my patients—especially as I'm treating them with this serum."

Marion closed her mouth. The man was right. But she didn't have to like it.

Elise came up behind her and put a hand on her shoulder. "Besides, you have a wedding to plan."

Marion started. A wedding? Of course, a wedding. She hadn't even thought about that, only the fact that she needed a husband to help save the guild. Did she still need one? With her father once again at the helm? Yes, absolutely. There was no way she could know if his return was permanent or just an aberration in the status quo. Before she could answer a young man entered, holding out an envelope.

"For you, my lady." His huge cap obscured most of his face. "I've been instructed to wait for your reply."

She turned to the workstation and tope open the sealing wax. She knew that crest. This was from Robin.

We need to talk. I have more information you need. Pick the time and place and I'll be there.
~R

Marion scribbled one line, *Old airship, one hour.* She handed the envelope back to the waiting boy. He seemed familiar and more of a man than a boy. He touched his cap and left. The others waited for her to explain.

"Robin has requested a meeting."

"And?" Tuck broke the silence.

"I've agreed to meet him." She turned around the room, taking in all the equipment. "How much of this will you have to take with you?"

"Not as much as you would think." Tuck moved back to the office and returned with a leather satchel. "Robin has most of the equipment. I'll need a few of my chemicals, but most of what I have to have to continue is already there."

"Is it safe for you to move about the city?" Elise bent down and began handing him notebooks and papers to load into the container.

"Should be. I told Robin not to send any of his men, but I spied one tailing me all the way over here. I assume he's still lurking about somewhere. I'll draft him as a pack mule if he is."

"Well, I for one am glad he did," said Marion.

Tuck kept loading supplies. "For a little while, I'll also need William to come with me."

William puffed with pride. "I'm happy to go." Then he caught sight of Marion and gulped. "If I may, that is."

"Of course, you may. That's where you're needed the most." Marion gave him a quick hug. "But you must promise to be careful and come home when the doctor can spare you again. I couldn't have managed this place without you."

He bobbed his head and hustled away to another room.

Tuck stopped and faced her. "Are you certain about this upcoming marriage?"

"It's the best thing for the guild. I can't assume Father's return is permanent." Marion stiffened her back and squared her shoulders. "I need a partner to help me with everything. Lord

Edward knows how to run a guild and under his tutelage, I'll be an asset instead of a liability."

"I know your reasons." Tuck's eyes seemed almost to bore into her soul, exposing secrets she'd buried long ago. "But I believe you've chosen the wrong man."

"Well, I didn't exactly have suitors lined up for the prospect of me as a bride." Marion forced a laugh. "We've discussed the matter and know this won't be a love match, but instead one of mutual respect. I'm certain I've made the best possible decision in accepting Lord Edward's proposal."

Tuck stared at her for a long moment before he turned away.

Robin studied at the slip of paper in his hand. The old airship? It had been eons ago when he'd last been inside that massive compound. He should have known she would use that as her escape. Her life hadn't been an easy one. In many ways, much worse than his own. Was that what had so warped her perspective toward Edward? Surely it wasn't love.

He crumpled the paper and hurled it into the fire. What did he care about who she loved and who she didn't?

"Bad news?" John had come into the room on silent feet. How did a man that large move so quietly.

"No. Not at all." Robin turned to face him. "Just an answer from Marion. We're meeting at her family's compound in an airship her grandfather buried years ago."

"I thought that was some sort of rumor. I had no idea there really was an airship there." John's face turned thoughtful. "She's been running her operation from there, hasn't she?"

"I don't know for sure, but I would suspect so. It explains how she was able to come and go without anyone the wiser. There's actually an entrance not far from the Pilots Guild."

Robin pulled his pistol from a drawer and slipped it into a holster that fitted across his shoulder and under his left arm. The contraption made drawing easy while keeping the weapon hidden. He then pulled on his workingman jacket, added a jaunty cap and turned to face John. "How do I look, guvnor?"

"Like you're expecting trouble." John turned his face heavenward. "One of these days your luck will run out."

"None the less, duty calls." Robin gave an exaggerated bow and quit the room.

Chapter Twenty-Four

Elise followed Marion through the maze of unused corridors deep under the Guildmaster's headquarters. They each carried one of William's electric torches to light their way. This was an entry point that Marion seldom used, so the cobwebs hung heavy and their footfalls raised small puffs of dust. At the last metal door, Marion handed her torch to Elise and turned the large steel wheel that unlatched the door. The hatch screamed an unearthly protest as she tugged the portal open.

"Can anyone hear that?" Elise peered into the darkness that lay behind them.

"No. We're too deep." Marion took back the torch and steadied the older woman as she stepped over the threshold and through the oval opening left by the door. After they were both inside, she tugged the door shut behind them, once again twirling the wheel to latch it.

"How do you know for sure?"

Marion crossed the room and reached for the matches and lantern she always kept on the mantle of what had once been her grandfather's onboard stateroom. "I once had Gretta test it out while I was in the more populated area of the compound." She struck a match and lit the wick, then set the chimney on the lamp and a flicker light illuminated their position.

Elise clicked off her torch and turned to take in the room where they stood. "Your mother and I were girls the last time I visited this room."

"I forgot you'd actually been down here." Marion led the way out into the corridor and toward engineering section.

"Oh, yes, we played down here as children." Marion could hear the joyful memories in Elise's voice. "And sometimes on the nights when I stayed with your mother, your grandfather would tell us stories about how it was when he'd been an engineer on the Her Majesty's flagship."

"Grandfather was a great storyteller."

"He would have been heartbroken to know your father sealed this place up."

"Well, he tried to." Now, it was Marion's turn to grin. "Even he didn't know all the ins and outs that Grandfather had built into this place."

They descended a once-beautiful brass circular staircase to the more practical area of the old ship. Here Marion once again tugged open a massive iron door and pointed to a more modern door set into the wall. "Robin will come in through this entrance." She began working the elaborate system of locks that held it in place. "It's not possible to enter here unless someone unlatches it from the inside."

"And how did Lord Robin come to know of this entrance?"

Marion was glad Elise couldn't see her blush. "You must remember that he and I played together as children?"

"I also think your two families were hoping for a match one day."

"I don't know about that. Perhaps." She bent to release the final latch and push the door open, revealing a vertical tunnel with a long ladder bolted to its side. She held the lantern aloft but its light was swallowed in the inky blackness overhead. "Like many other things, it was never to be."

"Ahoy below." She had been about to turn away when Robin's voice echoed from somewhere above them.

"I'm here." Marion peered upward toward the light that had appeared.

It wasn't long before Robin stood before them, slightly out of breath. "It's been many years since I've made that descent." He bowed to them. "I appreciate your faith that I could find the entrance again."

Marion pursed her lips. "I was certain you wouldn't have forgotten."

She turned to lead the way, but he stopped her. He reached for the lantern she held. "Let me see how much of this old ship I really do remember."

She motioned him to take the lead. "After you, then."

Unerringly, he walked straight to the base of the circular staircase and then into the once-comfortable sitting room.

"You did remember." She couldn't keep the warmth out of her voice. For some reason she was pleased to think he'd never forgotten their times here.

Robin inspected the room as Marion lit several more lamps in the cozy room. "You've kept her in better shape than I would have expected."

"What do you mean by that?" Of course, she'd kept her family's heirloom in good shape.

"I meant no criticism. Only that it's hard to believe she's in such good shape with the passage of time and only you to care for her."

Elise picked up one of the lanterns. "I'm going to reacquaint myself with this grand old lady. I'll be back after you two take care of business."

Marion perched on the edge of one of turfed chairs and Robin pulled a hassock up and sat near her feet. "What news do you have for me?"

Robin adjusted his position. "I haven't been completely honest with you about all that's happened since we found the children."

"Go on."

"You met the children, but what you don't know is that we visited the farm where they'd been held." Robin kept his gaze steadily on hers.

Marion's mind raced. Were there other children like those who needed help? The questions crowded in so tightly she couldn't verbalize them all. "When? Why didn't you tell me?"

Robin studied his hands. "We'd returned only a few hours before you came in with Addi. You were so upset, we ... I decided to wait until a better time to share all the details of our encounter."

"I see." Ice seeped into her bones and made her heart brittle. She'd known better than to trust him. "So you were fine with me baring my soul in front of everyone, but couldn't be bothered to share your secrets."

"Come on, Marion. That's not fair." Robin ran a hand through his dark hair. "You and Gretta were beside yourselves—with good reason. We all love Addi and were—are—worried about him."

"Yes. Initially." Her voice remained calm despite the betrayal she felt. "But afterward, in your study, you had plenty of time to give me these kinds of details."

Robin rose and began to pace. "All right, maybe I did. But I made the decision to wait until you would be open to what I have to say. Obviously, that was a misjudgment on my part. But here we are, and there are things you need to know. Are you ready now or do you want to continue to argue?"

She folded her hands in lap. "Continue."

"As I said, we—Tuck, John, and myself—scouted out the farm. It's one of those slated as fresh air therapy for the children being taken outside of the city." His voice stumbled. "But its purpose wasn't to make anyone better."

Marion leaned forward. The expression on his face warned her she wasn't going to like what she heard next.

"There were children there, in various phases of this ... illness. Some were just sick, like Addi. While others had been transformed into something like Tom."

He went on to give her details of what they'd experienced— the sights, the smells—everything. Then he took a deep breath. "And in the fields surrounding these buildings were livestock that had also been transformed. They were identical to the new equines that Edward has developed."

"Edward?" Her heart sank. Why couldn't he leave Edward out of this? "Did you see him there? Is there proof he's involved."

Robin took a deep breath. "Yes, I believe he's intimately involved. But no, we didn't see him on the premises." When she began to speak he held up his hand. "We wouldn't expect him to be there. He's much higher up than the day-to-day running of a farm like that. But the similarities are condemning."

"Does Edward own the property?"

Robin shook his head. "We can't unravel who exactly owns the property. It was once part of the Pilots Guild land, but was deeded out of the original land grant."

"Similarities aren't proof." Marion rose and closed the distance between them. "All you're telling me about Edward is based on assumption. You can't even say for sure he's even involved through land ownership."

Robin crossed his arms. "I can't say he's not."

They were obviously at a stalemate. Stubborn man, why couldn't he see the situation logically? She'd have to take action. "Show me. Let me see the farm for myself and draw my own conclusion."

"What exactly is it you want Robin to show you?" Elise had entered without Robin even noticing and now took a seat on the sofa.

He turned to her. "How much do you know about what's been happening?"

"Probably more than you might imagine." A frown crossed her brow as she took a seat. "Of course, I know Marion is the Maiden of Iron and all about what's happened to dear Addi. I've also been informed about the warrant for Dr. Tuck's arrest. You'll probably have to fill me in on the rest. Because I assume there is more to tell?"

Robin let Marion take the lead, more to hear how she presented everything than any sense of politeness. As she brought

Elise up to date, he watched Marion closely, trying to understand why she was so blind to who Edward really was.

"So," Marion finished up. "I've asked Robin to take me to the farm so I can see for myself what's really going on."

Elise turned to Robin. "Do you have anything to add?"

"Just that I think Marion is a blind fool when it comes to Edward." He began to pace again. "It's more than what he and his father did to my family, it's his ties to everything that's going on." He stopped in front of Marion. "You do realize he'll have complete control of the skies when the Pilots Guild and the Engineers Guild are merged. Don't you see the kind of power that gives him ... or whoever he's working for?"

Elise pointed at Marion. "Before we go down that path, I believe you also have some news for Robin."

Marion gulped back the hot retort and took a chair across from Elise. "I assume you know that Dr. Tuck came to guild headquarters this morning?"

"Yes." Robin joined Elise on the settee. "I didn't want him to leave at all, but he convinced me it was imperative."

"And so it was. William may have found the key to a cure."

Robin shot out of his seat. "A cure? This changes everything."

"No, not a cure," said Marion. "But a promising step toward one. Tuck is going to have to test his theory before they begin to replicate the serum. He left to return to your headquarters at the same time we left to come here." She paused and lifted an eyebrow. "He said you had facilities from which he could work?"

"I'd promise that man the world if he needed it." Robin touched his own right elbow. "I knew that if there was any hope it lay in Dr. Archibald Tuck."

"Well, he is certainly part of it. But it was our own William who made the actual discovery. The two make a powerful team." Elise lifted an eyebrow. "And you're about to find out firsthand because Dr. Tuck has drafted William to work with him. I hope that an additional person won't put you out too much."

Robin grinned. "I have plenty of room and look forward to meeting this amazing young man."

"Very well," Elise said. "Back to the conversation I interrupted. I'm glad that Robin has pointed out so obvious a point about Edward's possible control of the skies above us."

Marion flushed. "He won't have control. We've discussed the fact that I will be his equal partner in guild management."

"How do you know that he'll remain true to his word? Did you get the promise in writing?" Robin gritted his teeth. He had to make this girl see reason.

Marion fisted her hands in front of her, like she wanted to grab him and shake him. "It's not in writing, but don't you all see how this could be the beginning of a new age? With our union, we'll not only bring two guilds together, but there will be a woman in charge of one of them."

Elise locked eyes with Marion. "Did Edward actually tell you that you'd, in effect, be a Guildmaster? You know he doesn't have the authority to promote a woman to the rank of Guildmaster. The decision must be voted on by all the guilds. In addition, it must be approved by both the Queen and the Makers Guild."

"No. He didn't actually use those exact words." Marion rose and began to pace. "And we *did* discuss the obstacles to a woman becoming a Guildmaster, as well as how we would be equal partners."

"Do you love him?" Elise's soft question stopped Marion in her tracks.

"What on earth does love have to do with a union like ours?" She raised a questioning eyebrow as she clasped her hands in the posture of a child asked to recite. "I know my position as the only daughter of a major Guildmaster. I am to marry to the benefit of the guild. My search for a husband ends when I find someone with an impeccable reputation, who has the respect of the people."

Robin was gratified to see that she hadn't singled him out when she performed her recitation. He certainly didn't have the reputation to be considered. Although there had been a time ...

"Do you trust him?" Elise continued.

"He hasn't given me any reason not to trust him." Marion bit her lip. "And right now he's the only offer I've got."

"You do realize that's the exact same mindset that pushed your father into accepting Maylon's offer?" Elise's soft words set off an explosion in Robin's mind.

He gaped at Elise. "Surely Maylon couldn't have been the only offer her father received for Marion?"

"No, not the only one." Elise's face took on an expression he couldn't quite decipher. "But certainly, the only reasonable one. All the others were younger sons or lesser nobles without a brain among them. Instead of waiting for the right man, he rushed to get Marion settled so she wouldn't have to care for him." She turned back to Marion. "He knew the condition he was in with your mother's passing and wanted you well away from his grief."

"He wanted me well away, that's for certain." Marion's voice cracked. "I'll never believe he wanted the best for me. I was a burden and a continuing reminder of Mother."

"Whether you choose to believe it or not, the truth is still the truth."

CHAPTER TWENTY-FIVE

Robin eased into the sick room, searching for Dr. Tuck. Instead, Gretta rose from Addi's bedside and came to greet him, finger to her lips. "Is there someplace we can talk? He's resting now, and I want to know what's going on."

Robin led her back down the hall to his study. "Would you like some tea?"

"Heavens no." Gretta sank into the velvet sofa. "Annie has plied me with gallons, and I think I might float away if I had to force down another cup."

"Then what do you want to know first?" He leaned against the desk.

"Tell me there's hope for my brother. That William and Dr. Tuck truly have found a possible cure." Her blue eyes were red-rimmed but an inner strength shone through them in spite of the hand the past hours had dealt her. "Then bring me up to speed on Marion's plan to fix the this."

"From what I can gather, the outlook for this new serum of theirs is promising." Robin blew out air. "But it's untested, and the good doctor is understandably reluctant to test an untried drug on a person."

"Quit tiptoeing around. Between Bessie and Dr. Tuck, I know more than I wish about that dreadful farm." She gave a shudder. "The antidote will be tested on Addison."

Robin leaned forward. "Are you sure? If you know about the farm, then you also know there were animals there with the ... ah ... same affliction. I was thinking we'd bring several of those here for further experimentation."

"No." Gretta pursed her lips. "I've discussed it with Dr. Tuck. There isn't time. Addi is too old as it is. Every second that ticks by puts us further away from any chance of making him whole again." She bit back a sob. "There are already metal bits protruding from his left hand."

Robin moved to her side and took her hand. "We'll find a way. I swear to you, we'll find a way." With every fiber of his being he'd fight this evil and win this time.

"You sound just like Marion. Alone, you're each strong enough to make a difference." Gretta turned her red-rimmed us to him. "Together you're a force of nature. Why has it taken you so long to recognize that?"

Why indeed? Unfortunately he'd let the layers of hurt obscure the good parts of the past. Now he had two things to fight for. But would Marion be standing with him or against him? He met her unwavering gaze and chose to answer a different question. "As to what Marion plans to do—she and I will be going on an excursion tonight to visit that hellacious farm. She must see the place for herself to accept that Edward is up to his neck in this evil."

"And you truly believe he's behind all this?"

Robin stroked his chin. "Even with as much influence as his family has, I don't think he could pull this off without powerful allies. I'd be inclined to believe the Makers are behind a lot of what's happening. But yes, his mind is capable of planning this sort of evil. Of that I have no doubt."

Gretta gripped his hand tighter. "Then you must expose him or our dear Marion will be yoked with him for life."

Robin pulled away and rose. "I'm not certain how long her life will last if she does allow herself to become espoused to him. He would have nothing to gain by keeping her alive. And much to gain ..."

"Then it's up to us to save her from herself."

"Us?"

Gretta rose. "I'll speak to Annie about returning my clothes. I'll be joining you and Marion tonight."

"No." He faced her. "You won't. Your place is here. At Addi's side in case anything happens." All he needed was one more female to keep up with on this harebrained excursion.

"I'm not a useless female, if that's what you're thinking." She cocked her head at him. "You should remember that we've bested you in a fair fight once before." She gave him a grin. "Besides, you need me in case Marion won't listen to reason."

He hadn't realized how transparent he was. He leveled his gaze at her. "Very well. But on this little outing, I'm the one in charge, not Marion."

Marion awoke from her much-needed afternoon nap to the sounds of Matilda laying out her evening clothes. Was that woman actually humming? Marion stretched, feeling much more alert and able to cope. She could manage on limited sleep, but tonight she must be at her best. First was the conversation she intended to have with Edward, and then on to the foray with Robin.

"I have your bath drawn, my lady." Matilda appeared in the doorway. "It should ease the stiffness of an afternoon spent lazing in bed."

Her maid sounded more normal. Thank goodness that busybody didn't know the real reason she needed sleep. She allowed Matilda to help her into the bath and then into an elaborate gown she'd never before worn. It had been part of the trousseau provided by the Makers Guild when she agreed to the marriage with Lord Maylon. It was time to stop hiding from the past and use it to make a difference in the future.

"'Tis high time your ladyship began getting some use out of these beautiful gowns." Matilda carefully dropped the creation over Marion's head and onto her tightly corseted body. The décolletage was lower than she was accustomed to. She was thankful the gown had a matching choker, dripping with strings of jet and alabaster, to give her some coverage. She sat in front of her dressing table while Matilda piled her unruly hair into a mass of curls held in place by a jet comb that had been her mother's.

She drew the line at the dainty evening slippers Matilda had chosen. Instead she insisted on a pair of lace-up boots. Their pointy toes and low heel would be mostly covered by the dress in any case.

"You do look presentable," was her maid's only comment as Marion stared at the reflection of the sophisticated young woman in the mirror.

To her own eyes she looked far beyond presentable. She looked ... like her mother. Marion turned away to stop the moisture that threatened in her eyes at this observation. "Help me on with my cape. Lord Stanton should be here momentarily. I don't wish to keep him waiting."

Matilda draped the cape around her shoulders and handed her the small velvet evening bag in silence.

As Marion descended the staircase, she was conscious of Edward's eyes on her from below.

He offered her a hand as she reached the final step. "You are lovely this evening."

She took his hand. "Thank you, my lord. You look quite dashing." He did cut quite a figure in formal coat and silk top hat. His hat sported a discreet burgundy ribbon at the base of the crown adorned with the gold insignia of the Pilots Guild.

He offered her his arm and escorted her into his coach. "I thought we'd dine at my guild's headquarters. I hope you don't mind, but my father will be joining us. For propriety, of course."

His father too? That would make speaking with him at dinner impossible. "I do have something I'd like to discuss before we arrive."

"Of course."

She strained across the short distance between them inside the dark carriage, but his face was in the shadows. "I do have your assurance that as your wife, I'll be included in all the guild management affairs—especially with the Engineers Guild—correct?"

"Of course." He leaned forward and a passing gaslight illuminated the expression on his face. Joy, yes, but something else too. It made a shiver run through her soul. "You and I will be ushering in a new era. One where woman stand alongside men, exercising their intellects as well as their feminine wiles."

She grasped her handbag more tightly. "I just need to know that I can trust you."

"Something is troubling you." He reached across the space and took her hand. "We should begin now to learn to rely and trust each other. Let me share the burden you are carrying."

Her heart beat faster. She didn't have reason to mistrust him. Or, a small voice in her mind reminded her, to trust him. But if theirs was to be a true partnership, one of them had to make the first overture. She took a deep breath. "I have had some disturbing news about one of the places where the city's children are being cared for." She bit her lip. "And there have been rumors that you're somehow involved."

"I assure you nothing could be further from the truth." Edward squeezed her hand and sat back. She was falling in line with his plans. Now was the time to set the hook. "Tell me what you've heard, and we'll handle it together."

She shared her information on where the farm was located and the beasts that had been seen in the fields surrounding it. "So you see how bad it appears."

He brought a fist down on his knee. "Infamy. Who dares to blacken my family's good name?"

She shifted in the seat across from him. "I'm not at liberty to say. If I betrayed that confidence, I would find it difficult to continue receiving information I need."

"Loxley. It's that fiend Loxley." He again sat forward so she could see his face. This next part would require delicate handling. "The two of you were rather close before the scandal of how his father betrayed our Queen came to light, weren't you? Has he been bothering you with continued tales about my family's part in bringing Lord Loxley to justice? As I recall he took it rather badly and got himself branded as an outlaw."

Marion stiffened. "I still have my doubts about the former Guildmaster's involvement with that plot."

"I understand." He kept his voice soft and conciliatory. "And your loyalty to childhood friends does you credit."

She blew out air. "Regardless. I feel this latest information requires our immediate action. We should go there for ourselves and discover the truth."

"I'm afraid that would be quite impossible." He held up a hand. "My father is expecting us and such an expedition shouldn't be attempted without careful forethought and preparation. We could go tomorrow."

"Tomorrow? Tomorrow could be too late. What if something happens tonight?"

Did she know something was being planned for tonight? Hmm, that could work to his advantage. If he could catch Loxley, he'd have fulfilled one of the requirements set by Maylon. That would go a long in gaining him favor for his next request from the Makers Guild. "I cannot in good conscience suggest that we skip dinner or that we rendezvous for a midnight ride in the country. As your future husband, it is my duty to protect your reputation."

She sniffed, but allowed her shoulders to relax. Still holding his gaze, she continued, "I understand. However, I do want your word that you will not make the trip without me."

"Of course." He cocked his head. "But are you certain you're up for a confrontation, if such should be the case?" Would she confide the rest? This was the opening she needed if she was ready.

"Yes, I'm up to it." She snapped out the words, and he waited for her to continue, but she left it at that. So tonight wouldn't see her confessing her alter-identity. Soon, she would. And then he'd have her. There'd be no way she could get away then.

Chapter Twenty-Six

Edward saw Marion home, then rushed back to his house. "Send for Jeremiah." he told the butler who opened the door for him. "I'll wait for him in my study."

"As you wish, sir." The man gestured to a nearby footman, who hurried below stairs.

Edward was folding the note he had just written as his manservant entered. "You wish to see me, my lord?"

"Yes." He dribbled sealing wax on the folded parchment and affixed his seal with his ring. "Take this immediately to Simon. He'll know what to do. Then wake up Durstin and have him saddle Man O' War. I'm going back out."

Jeremiah paused. "Will you need me to help you dress?"

Edward came around the desk, frowning. "Of course not. You have your orders, see to it they're carried out."

"Very good, sir."

Edward ignored the other servants as he took the stairs leading to his rooms two at a time. Thank goodness, his father wasn't back from his evening out yet. He couldn't pass up the possibility of ridding himself of Robin once and for all.

He chose black riding breeches, black leather boots, as well as a black shirt and coat. If he planned to catch the scoundrel unawares, he'd have to use all the guile at hand. He stopped at the top of the main staircase, listening. Sure enough his father was back—he could hear him ask if his son had returned. In a flash, Edward changed direction and took the servants' stairs to avoid being spotted on his way to the stables.

Durstin stood in the cobbled yard, holding a calm Man O' War. "He's ready, yer lordship, and in fine spirits tonight." Steam rose from the gleaming black coat as the clouds rushed past a bright moon.

"Excellent." He ignored the groom's offer of help and vaulted into the saddle. "I'll be back in a few hours. I expect you to be waiting."

"Of course." The old man's face was hidden by his large cloth cap, but the tone of his voice made Edward look at him sharply.

"See that you are." With that, he wheeled the massive equine out of the stable yard and onto the main road. Excitement rose in his gut. He didn't care who saw his joy. Tonight would be the night, he was certain. For several miles, he let the equine have his head, stretching out his legs in a loping run. Only when he spotted the two shadowy figures, also mounted, did he rein in his steed. He took in their black garb and obvious weaponry strapped to their backs and saddles. "Good, I see you've planned accordingly."

"Yes, my lord, " Simon ducked his head, then smirked. "We've been waiting a while to get our hands on this group."

"That we have." Morris spit a stream of tobacco juice over his shoulder. "Tonight, they'll get what's coming to them."

"That's all well and good. Let's make certain your actions live up to your words. I won't tolerate losing again." Bravado was fine, but they couldn't go into this meeting with overconfidence.

"Everything has been removed except what's in the basement." Morris spit again. "That's an almighty large piece of machinery down there."

"It may work to our advantage to have it still there." Edward nudged his horse back onto the road. "Will the others be waiting for us at the farm? How much of the dismantling is finished?"

"Aye. We sent Neville on ahead. All will be ready when we arrive."

Robin paced around the gazebo as he and Gretta waited for Marion to appear. John had stayed with horses tied nearby. He'd had a time talking her out of finding a way to bring her own horse. It had finally taken a dare to get her to capitulate. Inwardly, he smiled. No, she hadn't liked it when he accused her of being nervous about riding a different horse. He'd known there wasn't an ounce of fear in that girl's body, but it had been the only way he could think of to minimize some of the risk for her coming with him. His horses were specially trained to return to his stables, even if the rider were unconscious or injured.

Gretta rose from where she'd been seated as the steps of the gazebo swung upward. Marion appeared, followed by Elise.

Robin strode forward, glaring at Elise. "What are you doing here? I don't have a mount for you."

"I'm not coming," she said. "I just wanted to make sure Marion wasn't waiting in the dark alone."

Marion narrowed her eyes at her. "And I told you I'd be fine, even if they weren't waiting—which they were are."

Elise studied them for a long moment. "Be careful. I don't have a good feeling about this."

Marion kissed her on the cheek. "I'll be fine. Quit worrying."

Robin watched Marion. Clad all in black leather, she mounted and calmed her horse with practiced skill and grace. How could one tiny woman be so strong? He moved his horse the front, hoping he was done with underestimating her.

They rode silently out of the city and through wooded lanes. After an hour, Robin slowed his horse near a copse of trees. "We'll leave the horses here and continue on foot."

He and John exchanged a look. "Stay here and be ready to move out, if you hear the signal." His long-time friend knew that Robin's paramount concern were the two women he had with them. He could count on John to take care of them first, and come back if he found himself in trouble.

Marion peered at Gretta. "Are you going to be all right?"

Gretta's face was a mask of determination. "I want to know what, and *who*, is at the bottom of all this."

Robin led the way through the trees until they came to an iron gate with low stone walls leading away from it in both directions. "We need to do our best to remain silent from here on." He vaulted the obstacle with ease then turned to help steady Marion and Gretta as they climbed over. Marion refused his hand, while Gretta allowed him to help her. He avoided comment and continued on. He was learning that her independence was part of the reason he loved this woman.

They stuck to the cover of trees as much as possible, until they reached the large expanse of open ground surrounding the dark house and buildings. Clouds scudded across the sky, making light from the moon spotty. He waited for a particularly large patch of clouds, then led them as they darted to the shadow cast by the main house. He made his way around the stone front to the back. They stayed close and didn't need him to check up on them. He paused and pointed to the fields laid out around the barn area. There several equines, obviously machine and flesh hybrids, dozed. Marion's mouth a grim line as she motioned for him to continue.

He kept glancing around. Just last night, this area had several guards patrolling. Now it appeared vacant. A pit opened in his stomach. Could they have already moved the entire operation elsewhere?

Feeling along the wall, he found the doorknob and twisted. It opened with ease. Now all his senses went into high alert. There was definitely something off. Before he could collect his thoughts, Marion pressed up against his shoulder and her warm breath tickled his ear.

"Is something wrong?"

"Very wrong," he breathed back. "I think we should go back."

"Not on your life." She pulled back and glared at him. "You promised me proof, and I'm not leaving until we know—one way or the other."

"Will you two stop hissing at each other? Let's get inside before someone comes along." Gretta sniffed. "This place gives me the willies, and that odor doesn't promise anything good."

Robin sniffed and his shoulders relaxed. No matter what, there was still *something* here. He'd be able to prove to Marion once and for all that Edward was involved. He inched open the door, but nothing moved in the darkness beyond. Motioning them inside, he unhooked a thief's lantern from his belt. When he opened one side of the four shielded window panes on the device Marion had a flame ready to light the wick. He eyed the contraption in her hand. It wasn't like any match he'd ever seen.

She grinned. "Another one of William's valuable tools. This is a fire-stick. One click and the spark lights the wick, providing almost instant flame."

He grinned back as he closed the sliding pane so only a sliver of light lit their way. "Nice. I may have to ask William to share some of his genius with my man."

"Not likely." The words were whispered and he couldn't tell if they'd come from Marion or Gretta.

They moved out of the back entry and into the hall. The odor seemed to gather as a fog at their feet. Would there be any reason to visit the wards with sick children laying unnaturally still in rows of white-sheeting beds? Probably not. Instinct told him they'd been moved. But the contraption in the basement would have taken time to dismantle and move. When they reached the top of the staircase, he handed the lantern back to Marion and began the descent into the madness of pure evil. He knew what to expect, she and Gretta were the ones who needed the light.

When he reached the floor, he raised his hand for Marion to take if she wanted help. This time she didn't ignore him. Her hand tightened as she took in the dim outline of monstrous metal chamber built into the middle of the room. He took the lantern and opened all the panes. There'd be no one down here to see them and they needed the light to see the villainy some men's minds were capable of conceiving and bringing to fruit.

"What is it?" Gretta lifted a hand to her mouth as if to cage the revulsion she felt.

They could barely see the inside of the metal chamber. A slight glow lit up the thick oval of glass set into the steel door. On the top were pipes and coils linking it to something in the ceiling. Off to one side was a smaller metal box covered with dials and switches.

"This thing is man-sized." Marion was moving closer and inspecting the hideous thing. "Or more accurately child-sized." She turned back to him. "Did you say Dr. Tuck was with you when you found this? Does he know its purpose?"

"He hypothesizes that it's used to finalize the transformation of those poor children into the machine-like soldiers who attacked you." Robin walked in front of her and swung open the door, pointing to a wall hung with gleaming ceramic and gold molds. As Marion studied them, an expression of dawning horror crossed her features.

"What kind of monster could conceive of such a plan?" Marion whispered.

"Don't you know?" Edward stepped from behind the massive machine with two other men flanking him.

Marion watched as Robin didn't hesitate. He threw the lantern directly at Edward and drew his sword in one smooth move. "Move. Back up the stairs," He shouted at Marion and Gretta. "Get to the horses. I'll hold them off."

Edward chuckled as the sound of boots on the staircase forced Robin to groan inwardly. "You don't actually think I'd leave you such a handy escape route, now do you?"

Robin still didn't lower his sword, even though he met her eyes and grinned at her raised bow, loaded with one of William's lightning arrows. In that one quick exchange, his love engulfed her. This was what she'd been running from for so long. How could she have been so blind?

"Come now." Edward advanced. "Do you really want to risk one of these lovely ladies getting hurt in a fight?"

"I could hold my own against you or any man here." She spit the words at her betrothed. The arrow notched in her bow and aimed at his heart didn't quiver.

As four more men entered behind them Robin lowered his sword and reached to push her arrow to the floor. "It's no use. We're out numbered ..." He mouthed the last few words, *for now*. His confidence strengthened her resolve even as she let him redirect her arrow.

"Yes, my dear, heed your comrade's sound advice." He closed the distance and wrenched the bow from her grasp. "Besides you have a wedding to plan."

Her jaw worked as she struggled with the emotions flooding through her. "I wouldn't marry you now if you were the last man on earth."

"I think you will." His eyes narrowed, and his voice hardened as he looked from Robin to Marion. "Or your new-found love will die a horrible death while you watch."

Her mouth dropped open. How could he possibly know? She'd only just know discovered her feeling for Robin.

"You are incredibly transparent and stupid, my dear." He grabbed her upper arm and dragged her toward the staircase. Another man had Gretta in a similar grasp and Robin was surrounded by three others as they marched back up the stairs.

When they were in the hallway, he turned to the man with Gretta. "You will take Miss Handleson back to where her horses are waiting." He tilted his head at Robin. "I do hope your man, John, doesn't give Morris any trouble. We'd hate to have to send him back in pieces with this young woman."

"You're letting her go?" Hope flooded Marion's chest.

"In a way." Edward grinned again. How could she have found warmth in his demeanor. "What we're doing is ensuring everyone's cooperation."

"I'm not leaving Marion." Gretta had been silent, but now her words struck with force. "My place is with her."

"Your place is where I tell you." Edward advanced on her. "If you want to ever see these two alive again, you'll do exactly what you're told. Are we clear?"

Gretta stared for a long minute, implacable hatred etched on her face. Finally, she dipped her head in acquiescence, and Marion released the breath she hadn't realized she'd been holding.

"Good. I'm so pleased everyone is now on the same page." He clapped his hands. "Again, you will return to your horse and make your way back with Robin's man. There, you'll proceed to inform Dr. Tuck that if he wishes the antidote for your poor brother, he must request it in person. When he appears, I'll send the serum you need to help your brother."

"What guarantee do I have that you'll keep your word?" Gretta wasn't ready to give up. Good for her.

"Why, none at all." Edward shrugged. "You truly have no choice but to accept what I say is the truth."

Marion's heart stuttered. Dr. Tuck too? She stiffened her resolve. This wasn't over. She'd find a way out, whatever it took.

Gretta hesitated, but finally allowed the man beside her to lead her out the way they'd come.

"Now for you two." Edward clicked his tongue. "Marion, you will return to my home in a closed carriage. For propriety's sake, of course. I cannot have my future wife's reputation sullied. I'll have your maid sent for and inform your father that you've decided to push the wedding date forward."

"He'll never believe you." Her words carried no force. Her father didn't care what happened to her. He'd be happy to get her out of his life and out of his house.

"Let her go." Robin strained against the men holding him. "You have me. You don't need her."

"Actually you have it backward, old man. It's you who are dispensable. I only need you—or more accurately your body as payment for a debt. The reason I'm keeping you alive is as surety for my affianced bride's continued good behavior."

CHAPTER TWENTYSEVEN

"Make sure our guest is comfortable." Edward thrust his chin toward Robin. "I'll be back down to speak with him after I've seen my lady safely on her way." He dragged Marion to the front of the house.

She wrenched her arm from his grasp. "I'm quite capable of moving under my own steam."

"Capable, yes." He let her move a few feet away. "But compliant ... that I'm not certain of."

"And well you shouldn't be." She narrowed her eyes at him. "Many are the men who have underestimated me."

"Oh, yes. Of that I'm certain. However, I've known about your alternate personality for quite a while. As have others." He eyed her Maiden of Iron attire. "I'm afraid it's you who have underestimated me—along with the Makers Guild."

Marion gasped. "The Makers Guild? What have they to do with this?" Then comprehension dawned. Robin had been right. They were involved in all of this. Then why was Edward part of it?

Her head ached as she tried to make all the pieces align into some semblance of order.

"Yes, the Makers Guild. Maylon and I have been working together for quite some time." He shook a finger at her. "You really weren't nearly as clever as you thought now, were you?"

She bit her lip. It was true. She had taken him at face value, refusing to listen to the wise counsel of those around her. Perhaps it was time to change her tactic. "Where do we go from here?"

He crossed his arms. "Assuming you're willing to listen to reason and behave—not much has changed from our original agreement. We'll marry, and I'll have full control of both guilds."

Blood rushed to her face. Marry this scoundrel? Over her dead body. She opened her mouth to speak, but he forestalled her with a regretful shake of his head.

"And if you don't choose to behave, we'll still be married, *and* I'll have Robin killed. No matter what, our marriage *will* take place. I have your father's permission, along with that of the Makers Guild and the Queen. It's up to you whether or not the day is one of celebration or mourning."

Breath left her lungs. Someone else she loved was in harm's way because of her own careless actions. Her heart ached and blood pounded in her temples. Could he carry out that threat? Probably. Unless she found a way to stop him. Without any concrete idea of how exactly to do that, her best course of action was to give in slowly and with much reluctance to make it convincing, of course. She glared at him. "I don't see you've left me much choice."

"That's a start." He studied her as if to see how sincere she was. "As I mentioned downstairs, we're moving up the wedding—to day-after-tomorrow. That will give us enough time to get you ready, without allowing time for you to cause mischief."

She allowed herself to be escorted to the door and handed into the closed carriage.

"See that you take her directly to my father's house. She's to be given the blue suite, just down from my rooms. And do it with a minimal amount of noise. I do not want my father awakened." Edward ignored her gasp.

"Am I not even allowed to go home and collect my own things?" If she could just get home, perhaps she could escape through the tunnels ... and what? Wait for Robin to be killed because of her actions? She gave a mental shake of her head. It was time to stop acting without thinking.

Edward's cold eyes pinned her to her seat. "No. Your maid is quite capable of packing what you need. I've already sent a man to inform her of the change of plans."

Marion frowned as the door was closed, and she heard the snick of a lock. How did he know whether or not Matilda was capable? Her mind raced. Was there a connection between the her maid and Lord Edward that she hadn't realized?

She road in silence to the Pilots Guild, through the main gate where the coach finally stopped in front of the Guildmaster's residence. Once out of the carriage, she was hustled into the house and left in the promised suite of rooms.

Marion paced around the confines of the main room. The suite was elegant, done in shades of light gray and robin's egg blue. Despite the feminine decor, it was nothing more than a prison. She'd tried the door, but it remained locked. She stood, peering at the night through windows blocked by an iron grill. The moon was just setting, but its pale glow bathed the grounds in an icy light, illustrating her situation in black and gray. How could she have been so wrong—about so many things? She bowed her head.

The sound of a key in the lock brought her around to face the door. In walked Matilda, followed by the footman wrestling her trunk through to the adjoining changing room. "That will be all," Matilda told him when he reappeared in the main chamber. "Lock us in. I have a duplicate key with me." She patted the pocket in her skirt. "There's no need to wait outside."

"As you wish, madam." The footman bowed his way out the door.

Matilda's eyes raked Marion from head to toe, taking in her Maiden of Iron attire. "I might have known you were that infamous outlaw. And see where it's gotten you."

Marion drew herself up. "You will not address me in such a manner."

Her maid smirked at her. "Do you really think it wise to take that tone with your future mother-in-law?"

Robin raised his head at the sound of footfalls on the staircase. His arms were pulled tight behind his back and secured with chains. His feet were shackled, and the guards stood a few feet away from where they'd dumped him in the corner of the basement.

"You may go." Edward said as he appeared at the base of the stairs. He glared at the guards as they quickly gathered up their weapons and scrambled up the stairs. When they left, he stared down at Robin. "Aren't you a sorry mess."

With some difficulty, Robin used the wall behind him to rise to his feet. "I'd say I'm in a lot better shape than you are."

Edward gave a bark of laughter. "Deluded as ever. When are you going to see that I hold all the cards? You should have disappeared when you had the chance." His face hardened. "Instead of coming back to irritate me. Now you're going to regret all the inconveniences you've caused me over the past few year."

Robin returned the glare. "I will oppose you until the day I draw my last breath."

"And that's why you won't be long for this world." Edward's voice rang with triumph. "As soon as the Lady Marion and I are wed, I'll have you killed and turn your body over to the Makers."

Robin's heart skipped a beat. He'd been right. "I knew you couldn't have been the brains behind all this. It figures the Makers recruited you as their little errand boy." He shrugged. "My father and I had long suspected they were moving toward a power grab."

"I sincerely doubt that you all had any idea what was going on." Edward's lips twitched. "Otherwise, your father would have been more circumspect in sharing his suspicions."

"Yes. Father did always trust too easily. It's not a weakness I have. I don't trust anyone."

He gestured to Robin's bonds. "And that didn't serve you well either, did it? Perhaps if you and Lady Marion had compared notes a bit sooner you wouldn't be in this mess."

"Perhaps." He refused to dwell on the wasted hours. It wouldn't do to let Edward get under his skin. He needed Edward to fill in the blanks, and this might be his only chance. "How did they manage to recruit you? They only had to dangle the promise of power and money, I suppose. You do realize they don't ever give away power. How do you propose to get around them?"

Edward shrugged. "Perhaps they're the ones who have fallen into my trap. Just like you and Marion, they have underestimated who they're dealing with."

"And how can you be so sure of that?" Robin feigned dawning understanding. "So it is your father who's masterminded this coup. I should have realized his outward appearance was just for show. Diabolical."

"My father isn't the genius behind this." Edward ground out his words between clenched teeth. "He's as much of a pawn as the guild. That old imbecile will have soon served his purpose and be gone. This is my doing. All mine. It won't be long before my father will have outlived his usefulness."

Robin grinned inwardly at Edward's angry response. "You expect me to believe that? You were barely out of school when your father engineered the guild takeover. How could that have been you? Why don't you prove your brilliance. Otherwise, I'm not biting."

"You'd be just like the rest of them in underestimating me." Edward pointed a finger at his own chest. "It was I who first began to plant the seeds of doubt in my father's mind. He'd originally been content as second in command. But I whispered to him about the unfairness of it all. How he was destined for greater things." He put his hand on his heart. "And how his only son would be so much better as an heir for the guild than you."

Robin winced. He *had* been a wild child, ignoring the warnings issued by his father in regard to some of his more daring escapades. He took a calming breath. His father had also come to his defense against those in the guild who'd spoken out, assuring them it was natural for a young man to sow his wild oats.

An evil expression crossed Edward's face at Robin's reaction. "You see now, don't you? You were just one of the pieces that fell into place when I began laying the foundation for what was to come. Your carelessness made it possible to sway my father with promises of stronger guild leadership. All of you were just pawns."

"To what end?" Robin forced down his frustration. "Yes, you'll be head of two guilds, but you're still subject to the Makers and to the Queen. You've traded one master for another."

"You're just like my father, unable to see past the way things have always been. The world needs someone to lead without the encumbrances of checks and balances." He waved his hand. "What's needed is a benevolent dictator. One who can see what's best for mankind—and has the courage to act on it."

Robin stared open-mouthed. Clearly, this madman saw himself as that leader. He swallowed and continued to push. "So you'll get rid of the checks and balances. How do you intend to remove the Queen without an uproar from the people who love her so much?"

"That's the easiest part." Edward laughed again. "She'll be assassinated by the Makers Guild, and my father will die trying to save her. There won't be any place the guild can hide from the irate populace. Then, in the confusion, since it was my own dear papa who sacrificed himself, I'll be the natural one to take charge." He rubbed his hands together. "It really couldn't be working out any better. Even the Engineers Guild will support me because the tragedy occurred at my wedding to their darling Marion."

Robin's gut clenched. He could see it all laid out, and it was diabolical—and attainable. "Then why do you need me?"

"You mean what do I need you for beyond the joy it will give me to watch you die? It's obvious that Marion cares for you. She has a distressing tendency to want to keep those she loves safe. You will ensure her good behavior during the wedding. But afterward ..." Edward shook a finger at him. "You've managed to irritate some very powerful people in the Makers Guild. I promised them you in exchange for help in this endeavor. You were my insurance there as well, securing the cooperation I needed."

CHAPTER TWENTY-EIGHT

"It's time you were up and about." Matilda's voice reached through Marion's nightmare-filled sleep and pulled her back into the world. "Lady Gretta will arrive shortly, and you're to be fitted for your wedding gown."

Marion rubbed eyes gritty from troubled sleep. She couldn't remember any specifics from her dreams, only the feeling of hopelessness. She watched her servant. No, not her servant, her future mother-in-law. Matilda was Edward's mother. Her eyes focused on her former servant.

"You remember don't you?" There was nothing subservient in Matilda's manner now. "It's been a long time coming, but the secret's finally out. And at my son's wedding, he'll be publicly acknowledging who I am." She threw back her shoulders, no longer mimicking the demeanor of a servant. "You're not the only one who'll be surprised then."

Marion searched through memories of how exactly Matilda had come to serve them at the Engineers Guild. She couldn't bring to mind where exactly the woman had come from, although the reasoning behind her father's choice had been abundantly clear. She could still hear his thunderous voice echoing in her mind. "You need a strong hand, young woman, and I cannot always be there to be sure you're looked after. Matilda will supervise your activities—and report back to me." No amount of tears had swayed him. With her mother's death, his heart had turned to stone.

"No, I didn't expect that." Marion was too exhausted to exchange insults. "What comes next?"

Matilda tilted her head as if trying to ascertain the motive behind Marion's surrender. "I told you. The Lady Gretta will arrive soon, and we'll be getting you ready for tomorrow's celebration."

At the mention of Gretta's name, Marion's heart rose. Gretta would have news. They'd have to find a way to talk in spite of Matilda's presence. She threw back the covers and swung her legs over the side of the bed. The aroma of chocolate pulled her upright and she moved to the table at the window. "Thank you." Her response was automatic, but useful. It wouldn't do to antagonize Matilda right now.

Matilda's pink face wore a frown. "I don't know why my son continues to spoil you. But he left orders that you be treated well—within reason."

"How kind of him." Marion couldn't keep the sarcasm from her voice.

Matilda's hand shot out and connected with Marion's cheek in a slap. "I won't tolerate that kind of talk about your husband."

Tears welled in Marion's eyes, but she refused to let them fall. She wouldn't even give that harridan the satisfaction of rubbing her cheek. "He's not my husband yet."

"Perhaps not, but tomorrow's ceremony will take care of that." Matilda locked eyes with Marion.

The key turning in the lock broke the tableau. Gretta walked in, looking beautiful and like she hadn't a care in the world. Behind her was Elise, carrying a satchel and a white cloud of tulle, lace, and silk. Marion would know that dress anywhere. Elise had brought her mother's wedding gown.

Gretta crossed the room and leaned down to kiss Marion on the cheek, but stopped and traced a light finger across what must have been the imprint of Matilda's hand. "Whatever has happened here?"

Marion covered her cheek with her hand. "I must have slept oddly." Her eyes begged Gretta to let it drop.

"No matter." Gretta kissed the top of her head then straightened. "We have much to do today to get you ready for tomorrow."

Elise busied herself carefully hanging the dress on the door of the massive wardrobe. "I knew you'd need us both." She turned to Marion, her eyes wise and filled with love. "Your mother can't be here, but we'll do our best in her memory."

Marion rose and crossed the room to touch the memory of her mother. They'd giggled together when Marion was young, imagining who she might one day marry. Now the day had come and was a disaster. She straightened her shoulders. No, she'd make sure it was *not* a disaster. Somehow she'd turn things around ... this time she'd do her duty ... even if it killed her.

As she inspected the dress, it occurred to her that this was a very clever copy, not the original at all. She leaned close and lowered her voice. "Elise, what have you done?"

Elise's eyes twinkled. "There was no way I'd let you wear your mother's dress—even briefly—for a fiasco like this. It's enough alike to fool almost anyone, even your father. But you won't have to worry when it comes time set things to right."

Gretta was inspecting the brushes and combs set out on the dressing table. "This will not do at all," she told Matilda. "You know I prefer to work with curling irons to make Marion's hair behave. Did you forget to bring them with you?"

Matilda looked bewildered. "I thought they'd been included, my lady. I'll find them." She bustled out.

Gretta grinned as she pulled two irons from the folds of her skirt and shrugged. "I had to think of some way to get that monster out of here." She moved to stand in front of the now locked door. "Although I don't know how long she'll be gone. Catch us up on everything that's happening, then we also have news."

"Matilda is Edward's mother."

"What?" Elise and Gretta spoke in unison.

Marion grimaced. "Yes, it's true. She informed me last evening. Since you obviously know that my wedding has been moved up, I think that's all I have to share." She took in the still closed door. "Now it's your turn, tell me what happened after Edward let you leave."

Gretta shoved the curling irons into a back corner of the wardrobe. "To make her think she overlooked them." Then she took a seat at the small table in the window alcove and motioned Marion to return to her chocolate. Elise drew up the dressing table chair and joined them.

Gretta poured herself a cup and took a small sip before beginning. "John and I returned to Robin's and found Dr. Tuck and William working on Addison. His fever had spiked again and they felt they couldn't wait to administer the serum." Her eyes darkened. "He's just on the edge of being too old for them to do anything at all for him."

Marion reached across and covered Gretta's hand with her own. "He'll be fine, you'll see. Between them, Dr. Tuck and William can work miracles. Is he improved at all since they began treatment?"

"He is. But he's got a long way to go." Gretta stared out at the cloudy morning. "His entire left arm and leg are in bad shape. It's like the virus has replaced his skin with metal. Tuck doesn't know how much of that will be reversible."

"We must have faith, my dear. He's a brave lad and strong." Elise gave Gretta a warm look. "Just like his sister."

"What about Tuck?" Marion twisted her napkin in her lap. "Please tell me he refused to go to Edward."

"Of course he went." Elise's brown eyes mirrored her concern. "He left as soon as he felt Addi was out of danger. He wouldn't do anything to put you or Robin in harm's way."

"Foolish man." Marion rose and began to pace. "Now there are two of them."

"Excuse me?" Gretta followed her with her eyes. "I don't exactly think you're in a place to be planning a rescue of anyone."

Before Marion could explain, Matilda returned.

Robin studied the cell from his makeshift bed. Even though the stone bench was hard, the hay hadn't been too old and kept him warm through the night. The rattling of keys promised someone was approaching. Hopefully, they'd be bringing him something to eat. He'd been transferred to the dungeon of the Pilots Guild. He gave a wry grin. He was home, even if in the dungeon. Even though he'd never been inside this particular cell, he'd spent much time exploring these mostly unused areas of the complex and knew several passages that led upstairs if he could get out of the cell.

The rusted hinges groaned as an old servant pushed through. A guard stood behind him, making the thought of escape impossible. "Be quick, old man." The guard was one Robin didn't recognize. Probably one of Edward's men.

But the old man was a welcome site. "Hagley, do you remember me?" Robin kept the words as low as possible.

The old man stopped and stared before his seamed face broke into a grin. "Sure and if it's not the old lord's son."

"No talking," the guard called from the doorway.

"Aye, sir." The man dipped his head and set the tray on another stone bench across from the one Robin had used for his bed. He rattled the dishes to cover his next words. "I'll be at your door when it's safe to come back down. We heard you was here, and we won't be abandoning you this time."

"That's enough. Leave it. He's not here to be waited on." The guard took a menacing step inside the cell, keeping an eye on Robin and a hand on his sword. Robin didn't doubt his ability to best the guard, but decided it would be better to wait and find out what was happening.

After the door clanged shut, Robin inspected the tray that'd been left. A hearty beef stew, bread and water. Not a feast, but more than he'd dared dream. He ate quickly, with one ear cocked for a sound in the hallway. Even more than food, he needed information.

After he finished, he took stock of his situation. There was one tiny window set high in the wall, and all he could see was the overcast sky. He measured the cell with his eyes. He guessed it to be about ten by ten. Nothing but stone, with one rusty drain in a corner. The solid wooden door was reinforced with iron and the hinges were on the outside. Set into it was a tiny iron grill, man high. He peered out, pleased to see there was no guard stationed outside his cell. He tried the door. Rock solid, as he'd expected.

He shoved the straw to one end of the bench and sat down to wait on Hagley's return. The old retainer had originally served in the stables. Robin relaxed as the memories sharpened into focus. Hagley had always been willing to cover for him when he was late or if he brought his horse in extra muddy or footsore.

After what seemed like an eternity, he heard a low whistle outside his door. He bolted to the door and sure enough, Hagley stood on the other side. "I told you I'd be back soon as I could. I should have a few minutes before the guard makes his rounds again."

"What did you mean when you said you knew I was here?"

Hagley's eyebrows seemed bristle. "There's been a lot of us who weren't none too happy about how your father was treated." He dropped his head. "But we was scared and uncertain. It made us slow to act. By the time we realized how awful the mess, your father was dead and you were branded an outlaw."

Robin put his fingers through the grate, wanting to reach out to the old man and offer comfort. "It wasn't your fault. And truthfully, I don't know that there was anything you could have done."

The old man reached gnarled fingers through the grate to clasp Robin's. "We made a pact after they murdered your old dad.

When it was time to come to your aid, we'd be ready and this time there'd be no hesitation."

"Thank you." Robin swallowed hard. He hadn't expected aid from this quarter. But he'd take all the help he could get. "I've got some men on the outside. You know John, and probably a few of the others. They left with me. I'm certain they'll be working on a way to get me out of here." He snapped his fingers. "The Lady Gretta. You know her?"

"Yes, sir. I know all them you mentioned." His eyes twinkled. "We been keeping tabs on you."

"Good. Gretta may be able to carry messages or possibly get the information you need. She's trusted by my men. And I suspect Marion will insist on having her at her side for the wedding." He choked on the last word. No matter what it cost, he'd prevent that unholy union.

"She's upstairs now with Lady Marion. Now that one's grown into a feisty one. We know who she is and what she's done for the children." He tilted his gnome-like face. "You could do a lot worse for a lady-wife."

Robin gave a bark of laughter. "You are right about that." He sobered. "First, I have to take care of the monster she's supposed to marry, once and for all."

"We're ready. Whatever you need, we'll back you all the way."

CHAPTER TWENTY-NINE

It was late afternoon, and Marion was weary of standing in front of the mirror while Elise pinned and stitched, remaking the counterfeit gown to fit her petite size. Matilda had been in and out often enough to make meaningful conversation nearly impossible.

"Stop fidgeting." Elise leaned back and stretched her back. "Why don't you have some tea while I sew some of what I've pinned."

"That would be marvelous." She stood still as Gretta and Elise pulled the dress down so she could step out of it. Matilda stood ready with her dressing gown, and Marion slipped her arms into the blue trimmed satin before plopping into a chair by the window. Gretta poured them each some of the restoring beverage.

Gretta peered at her over the rim of her cup. "I must say you've been extremely patient." She watched Matilda who appeared to be busy helping Elise. "All things considered."

"I don't see I have much choice. We've only today to get the dress ready. And if I make a move, Robin's life will be forfeit." She met Gretta's eyes. "I'll die before I allow someone else I love to be sacrificed because of something I did."

Gretta's mouth took on a grim line. "This one—no more than the last one—was *not* in any way shape or form, your fault."

"That's not true and you know it." Heat rushed to Marion's face. "The last time I balked at a marriage of convenience, and it cost me the life of my brother and the love of my father. This time, I will not make the same mistake."

"You know he'll kill Robin no matter what you do." Gretta's face was bleak.

"I know that's his plan. But if I find a way to free Robin before the wedding, he'll be able to make good his escape."

"He'll never leave without you."

"He will if I tell him I want to go through with this wedding." Marion again avoided Gretta's eyes.

"You can't," she began, then noticed Matilda staring at her and softened her voice. "You cannot intend to marry that monster. Look what he did to the children." Gretta grabbed her hand. "Look what he did to Addison."

Marion's eyes burned with unshed tears. Would this nightmare ever be over? "I know. But I have a greater chance of stopping Edward as his wife, rather than his prisoner."

"Why do you have to be only one of those two?" Gretta hissed. "We could get you out of here and the Maiden of Iron could save the day."

Marion thought for a long moment before she answered. "I think the Maiden of Iron has done quite enough already."

Before they could continue, there was a knock at the door. Matilda opened it and in walked Marion's father. He stood in the doorway, staring at Marion. She couldn't read his expression, but he looked older than she'd yet to see him and somehow caved in on himself.

"Leave us." His words were as strong as ever as he waved them all out. After a long hesitation, even Matilda quit the room.

He crossed the room to where Marion was seated, too weary to rise and fight yet another battle. "What have you done, daughter?"

"I have done my duty as your daughter." She stared him down. "I have found a suitable husband, and tomorrow, we marry."

He sank to his knee in front of her and took one of her hands. "Is this truly what you wish?"

She yanked her hand out of his. "Since when have my wishes been a relevant consideration?"

He used the table to pull himself back up and took the seat opposite her and turned his eyes heavenward. "It seems I've once again made a mess of things, my darling. You left our children in my care, and I've alienated one and gotten the other killed." He buried his face in his hands. "Why did you leave this task to me. You knew I wasn't worthy."

Marion stared at her father in dawning horror. He wasn't talking to her, but crying out to her mother. Was this yet another trick to manipulate her into behaving?

"I ..." Her voice failed her. She cleared her throat and began again. "I don't understand."

He lifted his head. "I don't either. I've tried to do right by you, and I've done you great injury again and again. Now, it may be too late."

Marion's thoughts chased through her mind. Could he be the ally she so desperately needed, or was this some elaborate subterfuge designed to destroy anything she might be planning?

She bit her lip. There was just too much at stake here. If he was somehow in league with Edward, like he'd been with the Makers Guild before, then confiding in him would destroy any chance she had of saving Robin's life. She chose her words carefully as she kept her expression pleasant. "I don't know what you're talking about. As I've explained, I love Edward. We've moved up the wedding because we just don't want to wait any longer to be together."

"I know you don't trust me." Lord Ravenswood pulled himself to his feet. "But I am here when you need me. Edward has requested I dine with the two of you, then meet afterward to sign the final papers. I will be there to walk you down the aisle, and if you change your mind at any point, I would give my life to help you escape this match." When she remained silent, he turned and left the room.

Edward sat behind his desk, waiting for Simon to escort Dr. Tuck in to see him. That fat old man would regret meddling in affairs that weren't any of his business. "Come in," he answered the discreet knock at the study door with a tone of impatience. There was still much to be done before the ceremony tomorrow.

"He presented himself at your door as requested." Simon ushered in the doctor, closed the door and stood in front of it.

Edward studied the doctor before turn his attention to Simon. "Wait outside. See that we're not disturbed."

Simon glared, but didn't offer a verbal protest. That man would bear watching. He was developing tendencies Edward didn't care for. He gestured for Tuck to take one of the leather chairs across from his desk. "Please, sit."

"You've forced me to come. May I know why?" Tuck's face reflected a serenity that Edward didn't care for.

"I'll ask the questions, thank you." Edward stacked the papers he'd been working with and then pushed back. "You've been a busy man. Meddling in things you have no business in."

"In reality, that's not true. Any mysterious outbreak of illness is exactly what my calling is all about." He pointed past Edward into the field beyond where Edward's altered equines grazed. "I see you've continued with your experimentation with integrating metal into living flesh."

Edward followed the line of his finger with triumphant eyes. "You and your guild did your best to stop me, but I have a writ from the Makers Guild allowing me the freedom to *tinker* with my little creations."

"Do they know you also tinker with children?"

How inconvenient. It had only been a matter of time before the full extent of his plan came to light. But tomorrow was when he intended to reveal it, and not a moment sooner. "You were such a promising medical man." He tisked. "It's such a shame you fell in with the wrong companions. You could have been an asset."

"You think to intimidate me?" Tuck chuckled. "Do your worst. My work is done."

Edward frowned. Done? Had he possibly discovered the antidote for the virus he so painstakingly created? "It doesn't matter. Plans are set into motion and there's nothing you—or your misguided friends— can do to stop me."

"Perhaps. Perhaps not." Tuck's face took on a solemn expression. "What you have tried to do is evil. It goes against all laws of God and men. All creation groans under the weight of what you've attempted."

Edward laughed. "You have a flare for the dramatic, old man. By the end of tomorrow we'll see who is right." He pointed a finger at Tuck. "And who is dead."

Tuck's face remained impassive. "Indeed we will."

Chapter Thirty

Once again, footsteps outside his cell brought him up and staring out the small square in the barred door. Inwardly, he groaned as Tuck came into view. Simon opened the cell door facing his and pushed Tuck inside. He secured the door, then turned to Robin. "You and your comrade can have a nice chat in the few hours you have left."

Robin waited until their captor's footfalls echoed away before speaking. "Why did you turn yourself in?"

Tuck peered out through the small opening. "Because, as I told Edward, my work is done. He can do nothing of consequence to me now."

"Done?" Robin's heart leapt. "You've found the cure? It works?"

"I believe it will work. I had just dosed Addison when John and Lady Gretta returned with Edward's ultimatum. I left William and Annie overseeing his care. He's in good hands." Tuck peered at him over his spectacles. "I had a difficult time getting details out of John and Gretta. It seems they were under the impression that you didn't want me to know what had transpired."

"Of course, I didn't want you to know." Robin locked his fingers in the metal grate, fighting to keep his voice level. "I knew that as soon as you discovered what Edward had threatened, you'd feel obligated to come. You were more valuable refining the cure than as an additional hostage."

"That, of course, is a matter of opinion." He fixed Robin with a stern eye. "I operate under the auspices of my guild and am not subject to the preferences of an outlaw like yourself."

"Oh, that's rich. You're as much of an outlaw as me. It was your guild that forbade meddling with artificial integration." Robin flexed his artificial arm. "I can't say I'm unhappy about your decision, but please don't go throwing stones."

"What I did prolonged and improved life." Tuck's face stiffened. "What that monster has done is worse than murder."

"That much we agree on."

"Come now, old friend. Let us not quarrel. Tell me what you've got planned."

"I wish I could tell you I have something planned. Right now, I'm waiting to see what develops."

Tuck frowned. "If you don't wish to confide in me, that's your choice. However don't try to pull the wool over my eyes."

A spurt of annoyance sparked the frustration boiling just beneath the surface. "What do you expect of me? I have no way to contact John. Marion's getting ready to marry a monster and I'm stuck here." He gave the door a kick, jarring his entire body when it didn't so much a quiver. "I don't suppose John gave you any indication of what he might be planning?"

"That man keeps his own counsel." Tuck chuckled. "I could tell he wasn't happy about my plans to pay Edward the requested visit. He actually went to great lengths to ... convince me to stay put. It took me several hours to pick the lock on the room where he left me."

"I bet he's almost as aggravated with you as I am." It was rare for someone to get the better of John. Somehow, that thought didn't bring him the pleasure it once might have. "I have discovered one thing."

"And that was?"

"From what one old family retainer has told me, there is a core of supporters here. It seems not everyone is pleased with the new guild leadership. They have pledged their support if I'm able to make a move." He shrugged. "Although I haven't been told how many—or how old—these supposed supporters are."

"Still any is better than none."

"True." Robin again gave a tentative tug on the door. "It appears that any plans I make must wait until I'm released from this cell. I assume I'll be invited upstairs tomorrow for the festivities."

"Festivities?" Tuck cocked his head. "Perhaps I'm a bit behind on the announcement."

"Edward and Marion are to be married tomorrow." Robin again laced his fingers through the iron grill. "I'm to be surety for Marion's good behavior."

"So I'm not the only one who's noticed Lady Marion's preference. Interesting."

Hope threaded through his veins toward his heart. "I don't know if it's that or the fact that all the world knows her to be tender-hearted."

"But tomorrow? How could he possibly arrange that?"

Robin gritted his teeth. "He supposedly has the approval of the Makers Guild, her father, and the Queen."

"I can see the Makers Guild and her father. He's become foolish since his son was murdered. But the Queen? I sincerely doubt she's given her permission."

"Perhaps not. But Her Majesty is in a difficult situation if the Makers Guild has truly aligned itself against her." He held up a hand at Tuck's noise of protest. "And I believe it has. Then add the support of the Pilots Guild, along with the Engineers Guild and the only other power left her is the Healers Guild."

Tuck frowned. "Yes, I'm ashamed to say my guild would be unwilling to take sides in such a conflict. The idea that the members have pledged an oath to do no harm seems to overcome all common sense regarding what exactly constitutes harm."

"Even if they backed her, the force would be hard pressed to seize back control from those three guilds." Robin began to pace. "No, we must rely on our own wits and take advantage of the opportunity that's sure to present itself."

Gretta and Elise filed back in after Marion's father left, thankfully without Matilda.

"What did he want?" Gretta plopped in a slipper chair. "Is he going to help you get out of the wretched marriage?"

"I told him exactly what I've told you." Why couldn't those around her see that this was the only way to stop Edward? "I'm going through with this wedding."

"Wedding or marriage?" Elise asked.

Trust Elise to see through to the heart of the matter. "As you say. The marriage is critical to stopping Edward." She rushed on to forestall Gretta's interruption. "No one has been able to stop this working against Edward from the outside. Only as his wife will I be close enough to him to stop his madness from the inside."

"I think you're delusional. There's no way he'll let you get close enough to endanger whatever he's got planned." Gretta's eyes were grim. "If he'll even let you live."

"He needs me alive ... for a short time." Marion turned away. "He's not stupid. He knows my guild is loyal to me. If he harms me, he'll lose them."

"Agreed." Gretta leaned forward. "If it looks like murder. But if you're injured—or worse—in an accident. Then he becomes a person of sympathy."

Marion swallowed hard. That couldn't be allowed to happen. "Then I'll have to be extremely careful, won't I?"

Gretta went to the door, opened it and peered out before closing it again. "I wanted to make sure we were well and truly alone before I gave you these." She pulled two tiny lightning pistols from her skirt pocket. "William gave them to me for you. He said you'd know where they'd do the best good."

Tears smarted in Marion's eyes. Indeed she would. One for herself and a second for Robin. What would she do without her friends? She took the pistol and searched the room for a reasonable hiding place.

"Perhaps this would be a good place for one?" Elise took up the wedding gown she'd been altering and brought it over for Marion's inspection. In the side seam, she'd secreted a small opening with a hidden pocket.

Marion threw her arms around the older woman. "You are cleverest of all." She dropped the pistol in the folds of the heavy gown before turning to Gretta. "We must get the other one to Robin."

Gretta grinned. "I thought that would be your preference. Give it to me, and I'll see what I can do."

Marion had just passed the pistol back to Gretta when Matilda burst in with three servants bearing trays. The aroma promised lunch. They were being fed well. The oldest servant was a man stooped with age, the other two were shiny automatons. His warm eyes caught hers. There was something in his manner that tugged at her memories of this place. Perhaps he'd been here when she played here as a child. That was it. He was the old Guildmaster's personal groom. How odd that he'd been enlisted as part of the house staff.

"We don't want to interrupt forward progress being made." Matilda bustled around, clearing off the morning tea tray to make room for the repast. As she worked, Marion watched the old man approach Gretta. At their whispered conversation, she kept Matilda distracted and busy. Whatever were those two up to?

"Of course, you and your father will be dining with Guildmaster Stanton and his son. I understand you have business to take care of." If the other servants found Matilda's familiarity with her mistress odd they knew enough not to question it.

"That is my understanding." Marion turned to Elise. "We should be finished with the fittings in another hour, correct?"

Elise stopped her work. "Yes. And at that point, I'll need to access a sewing room so I can finish my work."

Matilda straightened from setting out the final dish. "Go ahead and eat. I'll make arrangements for you to have everything you need." With that, she motioned the other servants out and followed them.

"The repast does smell heavenly." Gretta drifted over to the table. "And there's enough here to feed an army."

"They seem to be treating you well." Elise joined them and took a small plate for herself. She eyed Marion, who hadn't made a move toward the food. "If you're going to be any good to anyone, you must eat."

Marion joined them and filled a plate with things she was certain she'd never be able to choke down. She moved closer to Gretta. "Whatever were you discussing with that old servant?"

Gretta studied at the closed door. "He has been in contact with Robin. It's as you suspected, he's being held in the dungeon here on the grounds."

"He's here?" Marion's heart skipped a beat. "He's safe?"

"For now." Gretta frowned. "Hagley isn't sure for how long. He said they're hard at work erecting a double gallows in the inner courtyard."

"No." A soft moan accompanied her exhalation. Why had it taken her so long to admit what she felt for Robin? Then she stopped. "A double gallows?"

"Yes. It seems Dr. Tuck slipped away from John and is also in the dungeon. From what Hagley's heard, they're planning a double hanging once the wedding is finished."

"That scoundrel." Marion clenched her fists so hard her nails bit into her palms. "He promised Robin would be safe if I went through with the wedding."

Elise put a hand on her shoulder and turned Marion to face her. "All the more reason for you *not* to go through with it. He's not someone you can trust."

"No." Marion shook off her hand. "That's exactly *why* I have to go through with it. Only then, can I ensure he'll be stopped." She turned back to Gretta, unable to bear the worry in Elise's eyes. "Did you slip him the pistol?"

"I did, and he's promised to get it to Robin. And let him know you have one as well."

Now Marion just had to figure out what to do next.

CHAPTER THIRTY-ONE

Things were progressing quickly and falling into place exactly as Edward had planned. All the players were here under his roof, all except the Queen, but she would be here for the ceremony, of that he was certain. She'd not miss Marion's wedding. She would see that as a debt of friendship. He pushed himself back from the desk as the clock on the mantle chimed. However, he should have received her answer by now. He pressed the button on the wall to summon his servant.

The door immediately opened, and Edward bit back a strong rebuke as he noticed the hooded figure who accompanied him. All thoughts of the Queen fled as he faced Maylon for the second time in as many days. "Please come in."

"Will that be all, my lord?"

"No. Please check there haven't been any messages from the palace delivered."

Maylon pulled an ornate envelope from his robe. "I have what your master seeks. Leave us."

"How kind of you to bring it yourself." He motioned Maylon into an ornate chair flanking the marble fireplace. "Is there a reason the Queen didn't send her reply through the usual channels?"

Maylon took the seat and slipped back the hood. "She needed … ah, shall we say … persuading." His icy eyes bored into Edward. "When she was made to understand the situation, she sent her reply through me."

"Of course." Edward inclined his head. "You have my deepest gratitude."

"I hear you have something else for me. Is that true?"

Drat, was there nothing this guild didn't know? If he ever discovered who in his household was informing on him, they'd be drawn and quartered. "As I promised, the son of the former Guildmaster is currently in residence in my dungeon."

Maylon steepled his fingers, tapping them lightly. "And what is this I hear about a gallows?"

"You did stipulate dead or alive, my lord." The muscles in Edward's jaw began to twitch.

"So, there's the confusion." Again that icy expression. "What we said was you could *capture* him dead or alive. Now that he's very much alive, I expect him to stay that way and be delivered to us promptly after the ceremony tomorrow." He cocked his head. "You do have the details straight on that, I assume?"

"All I was waiting on was the acceptance of the Queen. Everything else is as we planned."

"The girl's father is still in agreement? He's known to be a free-thinker and cannot always be controlled."

Edward's jaw tightened. "As long as I have the daughter under my control, the father will fall in line."

"Very good." He motioned to the papers littering Edward's desk. "Is everything else in place?"

Edward rose and walked to his desk to pull a blueprint of the main ballroom out of the pile. Maylon joined him. "Here is where Her Majesty is to be seated." Edward pointed to an alcove that kept the Queen from being surrounded by the general wedding guests. "It looks easily defensible—important to General Easton. But those tapestries conceal alcoves where I'll have men stationed before she arrives."

"Excellent. And where will your father be?"

"Here on the front row, directly across from the Queen."

Maylon frowned. "If the Queen is assassinated from behind, there's no way your father will carry the blame."

Edward sneered. Did the man think him an idiot? "I'm not finished. The men behind the Queen will take care of her guards, while the kill shot will come from another series of alcoves across from the Queen and directly in line with my father's position. Don't worry, I've thought of everything."

"It appears that you have."

"When can I expect you and your men tomorrow?" He wasn't weaseling out of getting his hands dirty this time.

Maylon stared at him for a long minute. "We will be here before nine in the morning. The wedding doesn't begin until eleven, correct?"

"That should give us the time we need to add your men to those of mine in the alcoves."

"And have you decided whether or not your poor father will survive the initial assault?"

"He will not." Edward's face hardened. "It's important he not have any recourse to a defense."

"Agreed." Maylon pulled up his hood. "Be sure to convey my respects to the Lady Marion. I do believe we'd have got on well together. But perhaps this is for the best."

Robin had been pacing for who knew how long when footsteps finally announced the approach of someone. At this point, he didn't care who. He needed information, and somehow, he'd find a way to get it. He peered out the grill and noticed Tuck doing the same. Hagley rounded the corner and Robin let out a pent-up breath.

"I'm sorry, young master, for the time it took me to get back here." He grinned up at Robin. "But it's been worth the wait, that much I'm sure." Tuck peered out at them and Hagley leaned closer to the opening in Robin's door. "Be he friend or foe?"

"Friend," Robin told him. "Definitely friend. Surely, you've heart of Dr. Archibald Tuck."

Hagley sucked in air and turned to face Tuck. "You're the one who's working with the Maiden of Iron to fix our wee ones. I'd be honored to shake your hand, if I could." He backed up so he could view both men at the same time. "But we'll see you both out of here soon enough, if I know the young master like I think I do."

Dr. Tuck broke in, "It's an honor to see you, Mister Hagley."

Hagley slapped his thigh. "Don't that beat all. Tain't no mister in my name. I'm just plain Hagley, have been ever since I left me ma."

"What news do you have for me?" Robin asked.

Hagley turned serious and drew something small from the wide belt at his waist. "Lady Gretta gave me this for you." He groaned at the single window with the metal grill. "But I see now I can't give it to you yet." Then he brightened. "I'll be tasked with bringing down yer supper. I'll find a way to have it for you then."

"Was that all?" Robin appreciated this garrulous old man but was finding it a chore to keep him on task. "Did Miss Gretta give you a message of any kind?"

Hagley rubbed the stubble on his chin. "That she did. Lemme think a bit." He scrunched up his face, and Robin tried to assume a posture of patience. He caught Tuck's gesture that urged him to remain quiet and let the old man think.

Hagley snapped his fingers. "That's it. I got 'er now. She said to tell you that Lady Marion has one also."

Robin didn't know whether to cheer or groan. He knew she was a good shot, but would having a weapon inspire her to caution or recklessness? He'd just have to wait and see.

CHAPTER THIRTY-TWO

To Marion, the afternoon seemed to last year. The dress fitting—as much as she hated it—gave her something to do besides wait. Fairly soon after Elise left to finish the alterations, Gretta was also shown out by Matilda. Marion had been glad her friend was out of harm's way but sorry to be left alone.

She was still sitting, staring out at the sunset through the bars on her windows when Matilda reappeared with another maid. "It's almost time for your dinner. We can't have you looking less than your best." She pulled the young girl forward. "This is Agatha. She will be taking over my duties as your lady's maid."

Agatha curtsied, but kept her eyes downcast. "It's an honor, my lady."

"Come on girl, don't be all day about it. I'll show you the gown Lady Marion is to wear tonight." The two disappeared into the adjoining room, but returned moments later with an incredible mauve evening gown. The gossamer lace adorning the overskirt caught the light and seemed to almost twinkle with a million points of tiny lights.

Marion gasped at the work that must have gone into that creation. And at the money the dress must have cost. With that much gold, she'd have been able to get Tuck the supplies he needed to find the cure even earlier.

"You are a very fortunate woman." Matilda gave her a significant glance. "Your future husband's generosity seems to know no bounds."

"Indeed," was all the reply Marion could manage.

Matilda sniffed, then she and Agatha began the work of lacing her into the elegant dress. Twenty minutes later, corseted within an inch of her life, she sat ramrod straight in front of the gilt mirror while Agatha coaxed her hair into a masterpiece of curls.

"As you can see, you're in good hands." Matilda nodded her approval at Agatha's expertise. "Finish up and I'll return to escort you to the dining room. There are details elsewhere that I must see to." She scurried out the door, turning the lock from the outside.

Marion studied her new maid, pleased the girl didn't seem to have the same cruel streak as Matilda. "My hair looks wonderful. You did a magnificent job taming it into submission."

"Thank you." The girl bobbed another curtsy. "I've been training to be a lady's maid my whole life." She looked at Marion with an expression of awe. "I just didn't expect it would be a to a great lady like yourself."

"Great lady? I'm afraid that would be my mother, not me. I'm just a penniless Guildmaster's daughter."

Agatha put her lips close to Marion's ear. "No, ma'am. I'm talking about your *other* identity."

Marion froze. Was this girl an unexpected ally or part of a trap set by Matilda? "I'm quite sure I don't know what you're talking about."

The girl moved to the door and put her ear to the wood. "That horrible woman has gone."

She crossed the room to stand behind Marion again and spoke in a low voice. "There are many of us here in the guild who remain loyal to Master Robin. Hagley has us organized and ready to help when needed." She fixed an errant curl. "My job is to keep you informed on what's happening."

Before Marion could reply, the key turned in the lock, and Matilda was ushering her out of the room. In contrast to the bustle and hustle the night of the masquerade, the manor seemed quiet. Servants scurried about their business, pausing to bow or curtsey as she passed. They descended the smaller staircase to the main landing, then down the large, central staircase that led to the ballroom and dining rooms. Edward awaited her at the bottom, much as he had before—had it only been three days previously?

"We'll be dining this evening with my father." He ran his eyes over her ensemble. "Even though this isn't a state dinner, the Guildmaster is a stickler for evening dress. You look lovely." He turned to Matilda. "Well done, mother."

Marion's felt stones gather in her stomach. She hadn't really thought her former maid would be bold enough to lie about her true relationship to Edward, but she had so hoped.

Matilda's round face pinkened, and she dropped into a low curtsey. "I'm so pleased you're satisfied."

"Be patient for one more evening." He pulled her up. "Tomorrow you'll take your rightful place as the mother of the groom." He turned and offered his arm to Marion.

Marion's mind raced, analyzing the situation, and finally hit on a possible weak spot. "Doesn't your father know she's here?"

Edward turned. "Very good, my lady. No, he does not." He stopped and turned to face her. "And you'll be wise not to share that information. Your childhood friend's life depends on your conduct this evening and tomorrow."

Marion lifted her chin. "Take care you don't carry out your threat too early or you won't have a bargaining chip."

"Oh, I won't kill him for any misbehavior on your part tonight." Edward's full lips widened in the parody of a smile. "But I will make you both wish he was already dead."

Marion's heart grew cold, but she kept her face impassive as she gave a curt nod.

They entered the massive dining room where Lord Stanton rose and accorded her the honor of a slight bow. "Good evening, my dear. We're so pleased you'll be dining with us this evening. We've much to discuss before the celebration tomorrow."

To her eyes, the tiny grouping at one end of the enormous formal table was ridiculous. Her family had always preferred to entertain small groups in the less formal family dining area. Perhaps this was a symptom of insecurity. She'd find a way to exploit this weakness.

Edward held her chair. She was seated to the right of the head of the table and Edward to the left. Thank goodness she wouldn't be beside him. The first course was served, and she spooned up her bisque waiting for Lord Stanton to open the conversation.

"Are you all ready for the festivities?" Lord Stanton peered at her over his soup spoon. "I know you ladies always have so much to do, and I fear we've rushed the timetable a bit."

Marion gave turned her mouth into a pretty pout. "I did have so much I wanted to do to get ready. It's such an honor, and I did wish to represent both guilds in a manner that brings honor. Is there any way I can have a few extra days?"

Lord Stanton frowned and turned to Edward. "I'm afraid that's just not possible, is it?"

"No, it's not. I've been over this with my bride." He wiped his mustache on his napkin. "She understands what's at stake and will be ready."

She wasn't ready to give up yet. "I'm afraid I don't really understand the rush." She put her hand on Lord Stanton's arm. "It's not like I'm likely to back out of match with such a prestigious family. And we are making history with the consolidation of two powerful guilds."

"Ah, but there are those who wish to oppose us." Edward shot her a warning look. "We must keep you safe, along with our esteemed guests. We cannot have a repeat of the chaos from the other night."

"Quite right. Quite right." Edward's father signaled for the next course. "We are living in perilous times and must outmaneuver our enemies. Right, my boy?"

Marion had suspected that Edward was managing his father, but it was worse than she'd imagined. There'd be no getting around Edward by manipulating the senior Lord Stanton. "Of course, my lord."

"There are many things at work against the alliance of our guilds," Lord Stanton continued. "Even the Queen herself has been reluctant to give her consent."

"But we have it now." Edward's glare was for his father now. "And that of the Makers Guild."

"Of course." Lord Stanton gave a quick bob of his head, and his forehead creased in worry lines. "And you did say that rascal Robin Loxley is in custody as well?"

"Yes." Edward waved away a refill for his glass. "And with him in attendance tomorrow—under heavy guard—we'll be able to head off any mischief his men might otherwise attempt."

Marion put down her fork. "Speaking of Robin, I may be able to help with that as well."

"Really, my dear?" Lord Stanton's glasses worked their way to his nose and he pushed them back up. "Any assistance would of course be welcome."

She avoided Edward's piercing eyes and concentrated on his father. "I grew up with him. And if I might be allowed to speak with him, I could convince him that this union is my choice." She forced an expression that showed her dimple. "It might help keep him from ... uh ... acting out."

Lord Stanton slapped a hand on the table. "That's a wonderful idea, don't you think? You must make that happen as soon as we're through with dinner."

Edward glared across the table at her. "Of course, Father, whatever you say."

She took a sip from her water and let her eyes challenge him across the rim.

Robin paced, trying to keep his mind from all the possibilities that might have befallen Hagley before he could bring the pistol.

"You really aren't doing yourself any good with all that worrying." Tuck's voice carried from his cell.

Robin stopped and stared out the small grate. "Perhaps not. But I must release this energy somehow."

"Patience, my boy. Patience." Tuck chuckled. "You have waited this long, you can wait a few hours more."

Footfalls on the stone steps kept Robin from answering. Sure enough, Hagley, accompanied by the guard, came down the stairs. He carried two trays, stacked one on the other, and stopped first at Tuck's door. The guard unlocked the cell and Hagley entered. Robin lost sight of him as he set down the tray. He could hear a murmur of voices. The guard shifted his weight and glared into the cell. "Hey, there. No talking to the prisoners."

Hagley reappeared. "No need to get testy. Just getting things in order." He waited to one side as the guard locked Tuck's door and turned the key in Robin's.

Robin moved to the back of the cell, hoping to get far enough away to safely exchange a few words with Hagley. "Did you bring it?" He kept his voice as low as possible.

"That I did, young sir. You'll find your bread a might tough to chew, you know." Hagley's eyes twinkled under his bushy white eyebrows.

This man was a true gem. "Any other word?"

"The young miss now has a new lady's maid, my granddaughter." He frowned. "You did know her former maid is Lord Edward's birth mother?"

"What?" Robin bit back more of what he wanted to say.

Hagley cocked his head. "'Tis true. We've heard it from Lord Edward. But, the current Guildmaster don't know she's here or that Edward knows who she really is." He put a finger to his nose. "There's plans within plans going on. Evil's afoot and it's going to be up to you to make things right."

"That's enough." The guard stuck his head into the cell. "It's time to get to my own supper. Leave the trays. We'll pick them up later."

Robin sat and began to eat as the guard locked the door. He waited until the footsteps faded up the stairs before he grabbed the much-too-heavy-roll and moved to peer out the grate.

Tuck faced him across the hallway. "Did he bring it?"

"That he did." Robin held up the roll and grinned.

"Hey, I didn't get a roll?" Tuck's infamous love of food showed in his aggrieved tone. Then he grinned as light dawned. "I'm guessing you didn't get much bread either."

Robin tore at the roll and soon had the small pistol in the palm of his hand. "Nope, but it packs a powerful punch."

As he and Tuck discussed options, footfalls again echoed on the stone steps. Robin stuffed the pistol in his belt and waited. He was shocked to see Marion descending the steps with Edward and a guard close behind her. Surely, Tuck would keep Edward and the guard engaged so he could speak to Marion.

Marion waited at the bottom of the steps while Edward advanced to Robin's cell. "I've granted this request to my bride. Any betrayal of my trust, and you'll both live to regret it." He looked from one to the other. "So do I have your word?"

Marion's face was a blank mask. Robin's fists clinched. What had that monster threatened her with? "Yes," he growled.

"My lady?" He held out a hand to prevent her from moving forward. "I'll need to hear your agreement."

"Yes." Her answer was low and said through gritted teeth.

Robin wanted to grin. Thatta girl. His Marion wasn't cowed, she was blindingly furious.

Edward stared at her for a long moment, then motioned the guard forward. "You'll give them exactly five minutes. Then, you'll escort Lady Marion back up to my study." He turned to Robin. "See what a trusting soul I am. I won't even listen in on your heartfelt conversation."

Robin moved to the back of his cell while the guard unlocked the door and Marion entered. The guard relocked the door and then moved out of sight as Tuck engaged him in conversation.

Robin held out his arms and Marion melted into them. "Are you hurt?" He felt her arms, wanted to reassure himself that she hadn't been physically harmed.

"Harm his prize?" She gave a bark of laughter. "Of course not. But you ..." Her voice broke. "He plans to kill you, no matter what."

He held her at arms' length and studied her face. "You know that? Then why haven't you worked harder to escape. He has no hold over you."

"But he does." She stroked his cheek with her hand. "As long as you're still alive, I have hope." She dropped her hand and moved a step further from him. "And we need to make plans. Our only hope of escape will come tomorrow during the ceremony."

He reached toward her, but then let his hand drop. "I have no doubt that John is even now planning a way to get inside these walls. It would be so much better if you were already far from here when he arrives."

"No." Her voice was low, but confident. "If I'm gone, then he won't have an easy way in. The ceremony is key. It puts Edward in a vulnerable position. We must stop him. That has to come above any personal consideration."

Drat her logic. Robin began to pace, his emotions battling with the cool logic that he'd always prided himself with using. He stopped and faced her. "What do you know about his ultimate plan?"

"Know? Not much. But I suspect a great deal. It's my belief that he's going to not just consolidate our two guilds, but in process set his father or himself up as the monarch." She bit her lip. "I fear for the Queen."

"So do I." He once again drew her into his arms. "But together we'll find a way to stop him." It was an unusual feeling to know he had a partner he could count on.

"We will." Her face was white, but resolute. "But you must promise me one thing."

His arms tightened. He'd do anything for this tiny woman. "Anything."

"You must promise to see to the Queen's safety first and foremost." He started to protest, but she covered his lips with her fingers. "No. I can take care of myself." She gave him a grin. "I'll have time. The Queen won't. Now promise me."

He groaned and then touched his lips to hers—putting all his promises in that kiss—and prayed it wouldn't be their last.

CHAPTER THIRTY-THREE

Marion's wedding day dawned bright and clear, normally a good omen for a bride. Today, it seemed almost a betrayal. She sat in her wrapper in front of the window, sipping hot chocolate while Matilda, Gretta, and Elise bustled about. She'd dreamed about Robin last night, multiple times. Some were good, previewing a future together. Others were fraught with blood and death. By the end of today, she'd know which portents had foreshadowed the truth.

"I asked you what you wanted for breakfast." Gretta stood over her, hands on hips. She'd obviously asked the same question more than once.

"I'm really not hungry." Marion set down her barely-touched drink.

Gretta folded her arms. "It doesn't matter if you're hungry or not. You need to eat and you know it."

Her friend was right. But what could she possibly keep down? "Perhaps some dry toast and bacon?"

Gretta turned to Matilda with a gracious manner that didn't fool Marion or Elise. "Can you see to Marion's breakfast? We can't have her fainting in the middle of the ceremony."

Marion kept her expressions neutral as Matilda grumbled her way out of the room. Gretta wasn't supposed to know Matilda's true identity. Her friend was exploiting the knowledge by ordering the woman to death. But she was relieved they'd have a few minutes to discuss things. "What have you heard? Has John figured out a way to get inside the guild walls?"

"Indeed he has." Gretta plopped into the seat opposite Marion. "He's coming in with the Makers Guild."

Marion leaned forward. "What? He must be crazy. They'll kill him if he's caught."

Gretta cocked her head. "He'll be killed if he's caught no matter how he attempts to get inside. By using the Makers Guild as cover, he can disguise his men in those hideous black robes, and none will be the wiser."

Elise came to stand behind Marion and put a hand on her shoulder. "The risk is great for us all, but the gain is worth it."

Marion swallowed hard. "How is Addison, any change?"

Gretta grinned. "He's awake and out of the worst of the pain. William is by his bed night and day." Her grin faded. "But much of the metal has yet to leave his system."

Marion covered her friend's hand with her own. "He'll recover completely, you'll see."

Gretta stood and moved to the door. "I think someone's coming." The key turned in the lock, and Agatha appeared with her breakfast tray.

"I have your breakfast, my lady." She settled the tray in front of Marion and whisked the covers off the steaming plates. "Cook also included a bit of jam. She said her raspberry preserves were good for settling a nervous tummy." She leaned forward. "She adds a bit of ginger, just like my own mum."

"Tell her thank you for me." The dishes did have an enticing aroma. The maid leaned forward and kept her voice low. "I can carry any news to my granddad, if you wish."

Marion stared into those clear green eyes. It was now or never. Trust or not. "Tell him to get word to Robin that John has found a way in. His men will appear as part of the Makers Guild. Make sure your granddad knows to wait for Robin to move first."

The girl clapped her hands, then stopped, as if afraid her outburst would be overheard. "I know Granddad will be pleased." She blushed as she noticed Gretta and Elise staring at her. "We've waited ever so long to see justice done."

Breakfast was late, and Robin hoped that meant Hagley was waiting on word from John before he came down. Finally the familiar footfalls sounded on the steps leading to their cells. Hagley again carried two trays, but the guard with him was different. Hagley stopped between the two cells. "You might not remember the young'un with me. He didn't have much contact with the Guildmaster's family, but he was learning even then to protect those he served."

The guard grinned, but Tuck found his voice first. "What happened to Edward's man?"

Hagley clicked his tongue against his front teeth. "Something he ate didn't appear to agree with him. So they sent Samuel down to keep me safe." The guard opened Tuck's cell first and let Hagley enter. In the meantime, he reached into his belt and pulled out a knife, handing it hilt-first to Tuck. "I know it's not much, but it's the best I could do on such short notice."

"Thank you, my boy." Tuck took the knife and concealed it in his own belt.

Hagley came back out and waited for the guard to lock Dr. Tuck's cell and unlock Robin's. "We can't let you out now. There are just too many guards around to risk it. But Sam has something for you, too."

Again the young guard pulled a knife from his belt. "I wish I could do more. But I'm supposed to tell you we're ready when you give the word." He saluted, and Robin felt the sting of tears from the loyalty this man represented.

"Thank you." He moved aside so Hagley could enter. "Do you have any word from John?"

"Yep." Hagley showed a toothy smile. "He's found a right smart way to enter the castle unchallenged. He's coming in dressed as them Maker Guild members."

Robin whistled through his teeth. However had John managed to pull that off? Hopefully, he'd live long enough to hear the story.

"Yep. He said to let you know that he'd be there in force, but wouldn't make a move until you gave the signal."

"If you get a chance, let him know to be ready. His goal will be to encircle the Queen, making sure she's safe no matter what."

Hagley's eyes widened. "The Queen? They're after the Queen?"

"Yes, we believe she's one of their ultimate targets. You must instruct those loyal to you to make sure she's well-protected."

Hagley put his hand over his heart. "We'll defend Her Majesty to the death. You can count on us." His eyes clouded. "But what about the young miss? Who'll be protecting her?"

Robin grinned. "I learned a long time ago that young woman can take care of herself. I won't leave her alone, but Edward needs her alive as much as he needs the Queen dead."

"We'll be ready."

Edward stood by the window in his study while his father paced around the room. "I don't see how you could have kept this from me. My own son, betraying me in this manner."

"I didn't betray you." Edward turned to face the red-faced man. "I took advantage of the circumstances, and we've both benefited."

"But to have dealings with that woman. I've gone to such great lengths to keep her away from you." He leaned toward Edward and lowered his voice. "You'll be ruined when it's learned that your mother was a commoner."

"You didn't think me common back then." His mother had entered on silent feet and now stood, hands on hips, glaring at his father. "You appreciated my insight ... and my charms."

"Good morning, Mother." Edward pulled his watch from his vest pocket. Nine o'clock sharp. She could always be counted on to be punctual.

"Of course, I did. I meant no insult." He held out a placating hand. "I'm just taken aback at the fact that our son hid this from me." He glared at Edward.

"You wouldn't have listened if you'd known she was involved." Edward dismissed his complaint with the wave of a hand. "Now, we have to go over the final plans before the ceremony this morning."

Lord Stanton moved to stand by a large piece of paper laid out on the mahogany table. "You've got the seating finalized?"

"Yes." Edward motioned for his mother to join them as he pointed to different areas on the diagram of the ballroom. "We've arranged for the Queen to be seated here, in the alcove with the tapestries covering the niches high in the wall. Behind each of which is a bowman. When it's time, they'll cut down the tapestries and have a clear sight to the crowd below."

"Where will the Queen's guard be situated?"

"They will stand against the wall." Edward pointed to the place on the diagram. "It will appear she's well-guarded, but the real threat will be from above."

"But she'll remain safe, correct?" His father removed a handkerchief and mopped his brow. "It will only appear she's in danger?"

"Of course." How could his father be so dense? Why didn't he see that the Queen stood in their way and would never become the ally he sought? "I've told you about the Makers' plans to assassinate her and seize the throne. We must give them enough room to implicate themselves before we can move."

"Where does ... um ... your mother come into all this?" Lord Stanton was obviously doing his best to avoid Matilda's eyes.

"As the mother of the groom, I'll be seated close enough to ensure Lady Marion behaves when everything unfolds." Matilda folded her hands in front of her.

"There will also be bowmen in the tapestry-covered niches across from the Queen's position." Edward pointed to the place on the diagram. "They will provide extra coverage when the melee begins."

"Yes, of course." His father studied the diagram. "You have me on the same row as ... her."

Edward's jaw tightened. "I'm publicly acknowledging her as my mother. That entitles her to sit in the same row as you. We need her help." He put a hand on his mother's to keep her silent. "And we wouldn't be where we are today without her insight and knowledge."

His mother primmed her lips but remained silent.

"Yes. I see." Her father went back to studying the diagram.

"You know your part in this, right?" Edward moved to stand by his father. "We must have you as the hero who saves the Queen. That will ensure her support." He exchanged looks with his mother.

"Yes, I'm certain of what to do." Lord Stanton puffed out his chest. "Her Majesty will be in my debt after the events of today unfold. There will be nothing she can refuse me."

CHAPTER THIRTY-FOUR

"It's time, Marion." Elise's soft voice broke through Marion's chaotic thoughts. Elise stood close with Marion's bridal gown draped over her arm. The Wedgwood china clock on the mantle softly chimed ten. Where had the hours flown? Before noon, this would all be over.

Matilda cleared her throat. "I will be leaving you in capable hands. As the mother of the groom, I too must get ready. At Gretta's shocked expression, she drew herself up. "Yes, from now on you'll be addressing me as an equal."

Gretta inclined her head. After Matilda left, she giggled. "Not likely."

"I hope you're right." Marion rose and let Gretta and Agatha remove her wrapper. Elise set the dress aside and went to the armoire where she removed a satchel stuffed into a corner. From it, she pulled the pants of Marion's Maiden of Iron working attire.

"I cannot believe it." Agatha stood wide-eyed as Marion dressed in her working clothes.

"Last thing." Gretta pulled a wicked-looking knife from the top of her own boot where she always kept it and handed it to Marion hilt-first. "I believe this might come in handy if you lose that little pistol."

Marion hesitated. "You might need it yourself."

Gretta grinned and reached down to pull another from her other boot. "I had William fashion a spare."

Marion took the knife, hefted its weight. It was a blade she'd always admired. "I'll see it's returned when we're done."

"Nope." Gretta met her eyes. "This is yours forever. Use it to your good health."

There was too much of a risk it would be noticed in her dress pocket. Besides it might interfere with her ability to draw the gun when it was needed, so she tucked the blade into the calf of her own boot. "Thank you, my friend."

Elise stepped forward before things could get awkward. "I've left some room in the dress to fit over these clothes." With Gretta's help, she dropped the wedding gown over Marion's clothes and adjusted some ribbons. "You have easy access to the pocket, but be careful. The seams are loose." She stood back and inspected Marion. "When the time comes, you can pull free from the dress if needed by pulling these two tabs at the waist."

"Ingenious." Gretta blew out a breath. "You have truly outdone yourself."

Agatha brought out the shoes originally chosen to match the dress. "Will you be wearing these?"

"Oh, my, no." Marion searched the room with her eyes, finally settling on her boots. "I'll need those for what's ahead. The dress is long enough to cover them until it's too late for anyone to make me change."

Gretta turned to Agatha. "Can you modify whatever you had planned for her hair?"

"I can." The girl frowned as Marion seated herself before the dressing table. "It shouldn't take much to rethink the style into something a bit more sturdy." She pursed her lips. "And I believe a few sharp combs and long hairpins might be called for."

"That's a good girl." Elise watched the change in the reflection. "I know you'll find the right balance between fashion and practicality for our bride-to-be."

Robin wasn't really surprised when Edward showed up outside his cell, replete in morning coat and top hat. "Going somewhere special?" Robin didn't even bother to stand up and move to the door.

Edward glared at him, then motioned the guard forward with a bundle of clothes. "I've brought you something more suitable to wear to my nuptials. After all, the Queen will be present, and I wouldn't want you to embarrass me."

The guard unlocked the door and tossed the bundle to Robin. Robin didn't acknowledge the fact that the guard was the same young man from the night before. Things were definitely falling into place.

"What about my colleague?" Robin motioned to Dr. Tuck's cell.

"Oh, he will have his own personal guard during the festivities. I have plans for him after the honeymoon, and I want to make sure he stays put."

Robin met the guard's eye, and he gave a barely imperceptible shake of his head.

"You will put those on and be on your best behavior, or I won't be able to guarantee the Lady Marion's safety in the morning's activities." Edward held his eyes until Robin gave a curt nod. "When it's time, two guards will escort you into the ballroom. Any untoward move, and Marion will pay dearly."

Edward stood at his study window watching the parade of carriages and steam-powered vehicles waiting to disgorge their passengers. Still no sign of the Queen, but she'd be here. There was plenty of time. Maylon had given his word and could be trusted to follow through on what he promised. Even as he thought of Maylon, he watched as the first of the Makers made their way from several carriages. Edward smirked. Those ridiculous robes made them an easy target. After today, they'd either abandon them or risk being torn to shreds by an angry, grieving population. He turned at the sound of the door opening.

Matilda stood on the threshold. "I thought I'd stop by one more time and wish you the best." She entered and curtseyed before him. Her manner was regal without a trace of subservience. "I'm proud of the man you've become."

His heart twisted, but he ignored the urge to reach out to her. "Really, Mother? Sentimentality? I would have thought that beneath you."

Her face reddened. "Mock me if you will. I felt it necessary to tell you."

He inclined his head. "As you wish. Is my bride ready?"

"I'm going now to check on her. We'll be down shortly. I'll see her settled in the anteroom before I await your escort."

As promised, two guards came down to escort Robin to the ceremony. One of them was Samuel, although he gave no indication of his previous friendliness. Robin had no way of knowing whether the other guard was a friend or one of Edward's men. They manacled his hands in front of him, but left his feet free. Surely, that couldn't have been at Edward's request. At one point, Samuel stumbled slightly and grabbed at Robin's hands to right himself. The other guard frowned, but hadn't noticed the key Samuel slipped him. With his hands in front, it would take only seconds of inattention from the guard for Robin to free himself. The lightning pistol and knife would be easy to access once he had full use of his hands.

Marion heard the fanfare that announced the arrival of the Queen and her heart sank. She'd been so hopeful that the wise old monarch would stay away. Before she could share her observations with her companions, the door opened, and a transformed Matilda stood in the doorway. Her short, plump form was encased in dark purple brocade, and a discreet tiara peeked from her elaborate hairstyle. She was every inch the mother of a future Guildmaster. "It's time." She eyed Marion. "You appear suitable." She turned her eyes to Gretta who was bedecked as Marion's only attendant.

311

"You also are lovely." She waved to Elise. "After you see to Lady Marion's train, you may join the guests. Agatha, await your lady here."

"Yes, ma'am." The maid curtsied as they left the room.

Marion walked beside her future mother-in-law, careful to keep her boots from peeking beneath her skirts. It wouldn't do for Matilda to see them now, when there was still time to force her to change. The servants they met along the way stopped, but Marion kept her eyes focused on what was to come next.

Instead of taking the main staircase, they circled around to the lift that took them to the private rooms behind the ballroom. Here Matilda and Elise left them in an anteroom with Gretta. "Your father will be in shortly. See that you behave."

CHAPTER THIRTY-FIVE

At first, Robin was shocked that Edward had seated him in a corner of the Queen's alcove. He knew Edward planned for him to die in the attack to come. The fact he was this near the Queen confirmed that she too was in deadly danger. But in his over confidence, Edward had put Robin close enough to give him a fighting chance to save her. If he could deflect the first surprise attack, her royal guards would do the rest and he'd be free to help Marion.

He studied the room, seeing it through the eyes of one bent on assassinating the Queen. It had been years, but something was off. The tapestries. They were new. No, they weren't just new, they concealed the niches that had once contained artwork. He stared hard at one of the tapestries and could almost make out slight movement. That was it. Edward had concealed men behind those coverings. Robin gulped. They'd have any number of vantage points to not just take out the Queen, but her entire guard as well. He prayed that the majority of those men were loyal to him and not to Edward.

Edward took his place at the front of the ballroom, playing the part of a nervous bridegroom waiting for the woman of his dreams. Instead of focusing on where she'd enter, his eyes scanned the room. His eyes narrowed, the seats he'd reserved for the Makers Guildmaster and his heir were vacant.

He studied the tapestry-covered niches, doing his best to verify his men were in place and ready. He refocused on the guests. There were many more black-robed figures than he'd expected. Was Maylon planning a coup of his own? Had he been double-crossed? It didn't matter. They would soon see he wasn't an adversary to be toyed with.

Marion eyed the guards, but they gave no sign they even saw her. Impossible to tell if they were friend or foe.

Gretta went to the sideboard and poured a goblet of cold water. "Here, drink this. It will help you settle your nerves."

Marion gave a short laugh. "I don't think there's any drink in the world that could do that." She accepted the paper thin goblet and took a tiny sip. The water tasted off and she frowned. "I don't care for anything else." She turned away from the guards and mouthed the word, *drugged*, to Gretta. Perhaps Edward *was* worried about her. That thought lifted her spirit. She raised her chin. He had every right to be concerned.

Gretta's eyes widened, but that was the only indication that she'd understood. "I should have known that you'd be too keyed up for anything, my lady."

The two waited in silence until Marion's father appeared. He went straight to Marion and embraced her. "Tell me you're ready to let go of this nonsense and call off this farce."

Marion pulled back. "Now, Father, you're experiencing a bout of nerves. I thought only the bride was supposed to suffer from those."

A fanfare sounded, and Marion laid her left hand on her father's right arm. He appeared so miserable, she felt a pang for him. "It will be all right," she whispered to him. "You'll see."

He turned tortured eyes toward her. "No, it will never be all right again."

Before she could respond the doors were thrown open—time to go.

At the trumpet's fanfare, all eyes turned to the back of the room where Marion and her father stood. To anyone who did know her, she appeared impossibly tiny on her father's arm, but Robin knew the strength of that woman. In his eyes, she was ten feet tall. He forced his eyes away from her and to the front, where Edward stood alone. He appeared as any nervous groom might, gazing first at his intended and then around the room. But Edward was *not* a nervous groom. Every move he made was calculated and planned with precision. Somewhere in those feigned movements would be the signal that was supposed end the life of his Queen.

The music continued as Marion stepped closer and closer to the monster who intended to make her his wife.

Robin studied around the room. There were far too many black-robed figures, if anyone had taken the time to count. Good, that meant John had managed to get some of his men inside.

Marion's hand closed spasmodically on her father's arm when she caught sight of Edward and the crowd in the ballroom that rose to their feet at her entrance. So many people. She swallowed hard. There were so many black-robed Makers. Then she remembered John's plan and let out her breath. They'd have some back up when the battle began. Even with their added number she estimated far too many guests for them to protect. *How many of the guild members were loyal to Robin ... to Edward? Would it be enough?*

Her father put a comforting hand on top of hers. "Steady my girl. We'll get through this." She started as his words brought back familiar times from her childhood when he'd been the father who protected and guided her.

She noticed the lines that had etched themselves in his face, every one echoing the remorse of his words. Why hadn't she confided in him when she'd had the chance. "Yes, together we will." Her free hand slipped into the pocket sewn into her dress and grasped the lightning pistol. Such a puny instrument to protect so many.

While his guards had been preoccupied watching Marion, Robin had deftly unlocked his chains. He scanned the crowd and sure enough, close to the front, he caught the eye of John peeping out from his black Makers hood. Robin let out the breath he hadn't realized he'd been holding. If John was present, he'd have the backup he needed. They had a chance.

Keeping hold of the manacles with his left hand, he used his right hand to ease the lightning pistol from his belt and conceal it in his palm. His movement attracted the attention of Samuel who grinned when he saw Robin was free. Samuel shifted his body slightly to cover that fact from the other guard if he happened to notice. Robin's eyes narrowed. The guards weren't watching the him—or the bride—to a man, their eyes were locked on Edward.

He also locked his eyes on Edward. The guards' intense attention told him Edward's signal would come sooner than he'd thought. He'd expected Edward to hold off until the ceremony was complete and Marion under his complete control. His gut clenched. This meant Marion too wasn't completely safe.

The minister spoke words Robin couldn't hear, and Marion's father relinquished his hold on his daughter—handing her over to a monster. As Marion and Edward mounted the steps to a small dais, the seemingly nervous bridegroom reached up to tug at a too-tight collar. That movement screamed false, and Robin didn't hesitate. He leapt toward the monarch. "Protect the Queen!"

At his warning cry, her guards threw themselves on their Queen, providing a human shield as pandemonium erupted. Pieces of tapestry fluttered to the ground, covering some of the screaming guests as the whistle of deadly arrows sang all around them. From the corner of his eye, Robin saw John and his men throw off their hoods and begin to battle—some working their way toward him, others toward Marion. Good man. He'd anticipated Marion's peril just as Robin had.

Robin's attention returned to his own situation as Samuel blocked a sword the other guard thrust at Robin. He grinned his thanks and ducked under their clashing blades, intent on reaching the Queen. His knowledge of the compound could get her safely away long before her own guards could fight through the bloodbath around them. He used the chain in his left hand to knock aside anyone who got in his way, and was finally able to reach those surrounding the monarch. "Get Her Majesty out of here."

The commander of the guard lay to one side, mortally wounded by an arrow to the heart. Robin risked a look up toward the archers and was relieved to see chaos there as well. Fully half of them were wounded or intent on killing each other rather than pointing arrows at the Queen or the guests. He nudged the guard nearest him. "Get up, man. We've got to get the Queen to safety. This is a death trap. I know a way out." For a wonder, the man he spoke to recognized him and began to organize the human shield around the Queen. As he ushered them toward to back corner of the room and a little-known passage to safety, Robin tried to spot Marion, but the fighting at the front was too intense. Heartsick, he continued to lead the Queen and her defenders to safety.

Marion instantly recognized Robin's cry to protect the Queen. She, too, didn't hesitate, but pulled the lightning pistol from her pocket. Before she could get her finger on the trigger and point it at Edward, someone wrenched if from her hand. She stared straight into the face of a triumphant Matilda. "I knew you were planning something," the old woman said. "I was just waiting for you to make your move."

"Well done, Mother." In one movement, Edward took the small pistol from his mother and pocketed it while grabbing Marion by the arm. He locked eyes with his mother and pointed at his father, still standing in the midst of the melee. "See that someone takes care of that detail. I believe my bride and I need to leave—quickly."

Marion tried to wrench free from Edward, but the vice-like grip only tightened, cutting off the circulation to her arm. The man had inhuman strength. She stared at the arm that held her. Had he altered himself as well as the children he enslaved? "Be still or I'll rip your arm off." His mouth was set in a grim line and his eyes sparked with frustration and anger. She quit struggling, no longer doubting he'd carry out his threat. If only she hadn't decided to leave her knife tucked into her leather pants. Until she got out of this dress, there'd be no way to reach it.

She searched the room, hoping to see Gretta, and sure enough. she spotted the tall woman. As she feared, her maid of honor was in the thick of the melee, wielding a sword like any man and grinning for all she was worth. There were black-robed figures, sporting green headgear fighting with her. At least she wasn't alone.

Marion tripped and refocused on her footing as Edward dragged her toward the main staircase. If he'd only slow down a little she might be able to catch her breath and find a way to retrieve the pistol from his pocket.

CHAPTER THIRTY-SIX

As Robin and the guards closed in on the tunnel at the edge of the room, Hagley appeared with a half-dozen burly men. "We'll take it from here, your lordship. We'll see the Queen to safety. Your young miss needs you now." He pointed to the back of the ballroom where Edward was dragging Marion out the door.

Robin hesitated, torn, but the Queen's strong voice came from the midst of her guards, "Go, see to Marion's safety. I command it."

"Yes, Your Majesty."

Hagley put a hand on his arm. "Don't bother following them. Go straight to the airship dock. He ordered his own craft ready to fly just before the ceremony began. That one has a bolt hole and if he gets there, he'll be hard to find."

Robin didn't hesitate. He took off ahead of them into the dark tunnel. Blackness surrounded him, but he knew this passage well. There wasn't time to go back for a torch. He'd rely on his memory and feel his way to the side passage that led toward the hanger. It had been years since he'd come this way, and he'd be feeling his way in the dark, but he trusted his memories to lead him to the right path.

Rough stone under his boots felt familiar and his hand on the rock-chiseled walls reaffirmed his memories. It wouldn't be long now. Sure enough, a few more steps, and he felt a break in the wall. This was it. He worked hard to not break into a run, but he couldn't risk a fall. Slow and steady would get him there quickest. If only he'd be in time.

Marion feigned another stumble, trying to slow down Edward's progress without angering him further.

"Keep your feet under you." He refused to slow. "I'll knock you silly and carry you if you keep trying those stupid tricks."

Marion gulped. Unconscious would be the worst thing that could happen. She paid closer attention to her steps and kept pace as they left the main building and took off across the field. She gasped as she realized they were headed straight for the hanger. "Where are we going? We're not married yet."

"I always have a backup plan in case things don't go as expected. I have a quiet place to lay low." He chuckled at her look. "Already staffed with a priest, so we can finish our business while I sort out our options."

She'd die before she became his wife ... if she could make that choice. She could face anything knowing Robin and her friends were safe.

Robin pushed through the rust-coated door and stumbled out of the darkness into a dusty corner of the hanger. He blinked several times to adjust his eyes after the complete darkness. Movement in the corner caught his attention as a swaying craft was towed out into the sunlight. He began to run.

Several workers shouted as he sprinted by, but they didn't attempt to slow his progress. The small craft began to rise and he leapt, catching one of the mooring lines as it gained momentum. No one's head appeared over the edge of the craft, so he began to climb toward the lip of the elaborate basket perched below the brightly colored dirigible. It was the perfect size for a couple off on a honeymoon. He might have planned just such a send-off if he'd been the one marrying Marion.

Resolve tightened his grip as he swung in the air currents but still, he climbed. Finally, he was within a hand's breadth of the basket. No handhold, so he continued to use the rope for his ascent. If someone—Edward—noticed him, he'd be done for. All the man would have to do was sever the line.

Wind whistled in his ears. He thought he could make out voices, but he couldn't be certain. The craft was still rising steeply, and it made progress difficult. Two feet till he could grasp the side. One foot. And he reached out a hand and locked his fingers around an intricately carved railing circling the basket.

Marion needed to act. What she didn't know was what to do. When they'd arrived at the hanger, her betrothed had tossed her into the basket head first, knocking the breath from her lungs and making her eyes see shooting stars. Before she'd regained her composure and her balance, they were airborne. There were shouts from the men who'd helped them launch, but she couldn't hear what they were saying. Edward ignored them, intent on adjusting the dials that governed the heat that powered the craft.

The first order of business was to lose this stupid dress and get access to the knife Gretta had given her. She stood, swaying slightly with the motion of the airship and the bump on the head. Her hands fumbled at her waist for the two tabs that would rip away the dress. There. A quick yank and the dress parted. She bent and retrieved the blade, facing Edward, who'd whirled at the sound of tearing fabric.

"So this is the way you want it?" He eyed her up and down, a vicious set to his mouth. "I'd anticipated ripping that dress off you myself, but no matter."

She crouched slightly, kicking the tattered garment out of her way. "You might have tried."

Edward grinned and pulled the lightning pistol from his pocket. "We seem to be a bit mismatched. Perhaps you'd like to put down the knife before I shoot you."

From the corner of her eye, she caught movement almost directly behind Edward. It couldn't be? No, her eyes weren't playing tricks. Robin was silently heaving himself over the side.

As he tumbled onto the deck, Edward whirled. "How did you get here?" Even as he spoke, he brought the small gun up to fire, and Marion launched the knife at his back. Knife throwing wasn't her skill, but she hit him hard enough with the hilt to throw off his aim. That was all the time Robin needed.

The two men clashed together with grunts. Edward used his inhumanly strong right arm to swing at Robin's head, and Marion gasped. Instead of crushing his skull, Robin's arm had come up and blocked the blow. She blinked. The impact had almost sounded metallic.

She inched her way closer as the craft continued to rise, now encountering a low-drifting cloud, blurring the outlines of the fight. They were too evenly matched to give her a sense of who would come out the victor. As they grappled, she eased around and grabbed her knife.

The sun burst on the scene and Marion blinked, intent on finding a way to bury the hilt of her blade in Edward's back. The small craft bucked as a change in altitude forced them into a new air current off in a different direction. The movement had given Edward a slight advantage, and he forced Robin back against the railing, toward what Marion now saw was the gangplank.

Edward's hand snaked out toward the release, and Marion catapulted herself against Edward, knocking him into a vulnerable position just as he pulled the lever.

Edward screamed as he was hurtled out into the air. Marion felt her own momentum carry her toward the opening.

"Not today." Robin's strong arm wrapped around her waist and pulled her back against him. "You won't get away from me that easy."

She stifled a sob and buried her face in Robin's chest as Edward's scream ended abruptly. "I killed him."

He lifted her chin, forcing her eyes to meet his. "You only did what had to be done. With him gone, you're safe. I'm safe." He grinned. "All of Britannia is safe."

"Yes." She leaned into him. "It's finally over."

The craft swayed wildly again. "Well, almost." Still keeping one arm around her, he engaged the gangplank and moved to the helm. "What do you say we bring this baby down together?"

CHAPTER THIRTY-SEVEN

The skirts of Marion's mother's wedding gown—the real one—billowed out around her as she took the stairs two at a time. Why had the Queen insisted on seeing them before the ceremony?

"Would you slow down?" Gretta had to lengthen her stride to keep up with Marion.

Marion modified her pace slightly. "Do you think she's changed her mind or discovered a reason we can't be married?"

"Of course not." Gretta caught up, and the two continued to the study that now belonged to Robin, the reinstated Guildmaster of the Pilots Guild.

Had it really only been two weeks since she'd faced Edward in this same house? "Then what can she want?"

"She's had her men combing the countryside for Maylon and the remnant of Makers who escaped. There's probably word, and she would want you to know all was well before you left on your honeymoon."

"I'm glad they apprehended his father." Marion still couldn't believe all that had been revealed after they'd dismantled the

Makers Guild. Just a handful of evil men had come close to conquering all of Britannica. She slowed and took a deep breath as they approached the closed door of the study.

The footman stationed outside the door bowed at her approach. "Lord Robin is waiting for you."

"Has the Queen arrived?" Gretta asked.

He opened the door and admitted them. "Not yet, ma'am."

Robin stood by the window, the same and yet changed. Marion studied him and saw the confident set of his shoulders that had replaced the studied devil-may-care attitude of the man he'd been only a few weeks earlier. She'd loved him then, and she loved him now—even with his modified arm. Perhaps he'd be able to help Addi come to accept his own imperfections.

He turned, the expression in his eyes wrapping her in love. "Good. I'm glad you made it before the Queen." He motioned to one of the chairs flanking the fireplace. "There's someone here to see you."

Addison rose slowly, and Marion let out a cry as she ran to him. "You're here. I thought Dr. Tuck said you wouldn't be allowed to come."

He embraced her with one arm, the other unnaturally stiff. He smiled down at her—when had he gotten so tall?—but the joy didn't reach his eyes. "Tuck and William have done all they can for me."

Gretta moved to stand beside him, her hand resting on is good arm. "They'll think of something. You must be patient."

"No." Addison's face was grave. "What I must be is realistic. It's time to move on and learn to live with my disability."

Tears pricked Marion's eyes. Standing before her was the price of her failure.

"Queen Victoria," the footman announced, breaking the tableau as the Queen of Britannia entered.

All of them bowed and curtseyed their deep respect for this tiny monarch.

"You may rise." She moved immediately to Marion, taking her hand. "I'm so thrilled for you on this day." Her eyes clouded. "I only wish your dear mama was here to see you."

"Lord Ravenswood," the footman bowed again as Marion's father entered, his left arm still in a dark sling.

"I'm here." He joined the Queen in front of his daughter. "And this is a union I can whole-heartedly endorse."

They all laughed. The Queen seated herself and motioned for the others to join her. "As you may have surmised, I have news."

Robin and Marion joined hands.

"It's not bad." Although the Queen's face remained somber. "I'm announcing the formation of a new guild to take the place of the Makers Guild. I couldn't bear to honor them with the continuation of the name. Not after the evil plots they fomented."

"And a good idea that is," said Marion's father.

"I have designated the formation of the Tinkers Guild, in honor of your man William's tinkering. So many of his inventions played a major part in vanquishing our enemies. William of Worth will be designated as the first Guildmaster of this new guild."

Marion let out a whoop and clapped her hands. "I couldn't be happier. There's no one who's more deserving."

"I couldn't agree more." The Queen's face relaxed and she held out her hand to Addison who rose and stood before her. "I've also designated this young man as the assistant Guildmaster because of his courage and willingness to stand in the face of evil."

Addison swallowed. "Thank you, Your Majesty." He ducked his head. "But I didn't really do anything except get injured."

The Queen pinned him with a mock-stern look. "Nonsense. Besides you must never disagree with royalty." She turned to Gretta. "I'm surprised you haven't taught him better manners."

Gretta wiped at her eyes. "I promise I'll talk to him, Your Majesty."

The Queen turned to fix her eye on Robin and Marion. "I also have final, one hundred percent approval from the other guilds for the Engineers Guild and the Pilots Guild to remain autonomous, but under the union of your two families." She held up a hand when Robin started to speak. "And the Lady Marion will be designated as the first female heir to the Guildmaster position in the history of Britannia."

The room erupted and Marion felt herself moved from person to person for hugs and congratulations.

The Queen rose and the tumult settled. "I'll leave you all to a short celebration." She held up a gloved hand. "But see to it you are not late to your own wedding."

THE END

About the Author

Edie Melson's motto is simple—*find your voice ... live your story.* Creating characters who dig deep and find strength in times of adversity is her hallmark.

She has loved science fiction and fantasy since before she could walk. Some of her earliest memories involve being cuddled in her father's lap, watching Star Trek (yes, the original series). She attended college to become a costume designer which fed her love of all things Victorian and led to her fascination with Steampunk.

Edie's also a popular blogger, and her personal site, *The Write Conversation*, reaches thousands each month and has been named as a Writer's Digest 101 Tops Websites for Writers. She's the director of the Blue Ridge Mountains Christian Writers Conference, the Social Media director for Southern Writers Magazine, and the Vice President for the Advanced Writers and Speakers Association.

She and husband Kirk have been married over thirty-seven years and raised three sons. They live in the foothills of the Blue Ridge Mountains in SC. Connect with her on her website, www. EdieMelson.com and through Facebook, Twitter, and Instagram.

94844773R00187

Made in the USA
Columbia, SC
07 May 2018